THE LOVE BOX

JOHN OLIVER HODGES

Livingston Press
The University of West Alabama

isbn 13: 978-1-60489-110-2, hardcover
isbn 13: 978-1-60489-111-9, trade paper
isbn: 1-60489-110-6, hardcover
isbn: 1-60489-111-4, trade paper
Library of Congress Control Number 2013930865
Printed on acid-free paper.
Printed in the United States of America by
Publishers Graphics

Hardcover binding by: Heckman Bindery

Typesetting and page layout: Joe Taylor

Proofreading: Warren Enriquez, Carmon Hamilton, Alesha McNeese,
Melissa Lafond, Creed Robbins, Michael Kimberly, Hannah Riley, Joseph Seale

Cover design and layout: John Oliver Hodges

All photos, except for that of the author: John Oliver Hodges

Some of these stories have appeared in slightly different form in the following journals: "Canes," *American Short Fiction*; "Trained To Live," *Neonbeam*; "Crying Babies
In Heaven," *Iron Horse Literary Review*; "We Must Feed The Children," *Swink*; "Dtehshuh," *The Chattahoochee Review*; "The Coon," *RiverSedge*; "Arbus," *Cream City
Review*; "Health Nuts," *StoryQuarterly*; "Toothpick" *Southpaw Journal*; "Zooganroux," *Whitefish Review*; "Hurry," *Word Riot*; "Negatives," *Redivider*; "Troutsky's Parade," *The Literary Review*; "Earth Shoes," *eChook Digital Publishing*; "Boxwoods,"
Wrong Tree Review; "Oven," *Atticus Review*; "How I Supported My Habit of Collecting Scabs," *Washington Square*. Several of the photographs have also appeared
previously: photo for "Canes," *American Short Fiction*; photo for "Dtehshuh," *Ad-
ventum*; photo for "Toothpick," *Southpaw Journal*; photo for "Give Up, Woman,
Surrender!" *Shots Magazine*. Author photo is by Brady Miller.
Livingston Press is part of The University of West Alabama,
and thereby has non-profit status.
Donations are tax-deductible.

first edition

6 5 4 3 2 1

ONNÉ ET PORTATIF, CONSTRUIT PAR **BURON,** INGÉNIEUR OPTICIEN, A ⫿

Planchette

FIG. 10

FIG. 4.

Boîte à plaques.

THE LOVE
BOX

FIG. 3.

Glace dépolie.

F.
Boîte

fer
es.

C

for Tina Chang

CONTENTS

ONE

TWO

THREE

FOUR

"*The World Boxing Organization had a dead man ranked in the top ten of its super-middleweight division for four months. During that same four-month period, the dead man rose in the rankings from number seven to number five.*"

> Bert Randolph Sugar before the United States Senate,
> One Hundred Eighth Congress, First Session, February 5, 2003

"*Now, if everything has been arranged as it should be, your portrait will often be made, even in less than twenty seconds, and in the most satisfactory manner.*"

> M. Gouraud, *Boston Daily Advertiser and Patriot*,
> March 26th, 1840

One

CANES

Caramel says my lips make them want me. It's why Germs track me. Why Gum is the kid. Why we are candy. Canes. From Room 30 at the Land Shark. Those Germans—a man with his pregnant wife who smoked nonstop—had Room 30 decorated all Christmasy: twinkling lights across the ceiling, fake frost on the window glass, and festoons of plastic grass hanging. They had a plug-in Santa Claus who waved his arm as we took off our clothes. When we were naked, sitting side by side on the mattress that didn't have any sheets, the pregnant Germ handed us peppermint canes. She said, "Eat." We started sucking the canes, but the German said, "No! Eat," so we crunched.

We crunched the canes with our teeth. The Germans crunched canes too. The Germans crunched as Caramel and I fucked and Santa Claus waved his one red arm. All of us were crunching, and whenever Caramel or I finished crunching, the Germs fed us more. Our stomachs got filled with crunched-up canes.

That is why I say, "Hey Caramel. Will you be my cane?"

Caramel sticks out her fat red tongue. "Taint Christmas yet, silly."

Caramel's real name is Carrie.

Carrie sparkled in the sun that first day I saw her. She balanced the curb in red heels, tossing back her hair and pulling her fingers along the strap of her Minnie-Mouse purse. I was across the street with my pillowcase of things, just having come from the Greyhound bus station, and it was strange, this nearly naked girl stretching her stomach for the cars going by. She had a funny-shaped head that widened at the top. Her cheekbones were pointed and cute. It made her eyes look sunken-in, and her hair looked dirty to me, and her skin was oiled up and sent out rays. Her legs buckled at the knees. The whole world was a frying pan that day. I watched her climb into a faded brown Pontiac with tinted windows. A few hours later, at the boardwalk, she walked right up to me and said, "You're that boy who was looking at me. What's your name?" That's how we met. We played pinball at the Midway Funfair because we are the exact same height, five foot six and a half. We both have brown eyes and we're both seventeen. We hung out together all the next day, and I fell in love with Caramel like somebody falls down a well. I just love love love Caramel, from now until forever and then to forever again. Caramel is the best friend I ever had. Caramel is the best thing ever to happen to me.

But aside from that time in Room 30 of the Land Shark, when we did it for the Germans, that's it.

Because Caramel says we should never be like Germs. We are compassionate, Caramel says. The only reason we can serve Germs is because we are not Germs. If we were Germs too, what we do would have no meaning. I don't understand exactly what Caramel means, but I trust her judgment. Caramel knows what she's talking about.

* * *

My first Germ, before the Germans in Room 30 of the Land Shark, sold paper for a living, so he said. I was about scared as anything. The way it came about was like this:

Caramel and I were sitting in the bus bench in front of McDonald's on A-1A when he drove up in a cream Volvo. Caramel went to the window, but the man didn't want Caramel. The man wanted me. "If he pulls a gun on you," Caramel told me, "tell him you've had your tonsils out." She laughed like it was the funniest thing, then handed me something for my ass, making me promise to use it.

I got in the Volvo. The man drove the car south on A-1A. After telling me he sold paper for a living, he started talking about his daughter who was this beauty queen, he said, and kept smiling, pulling his beard and licking his lips which were purple and thin. "Do you believe me, Gum?" he said

"Yeah."

"Good," he said.

He pulled into a motel. A six was on the key in scrawly red. Inside the room he asked me to open my mouth.

I must have looked terrified because he suddenly squished his face up and wanted to know if I was okay.

I tried to answer him, and this noise came out of me. It didn't mean anything. It was just a noise, but I guess he liked it because he looked up at the ceiling with this look like he was thanking God. He backed me against the door. I was thinking I would run, but he put his hands around my neck. "Did I hurt your feelings?" he said, flaring his nostrils. He ran his tongue over my lips. A fat sandpapery tongue, and he acted normal the way he did it, like maybe he was watering a plant. "I'm sorry. Do you forgive me?" he said. "I'll make it up to you, Gum. You'd like a treat, wouldn't you, Gum?"

He pulled my shirt off, threw it on the floor. Contaminated. It looked like a blue rag, like trash. He took my ribs and I felt like crying. I thought of my dad, because that shirt was the only one I had left from the ones he bought me. I thought if Dad could see me now he might stop writing his book for a minute and tell me to walk on home. He might even think that maybe he was never very nice to me.

The man pulled me to the middle of the room and stood back to look at me, to examine me. He was smacking his lips, going "Ummm mmm mm," and he said I would make a great display at the livestock show in Deland. "Stand on your toes, Gum," he said. I stood on my toes. He grabbed the belt loop on the back of my jeans and led me around the room. "I'm serious," he said. "I think you could take a blue ribbon." Then he shoved me on the bed.

"Take off your pants," he said.

I just looked at him.

He leaned over and grabbed my nose and squeezed it. He put his mouth at my ear and whispered, "You're going to suck my cock you little faggot."

I needed to be somewhere else.

The man laughed then stopped laughing. "Say something sexy," he said.

I started to cry.

That's when he fell to his knees at the foot of the bed. "Oh, Gum," he moaned. His face was twitching. He was acting like he was in terrible pain, like trying to make me feel sorry for him. He put my toes in his mouth. His eyes bounced around all blurry-looking and sick. "Oh Gum. My dear dear precious Gummybear!"

His beard scratched my feet. He was in a rhythm of sucking and moaning, looking up now and then to show me that he was sorry. I think it was a trick, him trying to get me to say something and then as soon as I did he'd use it as an excuse to get mad at me. So I kept

John Oliver Hodges

my mouth shut. He nibbled harder. He was chewing my whole foot and it hurt. I undid the button. The man released some pressure. I did the zipper. He ran his tongue over my ankle and stood, grabbed the frayed ends of my jeans and pulled. It was the first time I was ever like that, in front of somebody like that. The man took off his clothes and climbed onto the bed next to me and I did what Caramel says my purpose is for. I blew him some. I was thinking this would be everything, but then Mack pulled up my leg. I remembered my promise to Caramel. "Wait," I said, and started to explain, but he did it anyway. There was a lot of blood. I think he liked it that way. I didn't want to think the blood was mine.

* * *

With the blood money I bought Caramel these nice black cowboy boots from Sundance Leather. I stuck the boots in a brown paper bag and folded over the top. Then I walked to the boardwalk to find Caramel. One of our favorite things is to sit on the bench in front of the Midway Funfair eating Snowballs hot afternoons. Caramel's lips go bright red. Mine go blue. Walking up with the paper bag, I said, "Is today the day?"

"Is today the day what? What's in the bag, Gum?"

"Just some groceries," I said, and I said, "Is today the day we tie the knot?"

Caramel rolled her eyes and shook her head. She stretched her leg out and wiggled her foot. "How you like my new anklet?" she said. "It's real gold, you know."

"You said the only way you would ever tie the knot with me is if I got with a Germ."

"I don't know nothing about no damn knots," Caramel said.

"You mean I did all that for nothing?"

"You got paid, didn't you?"

"But now we both—"

"Shut up, Gum. You're supposed to be admiring my new anklet.

Don't you think it's pretty?" She stuck her leg out and wiggled her new foot again.

"I don't like it," I said.

"Well, poo on you. Go bother somebody else if all you can do is say nasty things."

"You're the nasty one," I said, and handed Caramel the paper bag. When she peered inside and saw her present, her eyebrows went up into points. "Oh," she said. And her eyebrows were beautiful. "Damn, Gum," she said. "I can't believe you did this." She put the boots on right then and there. A perfect fit. She walked around on the boardwalk some to see how they felt, and she looked great in them, just boots and a bikini. When she came back to the bench she kissed me right on my mouth, right there on the bench in front of people walking by. It was so romantic with the sound of the waves crashing behind us and the seagulls in the salty air, all that hot Daytona sunlight raining down from the sky like a blanket of lovely pins. I wanted to keep kissing Caramel, tell her about how much I love her, but no. Caramel would have none of it. Love, Caramel says, is for Germs. That night we slept in the cemetery across from Boothill Saloon. That was the night Caramel started talking to my ear, it's the only place on me Caramel ever kisses. Caramel tells my ear all her secrets, whispering into it like for hours, like my ear isn't even connected to me. When Caramel finishes whispering to my ear, she rolls over and falls asleep.

Like a reptile sleeps.

* * *

My second Germ was also before the Germans. About a week after my first Germ, a car pulled over on Oleander and I got in with him and blew him as he drove around. I think he was a bodybuilder, something like that. He was large and blond and smelled like Lemon Fresh Joy and he kept saying that if his girlfriend weren't such a prude he wouldn't be doing this. After that I got in with a Germ who all he wanted me to do was suck his neck, leaving as many hickeys as I could. I wanted Caramel to be proud of me, and so I rarely turned them down. I was making money. I had like over three hundred dollars in the pockets of my jeans. I played a lot of pinball at the arcades.

Then we met the Germans, who'd been washing their clothes at the Laundrolady, hanging around out front with big branches of mistletoe in their hands. Caramel and I had been walking by when the pregnant Germ waved us over. "La la la," she said, acting all goofy, and she shook the green bush over my head. On a sudden impulse, Caramel grabbed my face with both hands and kissed me passionately. The Germans laughed with approval, and so did the black transvestites smoking cigarettes on the bench. "Yah yah," the pregnant Germ said, and everybody was clapping, and there were cheers even from across the street at the 7-Eleven.

Ever since that moment my life has been wet inside. Caramel says that it was a fake kiss, that she was only kissing me for show, but I don't believe her. I felt that it was real and special, that Caramel loved me just like I love her so truly. I don't know what to do about all this. I love Caramel so much, but all I seem to be to her is an ear. Caramel wants me to think of her as my sister.

* * *

Lately we've been sleeping in John Hardy's van, which is a junk Dodge parked in his backyard. I'd much rather sleep outside, or at the Catholic Mission, even though they separate us there, and I have to lie down with fifty bums who fart and grind their teeth all night. At first I hated the grinding. But it reminded me of Caramel crunching candy. So I started liking the grinding. Caramel says people lose their teeth this way, and in case I hadn't noticed, look around, Gum, open your eyes, don't you see all the bums have missing teeth? It's because they grind.

But John Hardy butchers at The Beef People, which means free eats for Caramel, who deposits her blood money at the First Security bank, and tries never to spend any. On occasion Caramel sleeps in the house with John Hardy. It hurts my feelings. I tell Caramel we should sleep outside. But Caramel doesn't listen. Caramel likes to have to pay for it. John Hardy, like them, is a Germ.

And it's the stupidest thing why they called Caramel Germ. In middle school, Germ was Caramel's nickname. I know because my ear holds all Caramel's secrets. They called Caramel Germ because her shoes didn't have light blue stripes on them, and because one time in Math a roach suddenly appeared on her arm. Somebody saw it. Then the whole class saw it, and everybody laughed. The roach flew across the room, and even the teacher laughed. I guess they figured roaches are attracted to germs. Now they are the Germs and Caramel is the one who is here to save them all, to take away the ugliness so that they don't have to feel bad about themselves. I only sort of understand it. It's like that feeling when something's on the tip of your tongue.

But I love her. I love when we are together in the van and she is whispering into my ear. She's been burned and beaten and raised into the air, fucked with bottles and branches and the toys of children. She was molested at all three schools, by a woman phys-ed teacher, a janitor, a counselor. As a senior at Deerfield High, within view of a Coach Morris who was pretending to be mending a tennis court net, she was held down on the hood of a yellow Fury. There were five of them that time, all football players, though only three of them did it to her. It was during lunch. The Germ made it to class on time after that, but word had already spread. Everybody knew. The Germ was free pussy. That night the Deerfield Devils beat the crap out of the Hillsborough Bears, ending the school's yearlong losing streak. The panties they'd pulled off her that noon were then tied to some fishing line that hung from a big oak branch beside the gym, right there for everybody to see. After that, Caramel says, she never said no to anybody, nor tried to resist them, though she did eventually have the good sense to start asking for money in return. Her life's purpose, she says, had become very clear to her. This was what she had to offer, to contribute to the community at large. What she was born for had nothing to do with going to school, so she dropped out a month before graduating. She hitched a ride to Daytona Beach where one of the old whores, upon seeing how beautiful she was, christened her Caramel, a name she readily embraced.

Everything Caramel says to my ear is holy to me, even though it hurts me to hear it. Such awful things. The list goes on and on. When she gets tired of whispering, she turns over and falls asleep. Like a reptile sleeps, on her stomach, with the sheets tangled up. Moonlight creeps in through the windows of the van, spilling all over her in glowing blotches. I want to pull her legs apart from each other, pour water into the backs of her knees and drink from the little bowls. But if I pull anything, if I touch Caramel or kiss her stomach, she squeals, kicking me, pushing me away.

She's careless, the way she gets into cars without even looking inside first. It makes you want to beat her over the head with a sack of potatoes. She's got these ideas. Community matters. Yes! If not for Caramel the world would begin to crumble. What a laugh. Caramel is here to save the whole world.

* * *

One morning, after sleeping by myself all night long in John Hardy's van, here comes Caramel prancing through the yard grass in her red-hot bikini as if she hadn't even been squatting on top of a Germ all night. I know that's how they do it because once I went to the kitchen for some water and saw them through the open living room door. John Hardy was flat on his back in the shag, all white and hairy, and Caramel was on top of him, bumping up and down as if she was galloping through a meadow. She even had on the cowboy boots I gave her. She seemed to be enjoying herself, which made all that sacrifice stuff she talks about seem like bullshit. But that morning, I was feeling real mean because my feelings were hurt bad. When Caramel climbed into the van, smiling at me as though she was happy to see me, I said, "Good time?"

That cut Caramel, I could tell. She looked so hurt. She spit on me and grabbed her purse and heels and took off.

I followed her several blocks. Before she reached Main Street I ran up and grabbed her shoulder. Caramel jerked around and shouted, "You're so stupid, Gum!"

Peanut butter was in her breath. I saw her teeth, what looked like sesame seeds stuck in there. Her face was twisted up hateful and had all these wrinkles on it that I hadn't seen before. "You're the dumbest person I ever met! I can read your mind!" she said. "I know everything you think before you even think it, so why do I put up with you?"

Caramel walked off, shaking her head, mumbling hateful things about me under her breath.

I let her go.

I walked to the boardwalk and met this guy who said he was a retired police captain. Did I want to go to his house and see his bulletproof vest? Sure. He drove me to his house in Port Orange. Once inside he excused himself and came back in a few minutes dressed in uniform. He gave me a joint and told me to smoke it down. I lit up, what the hell. On TV was *The Price is Right*. I thought, this is going to be easy, but then he smacks my arm with his billyclub, knocks the burning joint out of my hand. "Eat the evidence, damn you!" he shouts, so I pick the evidence off the rug and eat it. Then he starts telling me that don't I know smoking pot is illegal? His face is red, spit flying everywhere. I said, "I'm sorry." At that he whopped me over the head. I saw black, saw those stars, and in like a second my jeans were down at my knees, my face was mashed in the cushions of his couch, and he was fucking me. I really thought he was going to kill me, but afterwards he was very nice, drove me back to Ocean Avenue, and told me he'd be here next Tuesday morning so that we could do it again.

I waited at the Midway Funfair the rest of that day for Caramel to show up. I wanted to apologize so bad. But Caramel was nowhere. My head ached, I had bruises all over my body and my ass hurt, and I felt like I was dying, melting, dissolving into the world, but no, I wasn't, I was just this body of pain, nothing but pain. On the bench in front of the Midway Funfair I began to weep. I'm such a baby. I really hate myself. In middle school, I was known as The Scrounge, that's what they called me. I hated it then, but I like it now because it's one more thing Caramel and I have in common, that we both had ugly names given to us. They called me The Scrounge and they called me Niggerlips. And the way they moved, their faces, all of them walking around me, it gave me the creeps. It was like there was a joke everybody knew but me, and the reason I didn't know the joke was because I was the joke. Now and then they got out of hand, because they knew they could hurt me. I'm not the tallest, not very beefy. I'm easy to push around. They hit me, played tricks on me, always shouting SCROUNGE! in my face.

I asked Dad to buy me new clothes. I begged my dad, but, "Clothes are for rich brats," he'd say, looking up from his writing desk. "Go rake somebody's yard if you need money," he'd say, and shoo me out his study like a fly.

Finally, once it got dark, I went to the van. Caramel was there, inside, already sleeping. I was so happy, just to see her. I laid down beside her and passed out to the sound of her beautiful snores, feeling safe and sound just knowing she was alive. In the morning we made up, and the world seemed like maybe it was a good place to be after all. She let me buy her breakfast at Lonnie's Café, and after that we walked over the Halifax Bridge and spent the day in the park drinking beer with the bums and old whores who love us. They call us Candy Canes because of the time I said, "Hey Caramel, will you be my cane?"

"Taint Christmas yet, silly."

They thought that was the funniest thing, so we told them the story about the Germans, how they made us eat the candy canes, and how they kept hitting us with their mistletoe branches until the berries, which looked like pearls, popped off and rolled around on the bed. They thought that was hilarious, so now every time they see one of us they say, "Hey, Candy, where's your Cane?" because they think of us as inseparable, which I wish was the honest to God truth.

* * *

I get sick of it, but Caramel insists. It's necessary, she says. Without us the world will fall apart, she says. All the lawyers and governors and teachers and whatnot, all those people who hold things together in life, they would not be there if not for us. We are the thing that supports them. I would love to tell Caramel how crazy that sounds to me, but I'm afraid. What I want more than anything is for Caramel to love me. She gets mad whenever I say anything that contradicts her way of thinking. I just wish she would stick close by my side and never leave. She gets bored with me though. Always in the back of Caramel's mind is the need to go play with Germs.

About a week after that great day we spent with the bum, I got in a fight with some guy in front of the 7-Eleven at night. I'd been standing by the pay phone when Caramel, in a black Harley-Davidson halter top and silky black shorts, walked by in the cowboy boots I'd given her. It made me so proud to see them on her feet. She winked at me, and went into the store. That's when this guy with a ponytail who'd been standing there said, "I once fucked her on Maxine's couch for five hours, man. That girl can spread her legs like fuckin' spaghetti, I'm serious, her legs are like these rubber bands, man, they ain't got no bones in 'em." His friends chuckled and shook their heads. One guy said, "Yeah, man, Caramel is cool. Me and Donald put her in this old freezer one time and she was banging on it trying to get out and shit. When we opened the lid it was like a jack-in-the-box."

Everybody laughed, picturing Caramel like that.

"A bitch-in-the-box," somebody said, and the laughter went up a notch.

"How long did you keep her in there?" I said.

"Don't talk to us," the ponytail-guy said.

"Yeah, if somebody sees you talking to us they might think we're all queers."

"Go suck somebody's dick, ass-wipe," the pony-tail guy said.

"That's what you do," I said.

The pony-tail guy tried popping me, but missed. So I tried the same, and hit him. By the time Caramel slid back through the glass of the store, I'd already gotten a black eye, and my nose was bleeding. The pony-tail guy had me in a headlock and was leisurely talking to his friends.

"Get away from him!" Caramel screamed.

The ponytail-guy laughed and tossed me down on the concrete. "Look," he said to the others. "It's Miss Fridge!"

Caramel had a Pepsi in one hand, a peeled open Butterfinger in the other. She looked down at me like I'd betrayed her while all that mean laughter circled around us. "He was making lies about you," I said.

That caused everybody to laugh. I felt like a fool.

"Goddammit," Caramel said, and took off across the street while those guys made more comments.

"Hey, sperm bank, come back. I need to make a deposit."

I followed Caramel into the dark of Oleander Street. "Where we going?" I said.

"To a dumpster. We need to find a place to put you."

"I was defending you honor," I said.

"Shut up, Gum!"

My damn feelings were hurt again. My hurt feelings hurt way more than my busted lip and swollen eye hurt. I wanted so bad for it not to be true, what that guy had said. Five hours. I love Caramel more than anybody has ever loved her.

We walked in silence all the way to the beach. We sat on the ledge of a seawall, and Caramel held my face in her palms. She was looking at my bruises, pulling the hem of my shirt up now and then to soak the blood. She kept flattening her mouth with disappointment, shaking her head, and she said, "You're lucky he didn't break your jaw, Gum."

"You're lucky he didn't break your jaw too, Caramel. He told me all about his time with you on Maxine's couch. Five hours."

"Shit," Caramel said. "I been trying to get my jaw broke for about as long as I can remember. Billy ain't nothing."

"Oh, is that his name?"

"Gum Gum Gum."

"I'm not lucky," I said. "What's good for you is good for me. It can't be any other way. Isn't that what you're always trying to tell me? I wish he did break my jaw. I wish he stabbed me with a long knife."

"Oh, Gum."

"I hit him first," I said.

"So you did, but I really wish you would do me a great big favor and shut up."

Caramel knows everything, so I shut my mouth and we sat dangling our legs over the seawall. Caramel finished her Butterfinger. Didn't ask if I wanted any. She was not pleased at the moment, I could tell, and the huge moon hovered over the ocean, so pretty yet we couldn't even hardly appreciate it any. A river of sand scraped the beach. Caramel's hair blew against my face. I asked her if she thought we might buy a car some day, because I knew how much money she had saved in the bank. Over three thousand dollars. She was very proud of that.

"What a bright idea," Caramel said. "I guess you'd like to drive to the moon?"

"We could just drive. It wouldn't matter where." I looked at the moon, wishing for something different than all this stuff we had. I hated it, I just hated it.

Then Caramel said, "I been thinking."

That's all, and I said, "What? Thinking what?" I felt like I'd said something real bad that made Caramel start thinking, and I wanted to take it back, whatever it was. "Thinking what?" I said. But Caramel said nothing. I tried to get her to open up, but Caramel just seemed sad now, like everything had been drained out of her, but she kept smiling though, all these little smiles at me, looking at me fondly, different from how she'd looked at me before, like now she saw me, the me inside which nobody else ever sees.

Quiet like that we walked back to the van. We laid down on the futon and I put my ear up next to her face so that she could start telling it her secrets. Nothing.

"Why aren't you talking to my ear?" I said.

"I done told your ear all my secrets. That's the end of the list, baby." Caramel kissed my cheek and turned over.

I snuggled up behind her and kissed her neck. Caramel didn't squeak or wiggle uncomfortably like she normally did. I kissed her neck some more. After awhile Caramel rolled back my way and she didn't care that I was touching her. I put my hand on her stomach and my mouth on her mouth, mashing my lips against her lips. We stayed like that for a long time, and then we were kissing, just like we'd been doing in Room 30 of the Land Shark when we put on that show for those Germans, only this time nobody was watching us. It was just us alone together in the van. I could hardly believe it. I didn't understand it. I know that somewhere inside me I felt like I was doing something wrong, but I wanted Caramel so much that I didn't even care anything about what she thought. I was just grabbing her all over, pulling off her shorts and Harley-Davidson shirt and feeling her and licking her and it was just natural the way we ended up. I wanted it never to stop. I wanted it to go on forever. I felt like the men who had put their hands on me. Other times I felt like I was falling down a drain. Sometimes I felt like that damn ponytail guy, and other times I felt like I was me, and just so thankful that

Caramel was mine mine mine forever. I was afraid. I'd stop. I'd almost fall asleep and then start again. By morning I was still fucking her. We were locked together. The light flooding in through the windows made it even more difficult, for now Caramel's loveliness was magnified. Light. It rolled around her arms and her ankles and gathered in pools between her boobs and between her legs. My mind left my body and something automatic took over in me. I was possessed, had no control over my body. It sounded like I was beating Caramel up yet I could not have stopped myself to save the world. I exploded. We fell asleep. As one.

When I woke I was alone, half of what I had been. The thought that Caramel was off playing with Germs again was almost more than I could bear. Naked, I went up front and sat in the driver's seat. With my feet on the dash I smoked a cigarette while looking out at the nature of John Hardy's backyard, the squirrel and birds and the bark of the trees. As embarrassing as this is to say, I wanted to suck my own dick because of where it had been the night before. Not being connected with Caramel, I felt insecure, desperate, so terribly and unbearably alone. It occurred to me that Caramel had been right all along, that really, we should have kept ourselves separate, brother and sister. Now that we had committed incest, something had begun, I didn't want to know what. I slid into my jeans and walked to the boardwalk. No Caramel. It was Tuesday. The retired police captain had been waiting for me all morning. He drove me to his home in Port Orange. I was looking forward to having the crap beat out of me. I really hoped he would break my jaw. But this time he simply wanted a blow job. I kept biting down on him, hoping he would get mad, but he only giggled each time. To have bit any harder would have drawn blood. I was disgusted. I swallowed his sperm, counting the beats of his orgasm as he shouted out in pleasure.

Me and the police captain seemed to be friends now. His name is David. He dropped me off that afternoon at John's Family Supermarket, and I had the feeling that he really cared about me. Before I

John Oliver Hodges

got out of the car he squeezed my shoulder, slipped me an extra forty dollars. I tried to ignore the wish that he'd been my father as opposed to the father that I had. It wasn't the sort of thought that made a person proud of who they were. It was the sort of thought that made a person look upon their own self as a freak.

So I went into the supermarket. I was walking through vegetables when suddenly I got the strangest feeling. It was like, everything got quiet suddenly. I looked at the display of artichokes and felt panicky. I got some orange juice, paid, and then walking back to the van the feeling got stronger, a feeling like maybe the world got hit somewhere by a nuclear bomb. A little girl on a bicycle rode by me singing "Jingle Bells," and I started running.

I ran all the way to the van. When I opened the back doors, there, on the mattress, side by side, were Caramel's black leather boots and a note that said, "Keep on crunching, baby. Just don't try and find me. I don't love you and never will."

I sat and cried. I threw my orange juice across the yard. It was John Hardy's day off. Eventually he came out and told me that Caramel went back to Deerfield to be with her mom and sisters, that she had decided to try and get her G.E.D. He took her to the station himself, saw her goodbye and everything.

I just cried and cried.

I cursed myself. If I hadn't done what I'd done the night before, maybe none of this would've happened, I thought. I raped her, I thought. I'm a Germ, I thought. Fuck me, I thought. Oh fuck me.

It's only me now, just me. I play with Germs. Mean men. Even the men that are nice are mean. They wait for me in the shadows, they stalk me, because Gum is the kid. They all have something to prove to me. I let them prove it. Seeing me afraid, they are fulfilled. Open your mouth, Gum. Eat this, Gum. Look at me when I'm fucking you, damnit! Shit on the floor, bitch.

The wind blows. My feet carry me over sidewalks, bricks older than me. A voice floats through the arcade door: "Where's Caramel?" I walk. I know where certain cinder blocks lay, discarded treasures—I know their cracks and chipped corners. They are familiar things, like the sand I am so used to, and the air and the sky. I took Caramel's boots, tried burying them in the cemetery but the earth was too hard and dry. I finally threw her boots onto the roof of the Laundrolady.

I carry my things in a pillowcase. At the bottom of the pillowcase is a tampon I found while cleaning out the van. It's Caramel's tampon, used, with old blood and the cotton falling apart. When I found it I kissed it because it's all I have left of Caramel. My greatest most prized possession. I take it out sometimes in the day when nobody is looking, and kiss it, seeing her face in my eyes all the while. Even with eyes open, I see her face, her funny-shaped head wavering with bits of dust, glass, painted buildings, cars. At night I sleep at the Catholic Mission. The bums grind their teeth and I see Caramel in Room 30 of the Land Shark, crumbs of cane on her lips. Christmas lights twinkle in Carrie's eyes. I hear the sound of Santa's arm, the mechanical wave, then remember the pregnant German, how in her excitement to feed us more she tripped over the plug.

WE MUST FEED
THE CHILDREN

The girl was cut open in back but Suck June did not want to touch her. Suck June did not want to put her on but I knew how this was done. My mother sculpted stuff, so I explained, said first there was clay. Somebody poured hot liquid rubber over the clay. The girl was like the rubber monster faces they sold at Spencer's Gifts. There was nothing to be afraid of, but Suck June would not touch her. What made them look so real were the feet, the toes, you saw the toenails, the wrinkles and the prints, like on the toes and on their fingers. In their palms were the lines that come from when you were a baby inside your mother, making fists. And there was hair. Somebody had put hair between their legs before the rubber dried.

The boy was also cut open in back. I took off my sneakers and slipped my legs into the girl and put her on like a pair of pants. I brought her body up over my head, stuck my arms into her arms. I had already shoved a stick through the girl's eyes and mouth so that I could breathe and see. I walked around, making Suck June laugh. I knew I looked hilarious and gross. Halloween was three days away. I knew what I would be.

After seeing me like this, Suck June changed her mind. She poked out the boy's eyes and mouth, then pulled off her dress and shoes and climbed into him. We ran through the trees, up to the top of the Indian mound where trees didn't grow. Up there, in the sunlight, we saw each other. I had my own small pair of breasts and Suck June had a little dangly thing between her legs.

Suck June said she saw her dad washing his thing in the sink. Her dad's thing, Suck June said, was like a turkey neck that jumped off the ground and bit him there and wouldn't let go. Suck June said one time she saw her parents in their bedroom connected to each other at the turkey neck. Suck June was acting weird, not like the regular Suck June. Normally Suck June was shy and did not say much. Suck June did other things too that were weird, like scream-ing at the sky and waving her arms.

On Halloween, about the time it was getting dark, Suck June and I went down to the woods and stripped to our underwear and put on our costumes. We headed up to Windsor Way and rang the bell of the first house with a pumpkin. Trick or treat, we said when the lady opened.

Oh my, the lady said, and covered her mouth. Where did you get those ornery costumes?

These ain't costumes! Suck June shouted, and turned and ran. I ran after her, laughing. We ran several houses over.

Trick or treat, we said.

This time it was Jelly Belly. We knew Jelly Belly from selling mistletoe at Christmastime—we'd go around the neighborhood, Suck June and I, with a red wagon filled with mistletoe, dragging the red wagon from house to house, selling our mistletoe—but Jelly Belly did not recognize us. After looking us over he called into the back. Mary, come quick. You got to see this. Hurry, I want you to see this.

Mary came to the door, and she did the same thing as that other lady, lifting a hand up to cover her mouth.

We already said trick or treat, Suck June said.

Dear Lord, the lady said.

That's pretty good, Jelly Belly said, laughing, his belly wobbling. He was the fattest man we knew. We'd talked about his fat after selling him that mistletoe, how it must be a terrible pain to walk with all that fat hanging off of you. Suck June had said that she wouldn't want him to hold that mistletoe over her head and kiss her. That's when we made up the name Jelly Belly. Jelly Belly was not giving us our candy.

I believe these two deserve the blue ribbon, Jelly Belly said.

Who are you? Mary said. Who do you belong to?

We're dead children, Suck June said.

The lady brought her hand back up to cover her mouth.

Jelly Belly held out the bowl of candy. Go ahead, he said. Get your fill.

We reached in with our rubbery hands and grabbed up a bunch of Mary-Janes and Tootsie Rolls. They were still watching us when we reached the street, where the lamp shined down, making us glow. There were some other kids coming along—one was a queen of hearts, a walking card—and when they saw us the card tipped over and bonked its head. They got up and hurried by, very fast. This was fun. People were afraid of us. They did not know what to think about dead children.

Suck June said it was too bad we did not always look this way. Wouldn't it be great if we could go to school like this? Suck June wiggled her turkey neck and shouted, Suck my dick! I tried thinking of something I could shout about the new me, but I did not know the words. Lick my breast! I shouted, but it was not so grand as what Suck June had shouted.

A dozen houses later Suck June and I decided to make this the best Halloween ever. Our pillowcases were already heavy, but the trick was to get enough candy so that we didn't run out until the next Halloween. So we found some sticks and hid in some bushes. We waited for some other kids to come by and then, with our sticks raised above our heads, jumped out screaming our slogans: Suck My Dick! and Lick My Breast!

It worked like a charm. The witches dropped their bags and ran like hell. We chased Batman and Robin down and stole their plastic pumpkins. An hour later our pillow cases were filled. We left our candy in some bushes then went to the house on Hawthorne where we knew there was a big box filled with Butterfingers. Some of the people in our neighborhood were too old or lazy to keep answering the door so they just left the candy outside with a note: Take Two.

Suck June and I dumped the whole box into our pillowcases. We were getting close to the graveyard, so Suck June said we should feed the dead, that in doing so it would bring us great blessings and our dreams would come true. It sounded weird to me, but in Suck June's house was a little shrine with pictures of old people that were long dead. There was always incense burning around it, and sometimes I would see a slice of cake on a plate there as we walked by to get to her room and play card games such as Crazy Eights, War, and Go Fish.

The sky was huge with bats fluttering through the moon. The gravestones glowed, and so did we, our pale costumes ghostly and strange in that light. We went around setting Butterfingers on the tombstones and marble slabs. It was creepy. I felt like we were doing something wrong. There were these misty streams wandering around and it seemed like the dead bodies were in the mist, floating, watching us. When we entered the children's section of the graveyard I became scared and said we should keep trick or treating so that we would never run out of candy.

But we have to feed the children, Suck June said.

People can't eat anything when they're dead, I told her.

That's not true, Suck June said. Dead people are people too. We must feed the children. So we went down in there where the kids are buried, and set Butterfingers next to the Hotwheels and Barbies and dump trucks and flowers scattered above their bones. At the bottom of the hill was a fresh grave, the rise of red earth looking sad and lonely against the backdrop of rickety trees. Suck June dug a little hole in it and, after peeling the wrappers off several Butterfingers, stuck them in and buried them over. Hold your breath and close your eyes and make a wish, she said.

I wished that I would become invisible to everybody in the world but Suck June. I told Suck June about my wish, then asked her what her wish was.

If I tell you, it won't come true, Suck June said, and pulled the upper part of her costume down so that it dangled from her waist. Her breasts were in the moonlight. They weren't anything. I pulled down mine, and we sat next to the child's grave eating Butterfingers. We ate a whole bunch then got back into our costumes and started walking. As we reached the road a police car pulled over and the cop hopped out real quick. He sort of jumped in our direction, and we froze. Suck June dropped her candy. The cop walked faster, like he'd locked his focus on us, and I took a step back. The cop walked faster still. Run, I said. We turned and ran as fast as we could. I was entering the children's section when I heard Suck June shouting, Suck my dick! Suck my dick!

I stopped. I knew I should do something, but what?

Suck my dick! Suck June screamed.

I ran back to where the cop was holding Suck June down in the grass. I saw him yank the costume down to her waist. That's when she stopped screaming. We were in trouble. Running away wouldn't do, so I walked over there by which time the cop had taken Suck June's costume entirely off. He was holding it in one hand, looking at it, while pressing Suck June down in the grass with his other hand. When he saw me standing there he said, Take that thing off, goddammit!

I did what he said. He then yanked Suck June up by the arm and she flopped around like a Raggedy Ann doll with black hair. He grabbed my arm and hauled us both back to his car where he locked us up in his back seat. Suck June was crying. I told her don't worry, but in a few minutes there were three more police cars at the graveyard and the cops were asking us questions. They wanted to know where we found our costumes, and we told them it was down in the woods by the creek.

The cops took us to Suck June's house first. As soon as the car pulled into the drive, her parents hobbled out in their robes and sandals, their faces hard and afraid of bad news. When they saw their daughter get out of the car, wearing only her underwear, it was a true Halloween spectacle. Her parents turned into ghouls for a moment, their mouths hanging open and seeming to drip green slime from their corners. When the cop told them that nothing bad had happened to Suck June, that Suck June had been terrorizing the neighborhood dressed in valuable evidence needed for the solving of a double murder case, the ghouls dried up and disappeared. It was her parents standing there once more, and they did not look happy. We were, after all, only nine, and already a cop was bringing us home to our parents.

As the cop pulled out of Suck June's drive, I saw her mother, who was only a little bit taller than Suck June, scowling at her and scolding her. I turned my head to watch as the police cruiser headed up Lothian Drive. I like to think I imagined what I saw next, but in my heart I know it happened. Suck June reached up a hand as if to protect herself, and her mother slapped her, knocking her into the monkey grass. Just then the trees blocked them out.

My own parents were thrilled. My dad the famous communist took it as a metaphor for America, a Machiavellian switching of skin, he called it, where upper class children were gutted and used as masks to conceal the parasite eating away at the capitalist system. Those kids are better off dead anyway, he added, and said that Suck June and I were little miracle workers, weren't we? We'd raised the dead. As for my mom the sculptress, she wanted to know every little detail. She grilled the cops in our kitchen as I put on my clothes, and then the cops took my mom and me down to the woods where, by flashlight, I showed them where we found our costumes. The case was fresh still. Suck June and I had screwed up what would have been an informative crime scene.

The next night on the six o'clock news they said our names, mine and Suck June's. The newsman did not say a word about how we danced through Waverly Hills wearing the naked bodies of murdered children, nothing about the feelings we'd had, that strange power that we felt when dressed up in skins that were not our own, or the plastic pumpkins we'd robbed from Batman and Robin, or the Butterfingers we fed the dead children.

It was exhilarating, hearing our names mentioned on TV. I felt famous for a few days, but Suck June was barred from seeing me. She told me not to come over anymore, not to talk to her. Whenever I saw Suck June in her yard, she would not even look my way.

My wish had come true in reverse. To Suck June, I was invisible. I should have tried harder, but later, in high school, Suck June drove her mother's Honda to Lake Jackson where, using a length of garden hose and some duct tape, she fed herself the fumes that would break her heart.

THE COON

His old friend floats in the fix, a watery cemetery, his kitchen with sticky feet, a battered shack and swampy woods wearing dresses and pearls and trash pile hats. Wearing faded overalls patched with velvet cows she emerges elfin in a murky wind-whipped field, white violets in her hair. And here, a naked slave rope-tied between Grecian columns, the remains of a cracker plantation burned by Seminoles in 1836: she struggles and seethes, contorted and red-fleshed and Dektol-wet and adorable. In the steady safelight glow he watches her watch *Star Trek* stomach-down on her mother's bed, lazy-ankled and bronze with spaceships in her eyes; and acting dead in the dirt of a

John Oliver Hodges

peach-gut road in Georgia, selenium possums like clock-numerals all around her, their bright silvery tails reaching out to stab her, hurt her. He washes her in a plastic tray by the sink. He runs his fingers over the slippery surfaces of her skin, touching her. He puts her in his blotter book and goes to bed.

Near noon the door knocks and his new friend comes in, pale-faced and mildly hyper with lipstick on. "So how was it?" she says, bubbling. "Did you print any of me? I want to see them."

"They're damp," he tells her, thinking of the deadgirl clock, the possums, the fun they'd had that hot July day, stopping the car now and then to peel one, bloody, off the shoulder to put in his trunk for making pictures with later. And her mouth, always her mouth. And she takes off her clothes and spreadeagles in the dirt.

"Come on," his new friend says, and sits on the bed with him and bounces the springs, bristling all over, this enthusiasm. "Show me," she insists. "I want to see them."

He reaches for the ashtray and lights a cigaret. He tells her he needs to cure the pictures first, needs to spot them with toner and make them nice, give them the full treatment, all the TLC they deserve. She takes off her work clothes and gets under the sheet with him and they fuck.

After that, while she's walking through the house to get to the bathroom to wash, something moves in the corner of her eye. She looks through the window glass, and at first thinks it's a dog out there. It's huge, this thing, a large grey ball tapping the ground with narrow black-stained paws. "A coon," she says. "There's a coon in the yard!"

A coon, he thinks, and comes out in his boxer shorts and they stand by the window watching it. "Neat," he says.

"Don't coons come out mostly at night?" she says.

"Yeah, strange," he says.

"I wonder if it's rabid?" she says.

The coon stands on its hind legs and sniffs the air. Not liking the smell, it hurries away into the little woods.

She showers.

He smokes in the kitchen cutting garlic on the counter. He fries tofu squares in butter and makes them sandwiches which he puts on paper plates with Cheese Curls. They eat side by side on the couch, her in a red towel crunching, him in his boxers and bony feet chewing. When she's gone back off to work, he gets the blotter book from where he'd concealed it in the dresser, and opens it, and his old friend stares up at him again, flat on her back and surrounded by the decomposing faces of blanch-toothed roadkills. Immediately he wants to change dimensions, wants to shrink down so small, and smaller, small enough to crawl into the picture, into the paper, and be with her forever, not behind the camera-glass as it always had been, but there, by her side.

Disgusted, he shuts the book. He wishes he'd left those negatives be, sort of, but how could he? Impossible. Either way, he knows, it can only bring self-loathing and regret, this. Her mouth and flesh. Printing her. He really should have known.

He dresses, figures he'll drive south to Beeps now and drink beer in the music, and smoke and watch the halter-topped lesbians serve Purple People Eaters and flip burgers behind the bar. He'll even take some pictures for a change, put a semblance of passion into the business of chipping off little pieces of the world, processing things, preserving them.

He loads his Rolleicord. As he crosses the yard to get to the car the coon jumps from the tin shed housing his old motorbike that once worked fine. That bike, all that had been wrong with it was a fuse, yet he'd started taking it apart one day, trying to fix it. He lost track of what went where, and so now it sits through the seasons, the two flats melding with dirt. On that bike she first kissed him, pressing her warm lips against his neck as he carried them helmetless through time and space. On that bike he'd reached his hand back under her dress and felt her thigh as the wind curried the cheap tan fabric.

John Oliver Hodges

The coon runs a ways through the grass and stops, stands on its hind legs and stares at him, the two glassy eyes gleaming brightly within the dark furry patches. He thinks the coon might be angry, and he steps back, having the sense it might want to charge him. And he thinks this might make a neat picture, actually, and so he takes the Rolleicord out of his bag and pops open the viewfinder.

The coon snorts and takes off into the woods.

He follows at a distance, enjoying the sight of this big bushy creature outside in the daylight. The coon crawls onto the declivity leading down to the street, and he guesses the show is over. He turns, heads back to the car. He reaches for the door and there's this thump, a scream, then a woman's pained and sorrowful "Ohhhhhh."

He runs to the ledge and looks over, sees the coon in the middle of the street struggling to right itself, make things work, screaming as the approaching cars slow. The coon doesn't seem to understand what has happened, and as it hobbles to get away it throws its head back, as if looking for the larger animal with its teeth stuck in its side, but there's nothing there.

He can't look at this. He walks to the side of the house and lies down in the grass beside the garden, the ice-green sprouts of lettuce happy in the sun, and the frilly shoots of carrots that have survived the winter. Spiderworts sway in the breeze, and they hurt, the lavender petals clashing so sharp against the sick feeling growing in his heart.

It is his fault! He chased it into the street! He might as well have taken a spear and stabbed the thing through himself! So stupid, always, messing everything up. She'd said he was a hater of women for having taken her picture in such ways, for making her be lewd and do those things that she did. There was nothing artistic about a naked girl pretending to be a clock, she told him. It was obscene, a man exercising his control, nothing more, and really, it was clichéd and stupid. He'd even had her crawl down into dug ground once, a grave waiting to be filled and, as usual, take off her clothes and act dead in the wet red clay. There was something missing, she said, a piece of his brain must have been damaged at some point; and it was true, he had fallen many times as a child and blacked out; he did these things on purpose, diving off the roof, jumping in front of cars, and always, never, never crying. His parents took him to a doctor, complaining that the child felt no pain, but the doctor, after banging his knees and looking down his throat said the child was fine, nothing wrong with him. I was dumb, she said. I didn't know better. You took advantage of me, made me an object. She told him this in a letter that she'd sent from Sarah Lawrence College where she'd begun her education, on scholarship, and it was the last letter he'd received from his old friend. It didn't matter how much pleading and wishing and hoping he did after that. All his letters came back: return to sender.

Well, he never went to college, even though the money was there for him to go. Boo hoo hooey. Instead he used the money for cameras and film and took a million pictures. It all seems like such foolish waste now, but nobody ever told him better. Nobody ever told him anything, not really, not his father. His father was a writer, his mother a painter. They were always at it, typing and brushing. There was no time for lessons and guidance and walking in the woods. There was no time for anything but eating, and after that sleeping. In the morning they'd pick up where they left off the day before, typing and brushing, and he'd either go to school or climb a tree or throw a bottle against a wall, feeling blissful in the small explosion he'd created, in the shattering sound and beautiful twinkling glass.

He doesn't care much for sitting in the garden like this, thinking stupid things, remembering, so he gets up to go do what he'd started out to do in the first place, go to Beeps, but heading for the car he sees a woman's head there poking up from the ledge, level with the ground, a ball, a head with brown curly hair and glasses just resting there. The mouth on the head goes, "Did you see it?"

He thinks he's in trouble. Maybe this woman had seen him

standing in the woods? Maybe she'd seen him chase the coon into the road? Maybe she'd been looking at him when the coon ran in front of her car?

"I heard it scream," he says.

"It was me that hit it," she says, and smiles, embarrassed. "I just happen to be with the wildlife and game commission," she continues. "Did you see where it went?"

"No," he says, "I guess it ran off."

"Do you think it's okay?"

"I don't know," he says.

The head thanks him and lowers, disappearing, him having a pretty good mind as to where the coon has gone. There is a large drain built into the curb at the bottom of the hill, a dark square which leads into a dark room. He's seen people crawling down into it, homeless people, bums. Surely that's where it is, hiding from the light in the damp shadows, holding its pain to itself, doing the only thing it knows how to do. Standing in the yard under the big round sun he makes a promise. When he gets back from Beeps he'll make a fire and burn every last scrap of her, all of the negatives and all of the pictures and test strips. It's hardly a big deal, nothing to get all excited about, or bent out of shape over.

Still, as he drives, he keeps thinking, damn him, and damn her, saying that he never loved her! It isn't true! He did love her, and still does love her to this day, over three years later. Object! How dare her say those things, those lies, and he wants to get rid of her, hate her, and the sooner he forgets her forever the better, and so he turns the car around, no time to waste, and heads for home, angry, and angrier. He's going to burn her goddammit, take the scissors to her and cut her up, gouge out her eyes and stab her, stab her in the heart, in the stomach, stab her breasts and jam the scissors up between her legs. It's not fair that she should stick around in his head like this, and it's not fair to his new friend. He can't love her right. He thinks of his old friend while fucking her, and it's all such a sad stupid comedy that he begins to laugh, laughing, it's all he can do. He's thinking of witchcraft and voodoo, like maybe that stuff is real, that when he cuts off her feet, wherever she is in real life, she'll feel his pain. Her ankles will start to bleed. Oh, what's this, there's blood on my ankles! She'll panic like he panicked when he read her letter. No! No! Don't let this be real! But it will be, and he won't stop. He'll turn his back on her, knowing as he stabs that somewhere in this world a girl screams.

TRAINED TO LIVE

I'm starting to like Queens, love Queens, really. Queens grows on
you. Come live in Queens, you'll see. The people, the great diversity,
the families in the parks throwing colorful balls to each other, flying kites, roasting frankfurters over coals, it warms you, just seeing
all that happiness, all those people in fun-loving communion. I get
warm, but I'm filled with longing. I need to make contacts, get with
some of these gorgeous girls all over, but I'm shy. I'm screwy. I'm
about dying inside for intimate company, and crying over how terrible I am at getting it. I've got this nice apartment in Queens that my
brother is letting me stay in while he's on sabbatical in Finland, yet

look how lonely I am.

In Queens, this routine.

I ride the bus to work each morning early, teach my classes, then loosen my tie and walk the four miles home, stopping at Key Foods for a six pack of Natural Light beer and one of those large cans of Foster's, which I stuff into my knapsack, something to drink when I get home and am lonely and have nothing to do but watch TV and smoke cigarettes and eat and sleep. I used to spend a lot of time writing short stories, but finally just said fuck it. I couldn't get them published. I wrote probably a hundred short stories, thinking that I might have something to offer the world, but all of it, it just came back to me in the mail. That's my life. Nothing but loneliness and failure. I'm so lonely that I call my ex-wife on my brother's phone, tell her about Amelia Chong, how in class today she said, "Do you know Philbert Haws?" She was speaking of her academic advisor, but I replied, "Fill her bras?" Amelia said, "What?" and I repeat-ed myself nonchalant, like I was truly sincere and curious. "Fill her bras?" I said in front of the whole class. Amelia blushed. Her mouth started trembling. The whole class was laughing at her, and her cute hand came up to hide her lips from view.

"You were screwing with her," my ex says.

"No, I swear, that's what I thought she said, but I loved how she responded, you know, bringing her hand up to her mouth like that?"

"Does she have big ones?"

"I don't think so."

"She probably thought you were commenting on her size."

"It was an innocent mistake," I say.

"You should ask her out."

"Don't be ridiculous."

"She likes you."

"Are you serious? Are you really serious?"

"Yes, you idiot, she wouldn't blush if she didn't like you."

"That's crazy," I say.

"You're the one who's crazy," my ex says, "You complain to me about being lonely, but why don't you do something about it?"

"She's way too young."

"Don't be ridick."

"She's my student."

"That never stopped your dad. It never stopped your brother."

"It's absolutely out of the question," I say, and feel so sad suddenly.

My dad married three of his students. The second one, my mother, was fifteen years younger than him.

"Ask her out for coffee."

"Are you serious?"

"Fool, that's old. Everybody knows that. From what you've said I can tell she likes you, but you, just because you can't ever do the expected thing, ruin things for everybody. That's the big problem you need to try and overcome in life, your stupid insistence that everything normal is evil. That's why you always end up hanging out with degenerates. It's also why your stories aren't any good. You don't know how to not go against the grain. You need to write something that people besides degenerates can respond to favorably. People don't want to read about girls having fathers who are doctors who sew their assholes shut so that when they shit it comes out of their vaginas. You still haven't figured that out. It's really amazing, you know."

"I'm a piece of work."

"You really ought to try to get over this thing with your mother. It's very sad."

"Now who's being ridick?"

"You're a sad sack of shit," my ex says, and I begin to cry a little.

In Queens, where masala cashew sacks cost two bucks at Indian restaurants, and the June sun heats the streets to a fine mist that rises and flaps the green leaves of the trees, and pigeons coo, and Jewish beggars hold out their hands to you, and people honk their horns, they love it, honking horns, banging on their horns, holding their horns down while cussing. Once, I saw a woman driver get pissed and stop her car in the middle of the street. The driver behind her, the one she was blocking, stuck his head out of the van window and yelled, "You crazy fuckin bitch, whassa hellsa a matta witcha?" Saw the woman get out of her car and scream back, wagging her finger as she screams, in her Queen's accent, "Don't you tell me nothing you slimy bastard!" And the man in the van: "Oh, you're fuckin pregnant, kill your kid, you crazy nut, get back in your goddamn car you stupid fuckin cunt!"

That's Queens, it grows on you. At night I watch the news. A man slams his wife's head in with a brick, a man shoots his wife and children, a man starves his children, a baby is found on a sidewalk, an apartment building burns down because the Hassidic Jews are not allowed to turn off the stove at certain times during the month, yes, all manner of gruesomeness, a bus driver stabbed, a nun raped in her car, a female jogger stabbed in the reeds by the lake, and raped, and an art student gang-raped in a parking lot in broad daylight. So says the anchorwoman at night. According to the diagram she shows us, the crime was committed beside one of the wheel stops.

And The Barber, as my students call me, this for how I cut their papers to shreds, lives on. They know not that The Barber is lonely, that he feels like a thing on a schedule, a desperate ghost going through motions, trying not to feel while life's intensity bores deep, infusing his blood with hot agony, an overload of sights that drives him crazy nights, when his forgetfulness ebbs away and memory and lust creep in and he can't turn off his brain. The pictures, the details of his days roar, haunt him, keep him up, the smallest things: two birds on a sidewalk with locked beaks, the people on the buses that he sees, their faces, and the eerie stones on the slabs of the Jewish dead grace whose brain's convolutions? His—so many glittery yarmulkes in the gutters—and the girls, the Asians who break his heart every time. "This is my stop too, I'm trying to get off," one says. Another in Converse high-tops, black to go with her black ponytail, glides down Jewel Avenue on a skateboard with orange wheels. Standing between the yogurts and a table of bread, an Italian guy says to his old mother: "Would'ya shut up for a minute and lemme get a word in edgewise?" I admire how close they are.

Before I know it I'm at work again, the university full of nuns. I pass nuns in the halls, don't say, "Hi Sister," don't say, "Hi Brother" to the priests I pass, but nor do I say "Shalom" to the Jews I pass daily on the strip where I buy vegetables and limes and plastic boxes of salted nuts. Say "Hi" to people in Queens, they look at you askew, with contempt, like *What is wrong with you? Are you retarded? Are you sexually deranged?* It's no wonder my students are afraid to look at things, to observe things closely, to stare. I tell them that stare rhymes with share, that if they don't stare they might not have much to share. To show them that I practice what I preach, I mention that on Main Street where all the Jewish action is, a fancy shoe store was having a sale the other day. As I walked by I looked at the shoes on display on the table and noticed that all of them sported the word Adolfo in large silver letters on the insoles. I'd never known there was a shoe brand called Adolfo, but then I looked around and noticed that the Jewish men walking up and down the sidewalk were all wearing these very same shoes. That word *Adolf* was right there pressed against the bottom of their feet all day, was that strange? It didn't mean anything necessarily, but I felt as if I had uncovered a secret.

I'm affecting them, though, I know, infecting them, I see results.

They are learning to be not so afraid to look.

Today, in class, Amelia Chong, short girl, wears black flip-flops, and it's the first time I've seen her feet unshod. I gotta be careful. I so much as glance Amelia's direction, another girl student takes note, *Oh The Barber is lusty*. It's crazed, how they can be so inattentive about the magic of their own lives, yet notice a professor take note of a flash of gray in a weft-work of chair-leg and cross-peg. Good

Lord, Lord have mercy. It's the last day of school. We are having a party. One by one my students stand up front and read from their work while we eat egg sandwiches (Ljonja from Kosova brought those) and chew gummy bears (a gift from Azu from Afghanistan) and plow into doughnuts (Julius from Guam) and drink purified water from plastic bottles, what Amelia Chong tugged in in a heavy cardboard box, huffing into the room late with sweat on her lovely brow, The Barber noticing all: *The girl is magic.*

After class, I assess my performance for the semester, coming to terms with the fact that I may never see any of these souls, sure, call them souls, again—but Amelia comes back in. She confesses that her I-Search Paper, the one about the unisex alternative to the Boy Scouts and Girl Scouts of America, what I suggested she title "Goy Scouts" is not included in her folder. The Barber shakes his head sadly, tells her he's got to stick by the numbers. If the numbers aren't there, what can he do? Amelia's mouth trembles. Up comes the hand to hide it. "Will you take it late?" she wants to know, hushy hush, and The Barber, if there's one thing he hate's it's giving F's, says, "Grades are due next Monday. If you can get it to me before then, good. If not, all I can tell you is I'm sorry."

"Oh, thank you, thank you," Amelia says, and sort of curtsies, and I give her my brother's number, sneaking glimpses of her sacred toes as she, strange Mongolian, writes the numbers down in her Personal Organizer, me thinking, *If she only knew.*

Before Amelia Chong, I am nothing but a worm.

I'm horny. It happens. A time comes where you got to admit such things, no matter how disagreeable they are to you, no matter how much you try to deny the truth or just wish to hell God wasn't so clever in his cruelty. The truth is, I would love nothing more in the world than to hold Amelia Chong in my arms, to put my hand on the back of her silky head, to hug her tight and feel her heart beat against me all night on into the next millennium, especially now that my ex has pointed out to me that by not making the effort I simply ruin things for everybody.

I'm walking back from school, my knapsack laden down with student portfolios, and I stop at Key Foods, get my beer, leave. I'm on my way home, but a girl I recognize—she's the Key Foods cashier who looks exactly like Kate Moss—stands at the pay phone, talking into it in the Queens sunlight raining down on her, causing her to shine, just covering her all over and attacking her like crazy. She's dressed not in her work clothes, but in yellow Capri-style pants made of soft cotton, and wears cheap green flip-flops. Her tight pink shirt doesn't cover her bra straps, and she has pink butterflies in her blond hair all pinned up in tangles on the back of her head so that her neck too is beat by the sun.

I take it in, all that mess and mass of young woman, of yellowishness and pink, and she seems large to me even though she is skinny, her feet long and large and hefty and competent, and the swatch of flesh above her stretch pants, her midriff, seems large too, wide and unabashed. There is jewelry on her, in her navel, on her face, and she is frightening. My impulse is to walk on, be the ghost I know myself to be, just don't disturb shit. But she gets off the phone just then. She looks me straight on, and suddenly I'm an old hand at this. I say, "Hey Girl," like I know her. Her eyes brighten, she squares her shoulders, stands up straighter. I say, "Anybody ever tell you you look exactly like Kate Moss?"

Her mouth opens, letting in the light. Can she believe her ears?

"I've been looking for you on the sides of buildings," I say.

"Get outta here," she says.

"You off?"

"Yeah, but you're the guy who buys a lot of chips," she says.

"You must live nearby," I say. As long as I know I'm pretending, I can act any way, even if it's like an arrogant jerk, but it's weird. I say, as if to persuade her that I'm incapable of smashing her face in with a brick, "I'm a English professor."

"I suck at English."

"You want to get some coffee with me?"

She laughs. "Sure."

What a pro I am! Maybe I'm not the ugliest oaf ever to live on the planet. My ex always told me that women are attracted to me, that I am a tall olive-skinned God with legs sexy enough to drown a hippopotamus in. In fact, she used to become very mad because of how much she liked my legs. And my feet. It wasn't fair, she said, that each time summer came around I never had to do anything to make my feet presentable in case I wanted to wear sandals, presenting them to the world, which I never did. If you look closely at most women's feet, she said, you will notice calluses ringing their heels.

I say, "In case you're worried, I dropped my hatchet off at the sharpener's this morning. It won't be ready for a couple more days."

She looks me over, but lets it go. "Anna," she says, and lifts her skinny white arm my way. It's like a white wire.

We shake.

Anna walks with me down Main Street in her flip-flops. "I've got this nice apartment," I tell her, and mention that I always feel that it's going to waste because I'm the only one in it. I tell her of my bro the Psych professor now in Finland, how I've taken over his life since I divorced my wife. I say, "If you want, we can coffee it up at my place," and I'm thinking *Coffee it up? Did I say Coffee it up?*

"Yeah, I like that idea better," Anna says.

The word *better*, in Anna's Queens' accent, comes out as "bettah," and is kind of nasally, nothing at all like Kate Moss's cool British business going on. Tell the truth, I don't much care for the dialect of Queens. All truth told, the Queens' dialect has been wearing on my nerves lately. Anna's accent isn't as bad as most, though, and it sounds to me as if she's been trying to lose it.

I see a cab just then, so, ridiculously, hail it.

We get in it.

As we pass the Jewish movie theatre, I tell Anna I saw on the news last night that a beloved neighborhood tabby cat was found stomped to death in the alley behind it. The cat's name was Mister Pants.

"That's horrible," Anna says.

"Do you think the stomper-onner wore Adolfos?"

"What?"

"Nothing," I say, and say, "*Meet The Fockers*, that's what they're playing."

The cab lets us off in front of my brother's cul-de-sac, and we walk the walk together, some of my neighbors who I've never met—the obese one with tubes snaking out his nose and the woman with an orange dog—watching us from their stoops because what else are they going to watch from their stoops? They watch whatever walks in front of them; but I let us in with my brother's keys, in the kitchen pour Foster's beer into my brother's thick plastic glasses, each glass shaped like a nuclear cooling tower, I have no idea why—cups I guess you'd have to call them, they're the only glasses he's got. Then on the pull-out bed, in couch position, we toast the wordless toast of people too cool for school, and drink. We talk, becoming friends. I'm just happy Anna has come here. I'm impressed with myself. We are telling stories, admiring each other, but Anna out of nowhere wants to know how much money I can give her.

I think about this.

"You're blushing," she says. She puts her hand on my leg, rubs it up and down.

"Do you need a lot of money?"

"You said you were a English teacher."

"Adjunct," I say. "I bet cashiers make more. We don't get paid much."

Anna laughs. Her laugh is high and sweet, only a little bit nasally. "Now I understand why you live in this dump," she says.

"Really? You don't think it's nice?"

"This place sucks ass," she says. "All these co-ops suck ass. The walls are paper thin, haven't you noticed? There's no back door, the people who live here are useless lumps with nothing to say but who talk way too much. Did you see them hanging out there with nothing to do? The only thing that excites them are dogs and cats, they talk to them, you know, like they are children. You say your brother bought this place? Doesn't he have to pay like five hundred dollars a month for them to collect his garbage? He pays them to wake him up with the sound of their lawnmowers and weed eaters, right? Ha ha ha! On the ground floor, no less, that really bites."

"I didn't realize," I say. I think Anna has made some good points.

"I don't mean to be a rag here, but I need shit, you know what I'm saying?"

"I have a ten dollar bill and a few ones."

"Big spender. I bet you have some corn chips though, ha ha!"

"My wife was into diamonds."

"I love diamonds."

"And Jack Daniel's."

"Two things that go together."

"If you steal my brother's quarters I won't tell him," I tell her.

"What quarters?"

"What he uses for laundry, I don't know, I guess it's what he's saved up over the years. He's got a big case full of quarters, but come to think of it, I don't want you stealing his quarters."

"Let me see them," Anna says.

"I wouldn't feel right."

Anna rubs up against me, kisses my cheek, nibbles on my jawbone. "Kate Moss is the most beautiful woman in the world," she says, almost whispers. "This might be your only chance to fuck the most beautiful woman in the world."

I consider this. I could always replace the quarters.

"You know you want to," Anna says.

"I'm a English professor."

"Adjunct," she says. She says, "Touch me."

I feel around on her, sip more beer from the cooling tower, and we kiss. I love the sour flavor of her mouth, how it mixes in with the beer, and her mouth is a good fit with mine, very Kate Mossy and delicious. But:

"How much do you have in the bank?" she wants to know between kisses.

"Nothing," I say.

"Listen," Anna says. "I don't think you should lie to me. My boyfriends call me pushy, but it's better to be pushy than to tell lies, don't you think?"

"I don't like lies either," I tell her, and say, "All liars will burn in the Lake of Fire," and I say, "Nothing is a figure of speech."

"Okay, well, yes, okay Mr. English Professor, what is it a figure of speech for? Two thousand dollars?"

"Lower," I say.

And blow her. I'm on the floor before her, on my knees while she, on the couch, has got her legs up. It happened sort of out of nowhere, but her pussy is shaved. The tiny sharp hairs growing back stab my nose and lips, but she enjoys it, the feeling of my tongue soft on her pee-hole, and crazy in circles around on her secret pearl. I was never great at this, I don't think, but Anna whispers yes each time I do something she likes. My ex's pussy anyway never got juicy this way. When Anna's yesses increase I let loose on her and it feels as if she is peeing in my face. Her whole body turns inside out and she's just so wet that I think I could drink her down like a beer.

We drink more beer. Then in the bedroom, on my brother's bed, Anna says, "See what I mean, look at this shit."

I say, "You don't like this bed?"

Anna explains that even though my bro obviously paid a ton for it, it sags in the middle, has this thick-ass mattress that is supposed to be good for your back, Posturepedic they call it, but that's exactly what it isn't. He paid for a lie. The cheapest bed available would be better. Same goes for the "stupid" wood floors that are supposed to be the cheese, but this wood floor accentuates the bad acoustics, Anna says, and is shellacked pointlessly. The place is an echo chamber, haven't you noticed? You hear your stupid neighbors burp and breathe, and if you think it's mean to call your neighbors stupid, wait a bit and listen to what they say. They cherish their plants. What it comes down to is your brother, like most people in the world, Anna says, people who buy beds so heavy you can't even move them, beds so high up that you can touch the ceiling with your foot, puts appearance over common sense. "I'd rather live in a trailer," Anna says, and lifts up onto her shoulders to touch the ceiling with her long bony foot.

"You're absolutely right," I say. I say, "I never noticed that," and suddenly I'm angry sort of. Anna has given me a glimpse of myself as a man so devoid of self-respect that he submits himself to widespread incompetence and stupidity. It's not something I care to dwell on, so I forget about it pretty quick.

We fuck. Then in the shower I scrub Anna's back with a loofah. We sleep through the night on that stupid bed. In the morning I'm up early, deranged, can hardly believe Kate Moss is in there under the covers. She's pretty awesome, I think, but I had noticed, while I was eating her pussy, some weird blistery-looking carbuncle thing or whatever down there in the tender folds. It worried me, but what was I to do? I put on coffee. I scramble eggs in case she, unlike my ex, likes them. I'm worried. What if I caught AIDS from Anna?

While Anna sleeps, I sit on my brother's stoop smoking Camel Lights, watching the children in the cul-de-sac. One child, a black boy no older than eleven, has got a full grown burly mustache, strange. He's bouncing a ball, sending it periodically through an imaginary hoop. A puny white boy says to him, "You suck milk out of your grandmother." The black boy, unfazed by the comment, says, "You suck Coke out your father's wiener." The little white boy, greatly agitated, screams, "You have five nipples!" The mustachioed black child, cool and collected, says, "You look like you need a breath mint." He shoots the basketball through the air, listening, waiting for the sound of the swish.

I love the wonderful dialogues of children. Last week in the laundry room it was little girls in shorts and pastel sandals talking cul-de-sac scandals, their tongues filthy like the tongues of their fathers, their accents nasal in the ways of their mothers, their lungs full of lead and their souls full of dog shit sightings everywhere all over, and pacifiers crusted in sidewalk vomit, pigeon corpses, cockroaches, myriad cigarette butts ringed in shades of lipstick, the petrified orange peels and the river of yarmulkes—it all complements them, makes dewy their skin, the lusty humans roiling in garbage, scooping it on, smearing it on, swallowing it all, and loving it, being it.

Anna comes out and sits with me, says can I at least give her ten dollars for a cab?

I slap Anna my ten-er.

In Queens, the largest of the New York City boroughs. It's huge, Queens, with beaches on the Atlantic and two international airports. The planes scream overhead all night and day, yet I'm only just now beginning to hear them. The outline of Queens looks like a shirt with a flowing tail, Brooklyn its left arm, Long Island its right. Anna folds my ten, slips it into the tight back pocket of her soft yellow pants. We hug. I walk her up to Main Street, but her apartment is close enough, she says, that she'll skip the cab. She'd like to hang out with me again, she says. She loves to drink, and loves cocaine, mushrooms, whatever, and especially she likes going to the beach. We should head out next Saturday to Jacob Riis Park, she says, and says that she won't go topless unless we walk over to Fort Tilden first. In Fort Tilden, Anna says, nobody cares what you do.

I freak, though, because my ex told me I would get AIDS if we ever divorced. But screw it. Worrying about it won't get me anywhere. Besides, I've got forty-four portfolios to read. I'm a slow reader. I read too carefully, it's ridiculous. I step inside, thinking I'll get to work, but everywhere I look I notice flaws, see things I don't like, impracticality galore going on here, a party in stupidity and I, apparently, am the birthday boy. This apartment is not nice. It's dismal, cave-like, horrific, the view from every window plain obnoxious—but double-fuck it. Get to work, you bastard, I tell myself, and whip out Amelia Chong's incomplete portfolio. Her first piece of revised in-class writing, entitled, "Trained To Live," begins:

As soon as we are born and out in the world, we are taught to the age of seven crawling, walking, speaking, learning ABC and 1-2-3's, becoming potty trained, tying our shoes, manners on please and thank you, riding a bike, learning to read and write, learning how to spell our names, memorizing our home address and phone number, learning math equations and functions such as plus, minus, times and divide.

I feel bad, ashamed, like I've cheated on Amelia, this thing I've done with Anna who can fill her bras—Anna's tits hung down like a fresh pair of running sneakers and could be grabbed up and yanked around. She was proud of them, of her nipples that shot out like logs and were long enough to cut in half, had you a chainsaw.

I'm twisted inside, my heart melty. I like that Amelia's are small. See her crawl, learning ABC. See Amelia learn manners on please, and grow into the young CBA (Chinese Born American) wonder she is today.

In Queens.

Packed in, crammed in, stuffed in, squashed in.

I take a walk. See crap all over the sidewalk: paper scraps, crack sacks, a plum pit, a lime sliver. The two concrete steps of the Pizza Professor have been painted bright red, the paint wet still, smelling toxic and radiating.

I simply know I've got AIDS.

Pigeon shit, sewage.

When my wife dumped me for a richer man, one who could buy her diamonds and designer plates, beauty products and an unlimited supply of Jack Daniel's, it was rough going, but I adjusted.

I applied for credit, no luck; but at least I gave great haircuts. She said living with me was like having her own personal hair stylist on hand. Whenever she wanted she could strip down naked and stand in the kitchen, or out in the yard as she sometimes did, and I would cut her hair, snipping away until it was perfect, exactly to her liking. The severed tufts would glide down her spine into the small of her back, catch in the gullies made by her clavicles, and settle on her shoulders and stick to her chest. Whenever I was done she would close her eyes and I would brush the hair away from her body with my hands.

Once back at my brother's place the phone sounds off. I grab it, press the button. Thinking it's my ex, I say, "I know I'm a piece of shit."

"Hello?" comes the voice.

"Amelia?" I say.

"Yeah."

"Oh, hey," I say.

"I worked on it," Amelia says. She says, " 'Tenderfeet Scouts' is my new title."

Her mouth in my mind does not tremble.

"Boys and girls both have tender feet, see?"

"Okay, sure," I say, holding back the impulse to explain a few things to Miss Amelia Chong.

"Remember how you told us we should tell the truth?"

"Yes, of course."

"I wrote the true story of me in the Brownies in Schenectady when we lived in Schenectady. The girls said I ate cats."

"Great," I say, and Amelia wants to know how to get her paper to me. I give her my bro's address. Amelia says she'll take the bus up from the Bronx. "Great," I say, and pace my bro's apartment. The door jambs are made of steel here. The blinds suck. The coffee maker sucks and the microwave sucks. The lighting completely "sucks ass," to use Anna's term; but Amelia arrives. I let her in. She hands me her folder. "Your class was the best," she says.

"Really?"

"The only class I felt guilty missing."

Short girl, a black cotton knee-length skirt on her today, its selvage a bright light rollicky blue. Amelia's jade ox rests against her breastbone, her lips shiny, not sopped up but slimy in the way of the small gloss-dab, a protective measure, spread it on, no cosmetic ridiculousness going on here.

The most horrific thing in the world, I think, are fake boobs.

Painted toenails aren't too peachy either.

"I liked having you in my class," I tell Amelia, "but rats aren't known for having friends."

"I'm supposed to marry a cock," Amelia says. "I'm supposed to turn into a great parent."

"I wish you were my mom," I say.

"Really?"

"I would hug you."

Up goes the hand, covering her mouth. What Amelia doesn't know is I have AIDS. She also doesn't know that ever since I contracted AIDS from Anna, I keep hearing Freddy Mercury from Queens sing "We Are the Champions." I can't get the damn song out of my brain.

"Would you like a peanut butter sandwich?" I say.

"Actually," Amelia says, "I haven't eaten."

"Good," I say. "That's great," I say. My ex has said that Amelia likes me. The only thing stopping me from ruling the world, she has said, is my hatred for my mother. I say, "When I was in the Boy Scouts, I almost cut my finger off while gutting a fish."

"Ouch," Amelia says. I show her the scar. She is impressed.

I spread Amelia's bread over with Jiff, close her sandwich, hand it over, watch her mouth open, bite into it, short girl. I say, "Good?"

"Peanuts have lots of protein." She wants to be a pharmacist, and will one day be one, I am sure of it.

"Nothing wrong with protein," I say.

And we sit, sit, just sit here on my brother's fold-out bed, in couch position, Amelia chewing Chinesely, peanut butter in her stomach now. This may sound gross, but I feel an emotional connection with that peanut butter. How wonderful, I think, to be digested by Amelia. I watch Amelia's mouth now as she eats, kosher crumbs on her lips. Seeing Amelia calms me, but I have AIDS. I can smell her. You can fuck her, I hear my ex say.

"My dad," Amelia says, chewing, "said eating peanut butter made him feel good. Peanuts are close to the earth. Peanuts taste like dirt."

"You must've loved your dad," I say.

"He was my hero."

"I wish I was him," I say.

Amelia's lips tremble. A bread crumb floats down. She pulls her sandwich away. The hand rises. I grab her wrist. I say, "Why?"

Amelia drops her sandwich into her lap, tries yanking back her hand.

"Why do you hide your mouth?" I ask.

Her mouth opens larger, her lips trembling grotesquely, her nostrils flaring. The sight is ghastly. Can I use such a word? Whatever the case, I let go her wrist. The hand covers the show. I pretend she's saved me the burden of having to see her disgusting mouth.

"Disgusting" was a favorite word of my mother's.

I look at the blank TV.

After a moment Amelia says, "I think you are hurting."

"I'm sorry about your father," I say.

"In China, when a person dies, paper boats are set in the nearby streams."

I picture myself at the helm of a paper boat, floating downstream, in Queens. While I was alive, did I have the courage to bash my mother's face in with a brick, get my name spoken out loud on the news? I tell Amelia I'm sorry if I acted weird. I should not have grabbed her wrist like that. I tell Amelia that I have AIDS, and Amelia nods her head, really seeming to understand, to care. Amelia puts her hand on my arm, squeezes it, then begins to answer my question about her mouth.

John Oliver Hodges

DTEHSHUH

Kosher Cove; night:

Captain Boo (only just recently a captain, just recently having purchased the forty-year-old boat, never having sailed a day in his life before that!) kept looking at the shore, a bit worried, a bit confused, ask me. He thought the boat was drifting, the anchor dragging. It'd be shitty, waking up to the sound of the boat hitting a rock, death-cold water pouring in through a hole in the keel. Each time the captain looked the shore just seemed to be closer. Captain Boo had one of those global positioning devices, however (a GPS), so before long he decided it was only a trick of imagination.

Then the beer and wine were gone, drunk up, and all at once the happy spirit coursing through our veins dissipated, just fucking shrunk away. I wanted to keep on, you know, talking, having fun, but everybody went down to sleep and I was left alone on the bow. I ran the gaff through the water, watching the bright glowing light swirling mysteriously around the stick, green and beautiful with so many magic bubbles. I ran the gaff back and forth, wondering if those Jews, as they swam for their lives, if their bodies were haloed in this cold green fire.

Or their souls, could they be down there still? Calling out in drowning cries? If they were, I bet they were going: *Where art thou, Oh Lord! Where art thou?*

* * *

Kosher Cove; morning:

I wake to bright sunlight clear and perfect across the water, and in the sky, the silver boat bars sharp in the eye. The peaks of the towering Chilkats appear to be heaped with billions of tons of confectioners' sugar.

I zip out of my bag.

Guessing I'm first up, I squint around. It's warm, couldn't ask for better weather, a pleasant wind blows; *Captain Boo, it's time to raise the sails! Where art thou, Captain Boo?*

The pump-up rests over the hatch, bungeed to the mast with our packs and camping supplies. I push the stuff aside to look in through the plexi, wake our trusted captain from his watery dreams, but get an eyeful. Our beloved captain is pumping Robbi; her legs and arms come out of his orange backside, waving frantically; together they are a purple god from some backwoods country, the kind who sit on rocks all day waving their many arms. Only this god is faceless. This god jerks and flitters and wiggles and is twisted. I'm starting to feel guilty for watching them, but Jaura rises up behind me and goes: "You sick fuck."

"Hey," I say, "is Captain Boo up?"

"You know he's not up," Jaura says, lighting her first Drum of the day. "Why don't you reach in there and get his attention, I'm serious, we need to get moving."

"Can I get one of those?"

Jaura tosses me the Drum and I roll one and light it, and check out Kosher Mountain over there, trying to pick out bears or some other kind of neat wildlife. I blow my smoke and think of the drowned Jews, sixteen of them the story goes. I imagine their ghosts staring out at us from the shoreline, their eyes aglint with silver sparkles. Some of the Jews are in the trees, lounging in branches, while others are balanced on crags.

Silas in boxers fumbles along starboard with an empty yogurt cup filled with coffee, rubbing sleep out of his eyes—he looks like a two-hundred pound baby in diapers doing that—and he wants a Drum too, he says. So I roll Silas a Drum—he's my great buddy, Silas—and we smoke with legs dangling over the side of the boat, drinking his black coffee in the sunshine, no sugar in it, just soaking up the wonderful morning. His coffee tastes like strawberries.

Silas says that when he looks at the ridges of the mountains he thinks of skateboarding. "Wouldn't that be great," he says, "if the mountains were made of concrete and you were like this giant? Wouldn't it be great to drop in on that ridge over there?"

Jaura rolls her eyes for me to see only—she wants me to think Silas is dumb—and flicks the last of her Drum into the cold ass water.

"If we don't leave now," Jaura says, "the Brew Fest will start without us."

Jaura's real disgusted, it's all in the curl of her lips, her mouth filled with something awful bitter, a drop of battery acid maybe, or a handful of clover stems, if you've ever chewed on them. She's plain tired of waiting so starts yanking the pump-up out of the way, going, "This is getting ridiculous," in her smoker's breathing.

Such efforts won't be necessary, though, for Captain Boo appears on deck, shirtless and orange-chested, stretching his hairy arms in the light and smiling whitely, very much the gringo, Boo, not what you'd expect of a Spanish professor, but then, Boo's a bona fide polyglot too, speaks everything but Chinese, Japanese, Korean and all those types of weird languages. Right now Boo's face bespeaks contentment. His face sports a ball of orange hair on top, gives his face a clown-like look. Boo's face says it's fun acting innocent about what went down down there in the cellar, or the hull, whatever it's called, and his face says that within his bosom is a cherished secret, ha ha!

"We've been waiting," Jaura complains.

Captain Boo is about the most happy-to-be-alive guy you ever met. He just smiles at Jaura's impatience, yells, "Anchors up!" and soon put-puts us out of Kosher Cove.

I wave goodbye to the sixteen Jews.

We raise the sails, kill the engine, troll for King Salmon, Jaura complaining that we're not moving fast enough as Robbi in her yellow bikini tans on a slip of blue towel. Robbi's hair has been cut short and dyed pink so she's very colorful when you take her all in at once. "Anybody want some block?" she giggles, wiggling her bottle of lotion in the air.

That's pretty neat, Robbi, she's a self-contained wiggling party, all those wigglers, Captain Boo's offspring, wiggling up inside her. I can't help but wonder if those little wigglers, when viewed through a microscope in the habitat they are currently in, are surrounded by light brought into being by their motion. If they are, I bet that light is red.

* * *

Captain Boo has told us it's a ten-hour deal, but we've already

John Oliver Hodges

passed the twenty-hour mark, and Jaura's pissed, is out of tobacco. And speaking of piss, have you ever pissed off the side of a moving sailboat? There's something totally obscene about it, all those mountains around you, they're just too grand for words, not a cloud in the sky, it's all sun, and the sun is looking down on you too, the whole world opened up like a mouth, call it God's mouth, and what're you doing?

After a long ass fucking time we finally sail into Haines Harbor. It's after ten, not yet dark out, but the night is coming, it's getting dusky. I'm glad to finally get off the water, feel the safety of something hard and stable underfoot, but my legs are wobbly. I've got the wobbles. It's a feeling I've never had, this wobbliness. I'm not much of a boater. Captain Boo says it's good, I need *sea legs*, he says, and there's only one way to get sea legs, that's by sailing.

Jaura's off the dock lickety-split, propelled by her lust for nicotine into a frenzied search of a place to get that pack of Drum.

Silas wants to hit the bars.

Captain Boo says he'll kick back on the boat, nap some.

And Robbi, in a short-skirted blue velvet Devil's dress, with hiking boots on her feet, gray wool socks bunched around her ankles, when she jumps off the boat, I see she has the wobbles too, for she almost falls backwards into the slimy green water. That water is really nasty, with turds and trash floating in it. "I feel like I'm drunk," she says.

We've all got the wobbles.

* * *

The White Whale is packed. A five-piece band plays New Orleansy songs, everybody dances, frolics, drinks great beer as the pool tables snap. Even Jaura dances. Her mood has improved. She's no longer jonesing for tobacco, but the Drum company, she found out, has removed all of their items from the shelf due to a lawsuit going on in the industry. It makes Jaura happy, gives her something new to complain about for days yet to come.

Of course, the star of the floor is Robbi, she has a natural grace, a freckled face, and a flow that sets her apart from the other dancers. Perhaps I am exaggerating. Perhaps there is nothing remotely special about Robbi, but then why does everybody watch her? Even the women, I notice, watch her.

Silas wants another round. It's my turn, so I make to the bar for a pitcher.

This woman, fat and short with short black hair, has been looking at me all night. Whenever our eyes meet she makes this expression like she could eat me up, then shakes her head real fast and hard, peeling her eyes away as if mad at herself for dreaming. While waiting on that pitcher she scoots up close and grabs my arm. "I'm Kathy," she says, "my mother knew Sting."

"Sting?"

"The rock star Sting," she says, and grabs my hand. "My mother ate dinner with Sting three times."

"Oh," I say, "that's interesting."

"Can I buy you something?" she says, squeezing my hand with both of hers. "I'll buy you any beer you want."

"Hey, I appreciate it," I tell her, "but I'm just chilling. I gotta get this pitcher."

The woman flattens her mouth, sighs, throws up a hand as if to say Well, at least I tried.

I return to our table. The band has finished for the night. It's the juke box going now, a wonderful juke box they got, all kinds of great songs on it like "Ring My Bell" and "Saturday Night."

Jaura fills her glass. Silas fills the other glasses. We need to make another toast to our great trip, to all those killer whales we saw in Kosher Cove, to the seals and bears and other cool stuff we saw, but where's Robbi? Is she in the bathroom?

"She must've left with that guy," Jaura says.

"No, she would've said something," Silas says.

"Oh Sweetie," Jaura says.

"What?" Silas says.

"Nothing," Jaura says. "Just, you don't know Robbi. I went to school with her. You know what they called her?"

"You already told me," Silas says.

Jaura looks at me. "Her name was Slob-On-My-Knobby. She was, you know, kind of slutty?"

Silas shakes his head.

"Well," Jaura says, "she was. I don't see anything wrong in reporting the facts. Did you see her dancing with that guy? He was so totally gross."

"And what am I?" Silas says.

"What do you mean, what are you?"

"I've danced with her before."

Jaura flattens her mouth, shaking her head at the same time. "You're drunk," she says, looking at me when she says it.

"Stop ragging my ass," Silas says.

"I'm just talking, Baby, but seriously, did you see her rubbing her private against that dude's leg? I mean, maybe with jeans, but even then I wouldn't recommend it."

The pitcher shrinks, goes pop then is gone. I guess I'm drunk. That glass we poured for Robbi looks delicious, all golden. I'm thinking about it, but Jaura grabs it and draws it to her mouth and swallows a good one.

We get another pitcher.

The thickness of the bar has dwindled, people are leaving now and that woman, I notice, the fat one whose mother knows Sting, keeps looking my way, still doing that strange thing with her face whenever our eyes meet. When I hit the bar for another brewski she grabs my hand again, brushes herself against me and says, "I'm taking you home for a marshmallow roast, you don't mind, do you?"

I like meeting people, hearing what people say about themselves, their lives and mothers and all of that, but I don't know. There's a girl in Juneau that I love. We haven't gone out or anything. We've never even spoken to each other, but whenever I see her I become terribly frightened. I tell this woman, I say, "I guess I'm kinda hungry."

"Yes!" she says.

"I won't sleep with you," I tell her. "I just need a place to stay tonight."

She's really squeezing the hell out of my hand now, as if she's afraid to let go. I have to tug it to make it mine again. I tell her I'll say goodbye to my friends. This is a good arrangement. Now Silas and Jaura won't have to worry about me crowding them in their tent.

* * *

Kathy's van's old, a battered Econoline with a painting on the side of a pack of dogs attacking a bear. It smells like dogs, dog hair is everywhere, all over the seats, on the floor and the ceiling too even. "A dog lover," I say.

"Yeah, I love dogs," she says, and turns out of the lot and accelerates. "If you were a dog, what would you be?"

"A black one, maybe a retriever."

Kathy laughs. She's got a sucking laugh, how some people suck a lot when they laugh? That's hers. "No," she says, "You're a Dobie, definitely, a little baby Dobie."

"And what're you?"

"I've always been a Shepherd, even when I was little. You're Iranian or something, right? You're kind of dark."

"That's my Jewish side," I tell her.

"Hey," Kathy says.

Kathy drives up this mountain, a steep dirt road with lots of rocks and holes in it, and the road keeps getting steeper. It's the kind of steep road you dream of in your dreams, in those nightmares you get. The bunches of houses lining the road have dropped away. It's just woods now, spruce trees and hemlocks.

Kathy turns onto a driveway leading down to a house. A light on in the kitchen gives the place a cozy look, but I hear dogs. When she kills the engine, the barking grows louder. Within their barks I hear hard-rushing water, melted snow running fast down the mountain to the canal. "We're here," Kathy says.

"It's nice," I say.

"I wouldn't trade it for the world."

We get out of the van and she yells, "Ajax! Magenta! Shush!"

The dogs quiet at once.

The dogs are hooked up on runners, two huge German Shepherds standing side by side, their tongues hanging out thick and pink and dripping and catching the light from the kitchen window. Kathy says, "Aren't they sweeties?"

"Yeah. They look like some nice dogs," I say.

Kathy says, "Don't let them scare you, Dobie. They've got a lot of growl, but won't bite you, not unless I command them to. This is Dobie," Kathy says, and kneels in front of Ajax, or Magenta. She kisses each dog, runs her fingers through their thick fur, going, "This is Dobie," in a soft voice. "He's a friend, okay?"

When she lets them off their runners they trot over and sniff me out, poking me with noses that I don't find very cute, tell the truth, even though in the past I have thought fondly of doggy noses. These nose are just a little too big, I think, but the four of us then hit the steps and enter the house where Kathy swings wide the fridge door, pops a can of Guinness draft and hands it over. She pops her own can of Guinness draft. "To us," she says, and we knock cans. We talk about tomorrow's great event, the Alaskan Brew Fest, and she tells me that last year the man who won the Pilsner contest had his entry disqualified after they discovered he'd hopped it with Tlingit aspirin. She says, "They made him give back the trophy and they gave it to somebody else, isn't that fucked up?" I say, "What do you mean, Tlingit aspirin?" and she says, "Devil's Club, stupid, didn't you even know that? They have a new rule where you're not allowed to put stuff used in tribal ceremonies in your beer." The Shepherds are lapping up water from their silver bowls.

Kathy shows me through her house, the TV room, the library. She opens the door to her bedroom and we go in, and she indicates with her arm where I'm to sleep.

"I'll be glad to sleep on the couch," I tell her.

Kathy laughs that sucking laugh. I guess she's drunk. I am too, and I laugh with her. Not because I'm drunk, but because her bed is sunken in the middle and looks like a horrible place to try and sleep, and her bedspread is a dismal yellow, ocher more like, with some stains on it, and the lighting is bad, I don't know, but Kathy stops laughing. It's just me laughing now. She's standing there looking at me laughing.

Well, I cut that laugh short, not too abruptly so as not to draw attention to myself.

Kathy goes, "Don't be silly, Dobie. In the morning I'll cook you that great dinner you were talking about."

"I'm devoted to somebody else," I tell her.

"Of course you are," Kathy says, and then, after looking around the room a second, she says, "Listen, don't even try it with me, okay? I know people," and she's looking at me weird now, like she's angry. "I know people," she says, emphatically. "None of you are like dogs at all. If you were like dogs you'd be better people."

I'm thinking, Okay, well, I think I'll get back to the TV room now, but Kathy pushes me to the wall. She stands on her toes and tries to kiss me. When I slide to the side she yells, "Bullshit! Get back here!"

I hurry along through the hall on into the kitchen where the dogs, man, they fucking jump in front of me and bare their teeth, growling, their hackles up.

I hear a scream back there. Sounds like she's pulling her hair, having a total hissy fit, but then there's this banging going on, some stomping of the feet. When I look over I see the swinging door fly open, and Kathy, she's like coming at me with a branch.

John Oliver Hodges

I wake up outside, a collar on me, the light falling all around. I'm on the runner. I try getting up but she hits me. I grab the collar. She hits me. "No!" she screams, and hits me.

I turn over onto my back and she holds the branch up like she'll slam me so hard.

I'm completely naked.

"I told you," she says.

I grab the collar, but she smacks my knee. "Put your hands on the ground, asshole! What's the matter with you?" She raises the branch, so I do what she says, and then, "Hey," she says, "that's it, Dobie. Yes, hey, that's a good boy. Good boy," she says, and is petting me.

"Look," I say.

"Shut up! I'll hit you!"

Okay, is this real? I'm dreaming, surely.

The branch comes down hard on the back of my neck. I start to turn my face to look at her but hear the thing crack against my skull.

I wake again, and there she is over there, naked but for these thick strap-on sandals, all fat on the steps with her dogs, one each side of her, these big-ass bushy motherfuckers looking hungry and mean and nearly as big as she is.

She seems pleased that I've opened my eyes. She rises and strolls my way with her branch, and she sits down beside me in the dirt, says it isn't fair, nothing's fair, she says, and puts her hand on my ass and is feeling it. She says, "I'm lonely, Dobie. Nobody wants me. Anybody can have me, but nobody wants me."

I'm wondering what would happen if I suddenly attacked her?

She grabs my balls. "Wow," she says. "Nature's perfect hand-warmers."

The dogs would rip into me.

"God, Dobie," she says. "This is so sad, isn't it? Everything is so sad. When I saw you with your friends I cried. You all looked so happy together. I never felt that way before, the way you looked. It makes me mad," she says, tightening her grip. She pulls me onto my knees, and I shiver from the cold cutting under. "It makes me want to do something," Kathy says, and yanks the fuck out of me. "It makes me want to hurt somebody," she says, "makes me want to make things right in the world, make them fair!"

I guess I scream, so Kathy lets go. One of the dogs licks my hand, it could be Ajax, and then Kathy is crying. I taste blood in my mouth from when I bit my tongue. Her sobs grow louder, sounding more and more painful until finally she seems overcome with grief, and stands up. I watch her cross the yard in her man-sandals, sobbing and fat and wobbling in the white Alaskan light. She stumbles up the steps, the German Shepherds following behind her, and the three of them disappear into the house.

I grab at the collar, undoing the buckle and rip it off my neck and run. Then realize what I'm doing. I sneak back to her house where my jeans are wadded up on the steps. I dash up there and grab them. The dogs start barking, and I run, I mean, I am fucking out of there! I am flying down the mountain, my feet getting all torn apart on the ground but I don't stop running for a good long ways. When I do I slide into my jeans, my balls aching terribly. I've got all these lumps on my head and bruises all over from where she hit me with that stick.

Further down the mountain I step off the road down to a creek and cup my hands to drink the cold water. When I raise my eyes I see a moose looking at me, but don't even want to think about that. I just drink more water and then continue on my merry way, my legs wobbly still from all that sailing. I'm hungry and cold and am still somewhat drunk.

Thank God the sun breaks through the fog. It comes down and warms my back, and when I get to the bottom of the mountain I feel so much better. No shirt or shoes on, but fuck it, I'm fine. I stop into Brady's, known for their Brady Brunches, and buy some hazelnut coffee as the Indian proprietor tells a waitress to keep an eye out for dumpster-divers in back.

I walk down to the harbor after that, and stand at the rail trying to remember which boat, which boat is the boat we sailed in on? I think it must be the one over there in the far corner, but can't be sure. It seems like a long way to walk just to find out, and my feet are messed up, and I'd probably be wrong anyway, and I feel so stupid without even having my shirt on. I really feel like an idjit, and don't know what to do. An eagle lands on a lamppost nearby and spits something yellow out of its mouth. It seems to be watching me.

I feel a grab on my shoulder and am like, holy shit. I turn around, fully expecting to see Kathy with her branch.

But it's my dear captain. Captain Boo! The sunlight hits him full on in the face, this happy smiling orange clown who I wrap my arms around, telling him I just ran down the mountain fast as I could. Captain Boo doesn't seem very interested, but he likes patting me on the back. We head for the boat, walking down the floating ramp that is not so steep as it was last night. The tide has risen.

At the boat Captain Boo whips up French toast with maple syrup, celery sticks on the side. I put on a clean shirt, my jacket, some socks and these eight-dollar boots I got at the mall in Juneau. After breakfast we stroll over to the Alaskan Brew Fest where everything is going on, happy people from all over Alaska drinking, playing guitars, and having great times. Like yesterday, plenty of sun shines down, enough to where girls bare their shoulders, their feet, kicking back in the grass and basking in the smoking-grill-smells of dozens of chickens wafting the grounds.

Silas is here. Jaura. My great friends. They wear smiles. Jaura's had luck finding a pack of Drum. We roll our tobacco, smoke the fine smoke, so beautiful coming out from our mouths, and wiggling up in small blue streams from our cherries. Silas, when the awards are given, wins for his porter a pretty red ribbon.

Captain Boo's worried.

The world is very happy today, yes, but it's late afternoon now, and where's Robbi?

Captain Boo asks around, everybody he knows, have you seen her? Seems like all of Juneau is here. They've come out on the ferry, bringing along bicycles and mandolins, but Robbi is nowhere.

Captain Boo asks people he doesn't know, strangers, have you seen a girl in blue velvet?

Yes, a lot have, everybody saw her last night at the White Whale. She was dancing one minute, then she was gone.

Captain Boo is afraid. Haines is a small community. There are not so many places Robbi could have lost herself in. Haines is the end of the trail is what the locals say. The continent stops here. Everything beyond is foreign. The Tlingit word for Haines is Dtehshuh. It's a bad place, the Indians say, too close to the border every person must cross one day. Why do you think so many bald eagles hang around Haines? It's because they know about the other side, and are hoping that its carrion will spill over into the real world.

But where the fuck is Robbi!

A girl in blue velvet, short-cropped hair died pink, can't be hard to find!

An announcement is made through a bullhorn, but nobody says anything.

And we smile, it's the way of the day, but we are worried.

Night comes. Still no word from Robbi. Captain Boo gets mad at Jaura. Captain Boo says Jaura should have kept an eye on her. Jaura calls Boo a pig.

I sleep in the tent with Silas and with Jaura.

I sleep like a slobbering baby in their tent with them, my great friends. The comfort, it is comfort. In the morning I look through the screen to see a girl stepping barefoot through the yellow daisies. The grass is thick and green and her feet so very white and pretty as she makes her way to the toilet.

I laugh.

My friends wake, thinking maybe Robbi has returned, and I've got this feeling. It is embarrassing, really, but I feel as if all this is new, that I've never seen any of it before. The air is crisp and gold, the sleeping bag so good and warm as I eye the Portalet, knowing what she's doing in there, getting rid of the old, making room for the new. I feel as if something great will happen, and don't want to look away in case it should slip me by.

CRYING BABIES
IN HEAVEN

I'm grinding curbs when Bastard, backdropped in palms in purple clouds, clumps home from the labor pool. Yellow teeth show through his curtains of mustache and beard. "Ain't chore name Jessum?" he asks.

"Jesse," I remind him.

"At's what I said," Bastard says. "Jessum. I been meaning to ass. Know dat girl live up dere wi'choo? Is she Chinese?"

"She's a little bit Korean," I say.

"Well what ch'all do up dere and shit?"

"She's cooking supper right now."

"Sheeeit," Bastard says, smiling hugely so the hairy curtains billow. "I don't put up wi'dat now. I can't take dat cooking and shit. I have to knock'r one time."

"Oh," I say, moving off to grind the curb.

"Ass'a nice lil toy," Bastard says, admiring my footwork. "But I been to meaning to ass. What . . . You know dem long . . . I been seeing dem long skirts she got on. What ch'all do wi'dem long skirts?"

"Nothing," I say. "She just wears them."

"Nothing?" Bastard says, crossing his arms, stepping back insulted. Then: "I ain't never seen none like dem looooong skirts. You say she's Chinese?"

I skate till he gets bored watching and goes. A few minutes later, I go too, and Tina has got it all laid out on the red-and-white checkered tablecloth: lasagna, creamed corn, French bread and a bottle of Blue Nun.

Our pink-footed rat (Super Supper) is also on the table, sniffing and reaching his head up close as he can to the lasagna pan without burning his nose.

"This is great," I say. "What did I do?"

"Be you," Tina says, hugging me.

Tina lights the tall white candle and hits the lights. We drink and eat as the light outside the window fades and the yellow bulbs at Bastard's burn. We see him and Virginia now and then getting up from TV to hit the kitchen for beer.

The yuppie wannabes next door slip on a record, and the song plays. The walls are paper. They got a baby. It cries all night sometimes, making you feel like knocking through the wall to rip its throat out. But that song. It's that old seventies one about our house being very very fine with cats in the yard. Except for me and Tina, it's rednecks in the yard.

I give Super Supper a crust of bread and he snatches it off to the corner of the table and goes to town.

After dinner we sit on the futon looking at the pictures we print-ed earlier at school. We peel back the thick porous pages of our blot-ters. A forty watt bulb burns above us, and the pictures shine, are damp, the silver halides glistening in that special magic they have before drying.

Tina's are of palms. It used to be dogs. She loves dogs, but she quit dogs after what happened to Books, her bubbly brown poodle. She'd taken three rolls of him, doing all his little tricks. She processed the film the following day and hung the strips up to dry. That's when somebody came into the darkroom and jabbed through every frame with a pair of scissors. Books died that same week, making her scream and cry for hours. Books had done a head-dive off the balco-ny. But the palms: she's got beautiful, sick, peeling ones, dead ones, headless ones, lonesome tall ones. It's in the trunks, their personali-ties, a little curve here, a knot of indigestion there. Regal palms, an-gry palms. And triplet-palms, all three leaning in the wind, rustling the way they do. Now it's the palms Tina loves. She's got them dis-played all over the bedroom walls, held to the paint with four-inch strips of electrical tape crossing the corners. She takes their pictures with a Diana, one of those plastic cameras they used to give you at gas stations way back in the old days, for free, when you got a fill-up.

Mine are of people that I meet on the street, or in graveyards. I catch them on porches, in laundromats—people who by their pres-ence attack me. An alarm goes off, a weird lusting, and I've simply got to have them: bag ladies, tattooed ladies, blind men, tourists, kids with scabs. I want their lives. At the beach they wear bathing suits. I walk the boardwalk, through neighborhoods, flashing them harshly with my Vivitar, making their eyes jump out at you, the tones and textures of their flesh and clothes. An old man carries a sculpture of his head with him everywhere he goes. A paranoid look is in his eyes, like he thinks you want to steal it from him. He likes me. Most people do. I've got quite a few pictures of him. And women pull their shirts up for me, and I've got transvestites and hustlers, preachers, retarded people. The Daytona sky does neat things, always, the clouds and light, and everywhere you look are hotels and billboards, churches, roads and crazy wires going everywhere. It's a valuable collection. Someday it will be worth something because things are changing in the world. It will be proof. A time capsule of sorts, a preservation of great people and gone things.

After looking at pictures, we close our blotters and take off our clothes.

As night gets on, I tell Tina what Bastard said about her *looong* skirts.

"What the hell business is it of his?" she says. "I swear those people are such rednecks. That guy could be an escaped murderer."

"He did used to be in prison," I tell her.

"For what?"

"Oh, I couldn't tell exactly. I think it was for rape or something. I've been meaning to ass him a question."

"He was in jail for rape and you didn't tell me?"

"I've been meaning to ass him, you know, *Hey, Bastard, would you mind if I took your picture?*"

"I'm serious," Tina says.

"I was just kidding."

"No, you weren't. What did he say?"

Running my fingers through her silky black hair, I admire the muscles in her nostrils. When Tina gets nervous, her nostrils do funny things. "Just that he wondered what we did with your long skirts."

"My skirts?"

"Yeah, he's weird, I feel sorry for Virginia."

"Virginia? You should feel sorry for me, for having to live next to him."

"I don't think he'll do anything," I say. "He seems laid back."

I stroke her hair over her head, down onto her back, where I feel her vertebrae all the way to her tail bone. "I'll protect you," I tell her, feeling the little knob there. It's as if someone cut her tail off. "Soon as Bastard starts breaking in through that window, I'll be there with my hatchet to cut his arm off."

"Stop," Tina says. "You don't have a hatchet. Even if you did, you might not succeed. It might make him angry."

"Hey, what's that noise I hear? Is that Bastard? Oh, my God, I think he's breaking in through the living room window. Oh, my God!"

"Stop it! Stop it!" Tina cries, ripping at my arm.

"No, it really is him," I say. "I better get up. Don't you hear it?"

"Stop it!"

Maybe it gets me off, Tina's fear. Maybe she's playing, to make things romantic. I'm not sure. What I do know is it's a lot of fun. So I go on, threatening her in a high-pitched voice about Bastard breaking in. Then another voice, angry and growly, barges into the room, as if someone is standing at the foot of the futon, looking down at us. It goes, "SHUTUUUP!"

We cuddle into each other, holding back our laughter. It's that yuppie wannabe with bleach-blond hair. His bedroom is sandwiched against ours with nothing between us but a thin slice of baloney.

"What a asshole," I say.

"Neighbors," Tina says. She begins to sing softly as she can that song about the very fine house.

"I said, *SHUTUP!*" comes the voice.

This is going too far. I bang my fist once on the wall, starting up the baby. I think about saying, "Shut your own damn self up, you rich ass-wipe," but change my mind. The baby is really wailing.

* * *

In the morning we leave at the same time, me and the guy. He smiles. As if yuppies are beyond uncivil behavior. What crap. I don't smile back. I follow his bleached head down the stairs, mentally noting that, next time his baby keeps me up, I'm going to crash through the wall like the Incredible Hulk. He gets in his Mercedes. I start my bike, ride to school, sit through class, and go to the darkroom to print my negs from the previous week.

When you ask to take a picture, people so often act like it will break your camera. They insult themselves all up and down the street. "I'm too ugly," they say. And this one guy, just last week, he said, "Know that saying about *shit happens*? Well, that's what I think every time I look in the mirror." It's weird because more often than not they are so beautiful. Another thing is often they feel like they got to do something strange to make the picture worth it, like dropping their pants or screwing up their face. Once, this old lady that I met stuck a beer bottle into her mouth backwards. "Now you know why they call me Big Mouth," she said. I think, though, that overall they are so pleased somebody wants them, their lives, for the record.

I print a man with a billion wrinkles in his face. I print a drunk woman crawling on the sidewalk with a string of slobber coming out of her mouth. Then I print a little girl sitting on brick steps, smashing a telephone with a hammer. I wash them, squeegee them, put them in my blotter and take them outside into the sun, real people clasped between the pages, my treasures. I wish I could be them, all of them at the same time. I wish I could live their lives. I strap them under the bungee of my seat and ride home.

* * *

Tina's at school, in studio. I light a joint at the kitchen table and smoke it halfway before opening my blotter. It always amazes me that my people are still here, that they never find some way of escaping. Really, it's not fair I should able to sit here watching them without their knowing. Every detail shows—moles and stray hairs, the dirt on their toes. Slowly I scan them, head to foot and back, always lingering on their faces, admiring them, looking into their eyes and loving them, sometimes getting filled up with a nearly unbearable joy. As if I'm about to explode. This thing, it's in their eyes. Like I've collected proof of something other than what they look like, of the thing inside them, something eternal.

I shut them up, pick Super Supper out of his aquarium and play with him, letting him squirm from one hand to the other, a little road made of hand that keeps replenishing itself. The thing about playing with rats, though, is their claws always make you itch. You have to wash your hands in the sink afterwards. Another thing is rats love to eat negatives, and so I put my negatives away in the drawer before setting Super Supper on the rug to roam free.

Then I turn on my amp. Virginia's at the bottom of her steps with her two raggedy girls. I play a couple of hardcore songs from the band I used to be in, then, for fun, pluck out some notes from "Sweet Home Alabama." As soon as I do it, Virginia turns her head—God bless her—and looks up at me and Tina's place. I keep playing, watching Virginia come alive, tapping her long bare feet on the bottom step, tossing back her gorgeous auburn hair.

I open the fridge and eat me some cold Lasagna.

The door knocks. I open. It's Virginia. "You wouldn't have a couple eggs I could get from you, would you?" she says.

"Yeah, I got a couple eggs," I say, and get them and hand them to her.

She says, "I love that song. That's where I'm from, Alabama, all my folks live up there. Say, you wouldn't have a couple slices of bread to go with these here eggs, would you?"

"Yeah, I got some bread," I tell her. I open the fridge, rip a good hunk off the French.

When I hand it to her, she says, "What's that?"

"French," I tell her.

"I don't know," she says, turning it in the light. "I ain't ever seen no bread like this before. Ain't you got some regular bread?"

"That's all we got," I say. "It's good bread. Slice it sideways to get you some slices. You can put it in the toaster if you want."

"Yeah, I reckon that's what I'll do. You know, normly I wouldn't ask you for nothing, but it's them kids, you know. Shelly and Linder ain't had nothing all day but a couple two or three balls of gum."

"Yeah," I say. "Listen. I was wondering. You think you would mind if I took some pictures of you and your kids?"

"Pictures?" Virginia says, crossing her arms and taking a step back. "Hey, you ain't a cop or nothing, are ya?"

"No."

"Well, why you wanna take my picture?"

"So that a hundred years from now when you're dead, all the people in the future can look at us. Just natural pictures, every day kind of thing."

"Natural? Well, okay, I guess I could let you. But you ain't one of them perverts or nothing though, is you? I wouldn't want no pervert taking no picture of me and them kids."

"I'm a student."

"Bastard was telling me y'all was weird. Now, don't get me wrong. I ain't got nothing against weird people, just, Bastard, he was telling me y'all ain't from around here. Y'all from Australia or some shit, right?"

"No."

"Well, I reckon since you gimme these eggs, I'll let ya do it. You want me ta brang them kids up here?"

"I was thinking we could do it at your house."

"In the house?" Virginia says. "The house is a wreck. You don't wanna take no picture in the house."

"Yes I do," I tell her. "All the things on the wall and all the possessions of the person need to be there. You see a little more about who the person is. You know, like I was telling you about those future people?"

"Well, I don't know nothing about that, but I guess since you gimme these eggs."

I tell Virginia I'll be right over. I don't want to give her time to clean the kids. I like dirt-smeared faces. My flash batteries are dead, so I'll do time exposures. I screw my Bronica into the head of my Gitzo, grab my flood. I go down the stairs, climb Virginia's, and knock on the screen. "Might as well get this over with," she calls from the kitchen. I enter and the two girls run up looking at me with huge, round, blue eyes, studying me as the eggs I gave them sizzle in the kitchen. I tell Virginia to keep doing like she is. The French is in the garbage on top of empty beer cans. I plug in my light, flood the kitchen with it, and tell her to look in the lens and freeze. I take her picture, spatula in hand. Then pictures of the girls sitting on the crusted counter with cat-scratched legs dangling over the ledge. Shelly has a deformed upper lip. One half of it is fat as a grown man's pinky finger, while the other half is nothing but a bloodless hair. The other girl, Linda, has perfect lips. I get a picture of Linda looking proud about her lips, then we all go to the master bedroom. I take Virginia's picture standing on the bed—when you have a camera, people do anything you tell them—with a poster of a pirate ship sailing on the wall. Then her with her girls in several other places in the house. The girls have egg yolk on their cheeks, their hair is in tangles, and they look as if they all walked out from The Depression. When I leave, I step down their stairs feeling like a robber.

* * *

Tina's in the kitchen heating lasagna in a pan, breaking and stirring it with a fork. I nuzzle up behind her, putting my hands on her breasts. "I took some pictures of Virginia today," I say.

"I bet you were flirting with her."

"You know I would never do that. I saw her down there, and I played 'Sweet Home Alabama.' "

"Are you trying to upset me, Jesse? Get your hands off. You serenaded her."

Tina lets go of her fork to pull my hands away.

"It wasn't like that," I say, putting my hands back. "I see you're in a good mood."

"My Diana melted. I left it in the car and it melted. Then I ran a red, Jesse. Do you know what that means? Someone almost crashed into me. This truck was coming right at me."

"Baby," I tell her. I blow on her neck. "That's terrible," I say. "I'm so glad you're alive. Look, we'll keep a good lookout for Dianas. Maybe one will turn up."

As Tina stirs, I kiss her neck, feeling the weight of her breasts in my hands, and pressing myself against her. "The flame is too high," I say. "Your lasagna will taste better if you heat it slow."

She turns down the flame, and I undo some buttons on her shirt. I expose her breasts, feeling them as the blue heat brushes up around them and my hands. I love her. I pinch the skin around her nipples. She turns her head back to give me a hearty kiss, but screams when she sees Bastard staring through the window of our door.

Tina runs away. I walk over. "What is it?" I ask through the glass. "What do you want?" I ask, acting like I'm fixing to open the door, but really pushing the lock-button instead.

Bastard just stands there, staring, his mouth completely hidden behind the dirty brown curtains of hair. His large almond eyes are glassy and forlorn-looking, as if, while thinking of a beautiful lady, somebody hypnotized him. I knuckle the glass to say, *Hello, is anyone home?* He comes alive and doesn't look happy, says, "I think you better come out here 'cause I've a mind to knock down that door and I don't care if you is a cop. I'll still knock down that door, Jessum."

The best thing, I know, is to see what the matter is, talk reason, make right. I go out, quickly shutting the door behind me. The yuppie wannabe woman is coming up the stairs, babe in arm. Bastard very loudly says, "You thank you's real smart, don't you, Jessum? Thank I'm an idiot you can walk into my house trying to pick up on my Ginny when I ain't home!"

"No, I don't think I'm smart," I say. "She came over for eggs."

"Ginny said you was trying to make porno movies of her and them girls. If you wasn't a cop, I'd report your ass."

"I'm a student. I told her that. If you want, I'll give you some pictures when I develop them."

"Oh," Bastard says, and the curtains part, the yellow teeth shine, and a wave of alcohol blusters forth. As the yuppie woman scoots behind him to walk to her door, Bastard's eyes lower. He pulls his beard contemplatively, saying, "Damn, will you look at the shitter on that thar critter."

I look at it. Bastard puts his hand on my shoulder, patting it. It doesn't mean anything to me. My eyes will not pop out for yuppie-ass.

"I wouldn't mind getting aholt of her panties," Bastard says.

Her husband opens the door for her. The husband gives her a peck on the cheek, then looks at Bastard. He pushes his chest out, trying to make it look extra big. After closing his wife and baby inside, he says, "I need to have a word with you, uh, what's your name?"

"Bastard."

"Yeah, well, I have a bone to pick. Let's go down."

Bastard rolls his eyes and follows the bleach-blond head down the stairs. I watch. The yuppie shakes his finger at Bastard, telling him things not nice, things inclined to hurt a man's pride. Bastard doesn't take kindly to it. He backs up as if to hit the guy, but the yuppie is quicker, stronger. You should see the thickness of his wrists. He slings his elbow back and lets loose his thick-wristed fist into the hairy curtains.

"Aww, Gad!" Bastard shrieks, crouching down, bringing his hands to his face. I see the blood seeping through Bastard's fingers. There is blood in the curtains, blood on the ground.

The yuppie climbs the stairs. He squints at me, asking, "What are you looking at, loser?"

"Nothing much," I say, and go back in.

Tina is peeking through the slit in the kitchen curtains. "They were fighting," she says. "Did you see it? God, I knew this was a messed up place." She starts to cry.

The yuppies put on their favorite record.

"Why do they always play that?" Tina says. "I'm so sick of it. I'm sick of this whole place."

"This is heaven," I tell her.

"Why were they fighting?"

"Bastard wanted, you know, to get in the yuppie-wife's panties."

"Oh my God," Tina says. "I'm gonna start looking for a new place tomorrow. What's so funny?"

"You," I say, pulling my camera out of my bag. Before Tina came home, I had skated up the street for a four-pack of Duracells. I got the energy now, the snapping power. I slide my Vivitar into the shoe and flip the switch.

"There's nothing funny. I'm serious. We should get out of here, now!"

The green light comes on, and I throw the camera in her face, letting her have it, tears and all, her nostrils frozen in panic.

She runs to the bedroom. I set my camera on the table and follow. For a couple of hours we snuggle, talking, now and then crawling to the wall, putting ears against it. Our esteemed neighbors are fighting. She's letting him have it about how stupid he is because a lawsuit is on him for not having bought workman's comp for his employees. The baby is crying, but they speak to each other as if there is no baby. We find out the guy owns a landscaping company. All the while we'd been thinking he was a lawyer. Ha! A yardboy. Without workman's comp. From their argument we gather that one of his workers stabbed himself in the eyeball with a pruning saw. Amazing what a person does to get ahead. Cut corners, save twisters off bags of bread. Well, it backfired. They're gonna get sued, for everything. The Mercedes will get taken; the baby will wail for food, for love. It's a world. With ears up there straining to soak up every last bit. When their fight reaches its highest pitch, where I'm thinking the guy is at any moment going to lash out and attack his yuppie wife, he smashes something instead and storms out of the house.

Ha, ha, ha, it gives me a kick. Even Tina is amused. We're on the futon, and she pulls it out because she loves it, giving me love, yanking it around and putting it in her mouth. It gets her horny and she peels out of her jeans. She takes off her shirt and gets on it, looking like an angel above me, with her silky black hair growing out of her skull, flowing down around her face, and her breasts there, the way she moves as if suspended in air.

With the baby still crying and everything, and looking up at this angel, I have a thought. I think, *What happens to all the babies that die?* Perhaps in heaven there's a nursery, a place they can be closed away, so when they cry, all the other angels and heaven people won't have to hear it, because what an awful sound that is, that needful anguish and slobbery pain, enough to destroy a perfect world. Otherwise, I guess babies are all over, floating around, crying in the clouds, wailing at the tops of their lungs, pissing everybody off.

There's a noise through the wall, a hollow scream, not too loud. Half a scream, like the way the light in the room is half, and the way I've still got my socks and shirt on.

The scream continues, sort of blending into things. Is it real? Tina stops fucking, tilts her head, and then, as the scream slithers into other sounds, sounds like a woman frightened, she rises off me as if I were some kind of launch pad for angels.

Tina crouches on the floor with her ear to the wall.

"What? What is it?" I say.

"Oh, my God. It's Bastard. He's in there. Bastard is in there, Jesse. My God, do something. Get up, go over there, hurry!"

I jump up, jumping into my jeans at the same time. I run through the front door and remember, *Oh shit, I forgot my camera.* I run back in the house, turn on the flash, and stand there, saying,

Hurry up, Hurry up, to my flash. The ready light pops on, and I bolt onto the porch heading over.

It's a weird feeling crossing someone's threshold uninvited. Especially without your shoes on.

I make into their bedroom, and sure enough, there's Bastard. I don't have time to think. I'm an eyeball. Eyeballs don't think. I'm a watcher, a looker, a recorder, a witness, and this, I know, somehow, is important. I snap a picture of her, of the yuppie woman backed into a corner, Bastard standing taller than her, his fist balled up like he's going to hit her.

And then Bastard turns, looking to see what the commotion is. When he sees it's only me, the hairy curtains part, and I flash it, his yellow teeth lighting up brightly. "I told you I's gonna get her fucking panties, didn't I, Jessum?"

This is a man in a house not his. A busted flower pot is on the floor. The fern that was in the pot—the soil, too—is all in the rug. Look, there's a baby! A baby in the rug.

I flash Bastard grabbing the woman. I flash the woman falling down then lurching through his legs, a look of horror now permanently burned into her face. I flash Bastard getting a hand under her skirt. It's a wonderful sound the camera makes, the dropping of the mirror giving way to an image, the tic of the flash, the winding friction of gears as I advance the film, as Bastard yanks down her panties. He's got them in his mouth now, and he looks at the camera, shaking his head so I can flash it, which I do. Then she's on the floor on her stomach. Bastard sticks a hand into her ass area, and the baby kicks. It's a him, I see, kicking the air with fat white legs, his mouth wide open. I flash it, filling his mouth with light.

A thunderous shout pushes in, as if God is coming into the garden. I've heard about God's anger, his jealousy, how he made people eat meat until it came out their noses. His rage covers everything: the screaming baby, the woman, Bastard chuckling, the fern. But it's not God. It's only the mass of man, the husband, the wannabe. He gets his hands around Bastard's neck, tackling him, and I flash it. He chokes Bastard, turning his head to see his wife now scooted over into the soil and broken shards of the planter. The leaves of the fern sprout out from behind her head, giving her an added dimension of hair. I flash it. And the baby, now strangely smiling with wet lips—I flash that. I flash and flash, and my heart is pounding so hard, and I'm scared as shit, it's bad, this, but I have to have it. I step back and flash the whole scene, and there's this place inside me where, inside of that sick feeling going on, there's another feeling telling me I'm lucky and that I'm rich.

I don't want the wannabe's attention switching over to me—I can tell he's about finished with Bastard—so I split over to ours. As I roll my film through to replace it with another, Tina grabs hold of my shoulder, shaking me, wanting to know what happened. "What did he do?" she says. "What was going on over there?"

"Not now," I tell her, but she keeps on.

So I push her a little, just a little, nothing mean, but she falls on the floor as if I just knocked her upside the head.

And she starts sobbing.

But I don't have time, not now. I set the exposed roll behind the stacked books against the wall by the TV. As soon as the new roll is loaded, I hear a sound—Bastard tumbling down the stairs—and another sound—Virginia running across the lot, crying. Then Shelly and Linda screaming, "Daddeee!" Yes! I will take more pictures. But there's a yanking on our door.

"God!" Tina shrieks.

I open the door, thinking I'll reason, but the guy charges in. I see he's about ready to break my nose, so I back away, watching him pick my camera off the table, fiddling with it like he wants to get the film out. But he's too stupid for that. He lifts the camera over his head, and throws it on the floor. My $2,000 Bronica SQ A breaks into three distinct pieces. The film unravels onto the linoleum, and he picks it up, the ribbon, all those latent pictures of his wife getting something or other done to her. He even smiles, as if he's so clever, so smart that nobody in this world could ever pull a fast one on him. When he leaves, he slams the door so hard the window in it shatters. As for my camera, those pictures are worth a couple grand. More than a broke nose, too, if that's what I'd gotten. God must be blessing the shit out of me tonight.

I go to get my film from behind Tina's Richard Brautigan collection. I'm thinking I'll develop it now, but it's gone! I look at Super Supper's aquarium.

"I let him out," she says.

She starts explaining she did it because he was upset, but I don't care. He's a rat! I rip through the house, tearing things aside, throwing dirty clothes up in the air, panicking. I feel as if everything has been lost. The most important thing in the world—because of a rat. I sling open the closet, and there he is, in the corner, holding my roll of 120, gnawing it.

I grab his ass up, and I guess I squeeze him too hard because he bites me. Those long orange teeth go way down into where my blood is inside my hand. It's a knee-jerk reaction what I do, throwing him. He slams against the wall and sort of sticks there a second before falling into the rug. He tries to get up and run, but his head keeps twisting sideways, his tail spinning and flapping, thumping the floor. He rolls over, not dead. He's done with, though. In pain. But the main thing is my film is only damaged—that's what's important. It isn't ruined. The pictures are there. The pictures will show. The pictures are blooming like flowers in my head, how the baby cried while kicking his legs. There were strawberries printed on his mother's panties.

Tina—she's on the futon softly crying, her delicate brown feet motionless in the shag. I stand in the doorway looking down at her, feeling like a jerk, clutching in my fist my roll of 120. And God, she's pretty like that, when she cries. She looks like a Slurpee I could definitely drink—strawberry. I'm thinking I'd better get my Pentax quick and start snapping pictures in thirty-five. That's when she looks up at me, her eyes all red and her face wet and tender with tears. I've never seen anything so lovable and great in all of my life. With Super Supper dying in the rug. Squeaking. So loud. Flapping his tail against the floor. And the baby, that future grown-up person, he finds his queue and that slobbery wail of needfulness, of being cast to the side, of not having what it is you got to have, rains down from the ceiling, sideways from the walls. It's a blender in here, a blizzard of crying and screaming and thrashing palm trees taped to the walls. A paradise. It is absolutely the best thing anybody in the world could ever wish so hard to have.

John Oliver Hodges

TWO

HEALTH NUTS

Tough men stop for lunch to gobble our spud salads down: Mutinous Mustard and Mad Mayonnaise. Construction workers, plumbers, they stop for a dose of Lunacy Noodles with Vegetable Sauce, say, or Brainy Burgers with Doodle Sticks. Maybe they're in the mood for some Touched Tofu? Some Cracked Cookies or Moonstruck Minestrone? We've been at it three years, a family-run funhouse, everybody snappy. When our daughters get off the bus, they help us till closing. We're adored, the charmed cheese. Vitamins, snacks, we stock them in prettified rows and dish out the best chow south of the Georgia line. We have a jukebox to play Loony Tunes off your quarters. We're good for a dose of hilarity. We give people cud to chew—that's organic cud, friend—and shit to shoot. My how we Chattahoocheeans love to gossip, to storytell.

Take yesterday. Now this is typical: Jeanne, the skinny chickadee from Floor One comes in, orders a order of Booby Balls—that's our term for falafel smothered in our special tahini concoction. Jeanne was initially hospitalized through the power of her momma, Baker-acted and branded the drooling fool. Girl was too much of a slut is what we gather, chafed her mamma's refined sensibilities. That's what started it, only Jeanne was a model crazo. She made it down to Floor Zero quickity split, but like many of our patients, once they're given the all-clear, it's vacation time's all it is. Soon they're back for some new little crime of smallness. Poor Jeanne, she'd been away less than a month before she up and escaped her Tallahassee halfway house, got bonkers in a crack-house. As we get it through the trick-le-down, Jeanne started smoking boric acid when the crack run out. That's what made her Kooky with a capital K. Whereas before, she'd only been, now forgive me for saying this, but Slutty with a capital S, or to put it another way, an insult to her momma. Now she was unalterably changed forever for the worst, like way down deep in the DNA jungle of her girl's private soul, daffy, as they say, no lie.

So Jeanne comes in yester's prelaunch, her pleasantly plump home-girl in tow. Dee preps Jeanne's Booby Balls, for which this in-timate-made Abe five dollar bill is proffered. Dee just looks at it, the dangle of her eyes in Jeanne's been-there-done-that fingers quite lovely still despite having rid life's cruel tides. "It's wet," Dee says. "Why's it to be wet?"

"I peed on it," Jeanne giggles, and Jeanne's home-girl giggles.

Dee pulls back the Booby Ball plate, sets it on the counter be-hind her. That's when Jeanne starts wailing out like a heartsick hound over she wants her Booby Balls. Everybody is looking at her, soaking up the details for the telling of a good tale on it later to whoever is willing to listen.

There's another customer in line, an older dude with a nose I've not seen the like of. It's a screwball nose, a S-nose, call it a snose over that it first goes one way then the other, makes you to think of a snake when you look at him. He is waiting to get his own order.

"What's the deal?" says he.

"She pissed on her money," says Dee. "I ain't taking it. She's got to give me some dry money. Would you take a five dollar bill had pee all over it?"

"I'll wash it!" Jeanne shrieks. Jeanne's home-girl flops out her tongue and Jeanne rubs old Abe back and forth over the girl's taste buds, as if that will remedy the situation here. With tears in her eyes, Jeanne tries handing the bill back to Dee, who says, "I don't take no wet bills, baby."

That's when Mr. Snose, our Good Samaritan, offers to pay for Jeanne. She's a good-looking gal, Jeanne, a chickadee in all the right places. That's part of it, the why of how she ended up back here where her momma first put her, Baker acted and branded the drooling fool. Once free, all male no-goods—there's an endless supply of those—wanted a piece of her to chew on. I can't say I blame them. Like I say, Jeanne has got it going on in the body department. But Jeanne, poor gal, she likely thought she had not a thing to lose in the world. She give it up to whoever wanted a bite, have at it. When your All means nothing to the One whose All means All to you, you become worse than worthless, odious unto yourself. I understand that mental frame.

Take back in the day, this of the time those goosers, my peers, took live girls dam-ward to learn the smooching business. That would be about the tenth grade, the eleventh grade, and the twelfth grade. All those grades passed me by like opened windows flapping gloriously, but I could not hear them, could not see them. I missed out on the fun stuff guys do as they grow up to be men of this world. I was like how I imagine Jeanne was before she knew she wanted to get high, a nothing human being who suppressed the desperate wanting. What I wanted, only, was for Momma to be happy. For that, I hid things from myself. I appeared healthy and happy, and I might even have believed that I was. The difference between Jeanne and me was many a man saw her, admired her, wanted quite clearly to partake of the livid wet thing her skin concealed, and with some effort, did so. Jeanne, I can be jealous of her in my times of weak nostalgia. Me, I was invisible those years of no return, daddy-less, without a girl's crush, unwanted by all. What I knew of the gleaming windows were sharp flashes that burned me in my sleep.

Yet who is the wiser today?

Hell, I'm in foods!

It is me, against the boys who defiled the temples of their prey, who shines most happily and with a general bearing of peace and ease. By my own opinion, I would say so. It is me to live the happier of lives now. It's not so strange. Jeanne's window got bricked over, slam-dunked in her face. The many boys of yore now-drugged-out or drunked-up, the plumbers and the concrete pourers, their windows too got slam-dunked. You go hopping through open windows it's bound to happen. In my sizable emptiness refocused, I've had to face things, "get over it," as I've heard so many say of the daily life dramas. My small-peaness, as I now understand it, was akin to a boulder I stood in the way of as it rolled over me. How else could I unburden myself? I stood in its way, the guilt roped about the shame not the least sigh-giver, that tandem high-roller of serious dung. One need not wonder much as to the color of mine eyes.

* * *

Now, I was born in the Florida panhandle in a place made famous by a sprawling institution. My momma nursed there, "cared" for the crazoes, fed them drugs, and strapped them down in their beds when they got out of hand. She told me stories of it when arriving home from work, a real complainer, my momma, and tough, strong. My daddy, she always told me, had been a criminally insane patient, and there was a good chance I would grow up to be her charge. "Rat can't run from rat," she said. "All rat does is hide, like you're doing right now. When his rat's blood finds you, I'll commit you." It scared me. "You're crazy!" she screamed if, say, all I did was opinionate. It didn't matter what the opinion was. All opinions coming from me were out of the picture, her picture. My punishment more often than not was a physical thing, like push-ups and sit-ups. My momma was big on calisthenics and all things healthy. "Run around the block ten times," she'd say, or, "Drop down and give me forty." Other times when my crime was more severe, if I, say, made a facial expression of self-assurance, she'd suddenly pretend like I was more trouble than I was worth, like she'd tried everything, had done all she could for the rat that I was, but the time had come to send the rat to the devil. I'd be left alone to do as I pleased, which you'd think I would have liked, but I didn't. I felt slimy, guilty, rejected, worthless. She wouldn't acknowledge me in any way till I started begging. That little boy of twelve, I see him, I feel him, he breaks. The last drop of self-love he took it upon himself to try and stow away in secret is thrown out—that is his gift to her, laid sorrowfully at her slender feet—and she stares down at him contemptuously, her arms crossed, waiting for him to try and hug her leg so she can kick him away. No, she will not consider absorbing him back into her loving fold till he says the magic words, till he delivers everything, all. "Stop mumbling!" she says. "I can't hear you." And the little boy declares it loudly: "I am a rat, Momma!" The special words have been spoken. What follows, the seal on the deal, the act, the what it is that's got to be done for life to go back to normal, then happens, but I don't want to think about that now. What I want to do is focus on the good things.

Me, now. Jumping thirty years up to now, to my life as I live it today, you will see a happily married daddy of two towheaded girls of nine and eleven. They're the prettiest things you ever saw, just precious beyond belief. And my wife, oh what a beauty! My wife and I, throughout our fifteen years together, have worked hard in the pursuit of our dream. We have cut corners, denied ourselves the artificial pleasures that give people so much satisfaction in life: travel, education, things and more things: boats and guns and tools from Sears and rings. In fact, I've never worn a wedding ring, though I did buy one for Dee, got it for forty dollars at Cash City. Dee, like most women, and little girls too, I have found out, is a sucker for jewelry. But the two of us did some saving, Dee her money from secretarying at Chattahoochee Electric, and me, the money I saved, the bulk of it, came from years spent working for Harvey the Happy Plumber, everybody always asking me was I Harvey, even though my name, you know, it was sewn into my shirts plain as day. We pooled our resources, Dee and I. We did what we needed to make our family life perfect. We purchased our dream, opening the first health food store and eatery ever to be opened up in Chattahoochee: Health Nuts.

* * *

The crazoes, those given passes to leave the nut-house till curfew, visit us, bring us their Abes, Georges, and Andrews. They buy sandwiches and cartons of chocolate milk, them from Floor One, labeled harmless by the folks in charge over there, the psychiatrists who are greatly influenced by what the nurses tell them. If a nurse don't like you, you might as well hang your soul out to dry, buddy. They'll drug you and belittle you and lock you up, and they might even, like my momma did to some such inmates, run off with your seed! Lucky for me, that is one story about my mother that has not yet been circulated throughout our populace.

Only today, that man comes back in, the Good Samaritan with a screwball nose. He devours a Sanity Salad and washes it down with a medium Loco Cocoa. He returns to the counter, says, "Let me see Jim."

"What you want Jim for?" Dee says.

I am in the office doing paperwork, but I can hear.

The man clears his throat. "I'm his daddy."

Call it horror, what I felt then. Momma, she told me my rat's blood would find me one day. By that, I thought she meant that I would go crazy, not meet my goddamn daddy in the flesh!

Now, it was me to throw together the Sanity Salad for him to eat, hold the cheese. He hadn't struck me in any amazing way, like what you hear about on TV, how long lost relatives recognize each other in crowds of strangers without even thinking about it. He was just a man, quite ordinary but for the snose on his face, a snose that was caved in at the tip with pink and green veins crackling out of it like lava. Not that there aren't plenty of folks around here with messed-up noses, just this man's nose, his snose, was not of the local variety. My first impulse, after hearing him speak that craziness about him being my daddy, was to close the door and hide under the desk. I didn't want to mess with this. Whatever it was about, I wanted it to go away, only before I could motion for Dee not to speak to me, to pretend that I'd gone out the back door to get some scallions from the farmer's market, she spoke up. "Jim, there's a man out here says he's your dad."

I went out there and we looked into each other's eyes, and I still didn't recognize him from did. I said, "You made it down to Floor One, that it? I don't recall seeing you before today."

"I was released years ago," the man said all soft in the voice, and he said, "Your ma sent me a letter before she died."

My heart was beating real fast but I played it cool. I said, "You're crazy, you know that?"

"I'm a hundred and fifty percent serious," he said. "You wanna see the letter? I'm shy, that's why I didn't catch up with you. I'm off the booze though."

What does a man say to that?

"When were you released? " I said. "What year?"

"That would be nineteen eighty," the man said.

That was twenty-five years ago.

"I'm sorry, Son," he said.

I said, "I ain't your son, you crazy bum. Get outta my store fore I call the cops!"

"Jim," Dee said.

"I didn't mean to upset you," the man said, and I about popped a brain cap. I picked up the closest thing at hand, the plate he'd done ate his Sanity Salad off, and made like I was to bust it over his most-bald head.

He focused his eyes down hard on me.

"I will!" I shouted, raising it up to slam.

"Jim!" Dee said.

I was walking at him. He backed up out of the store, and it's a good thing he got away, cause I don't know what I might would've done. My heart was beating so fast. My heart never beats like this, not no more it don't. I figured in my head right quick-like that he was released when I was twelve. Twelve, I thought, and busted apart like a damn baby. I felt sorry for my wife seeing me like this, but what could I do? This man had come in here and stuck a fork in my heart. All this gooey goo was flying out of my heart where the fork went in. The goo kept flying and flying and I hid myself and cried. I needed it out of my system before the girls came in. I didn't want them to see me upset. When I left the office I wore a smile. Poor Dee was glad to see me back to normal now, but she had a few questions.

* * *

I do see the dumb boy that I was, Lord have mercy. I'm eleven. I'm off the bus from school. I feed the rats in the large aquarium, then watch *General Hospital*. I do my homework. I read the instructions Momma has left me, what exercises to do, what record to listen to while I'm exercising, what chores to do before and after my shower, which is at five o'clock. Before showering, I clean the sinks, the toilets, the tiles in the kitchen, and the rug in the Peace Room. After showering, I begin dinner, putting the roast in the oven, if that's what's on the menu, or starting the soaked beans on the burner, whatever, making salads, peeling potatoes. When Momma gets home, I say, "Welcome home, Momma," and hug her, and kiss her once on the cheek, then return to the kitchen to check things, make sure all's in order, prepare our plates. By this time Momma has showered, and as we eat, she quizzes me on my day, and I ask her questions and she tells me about her job and we have a nice dinner. Then we watch TV, and I massage her feet, or maybe we play Scrabble. Sometimes we go in the back yard and play horseshoes or take a walk down to the river. When Momma says things to me that require a yes or no answer, I always follow it up with Momma. Yes, Momma, No, Momma, no variation, always Yes or No, Momma. I keep a straight face. Momma don't like no laughter. If I giggle or snicker, I have to do push-ups. Yes, Momma. She stands over me counting, and when I'm done, she's upset for the remainder of the day. I am afraid of her often, but mostly I want Momma to love me. I even, sometimes, as amazing as this sounds, giggle just to put myself in her brain. Momma knows when I do that. She has me run around the block ten times, rain or shine. Momma says I like to push her buttons. She says I try to get her goat and asks me please to respectfully stop messing with her. Finally she reaches her limit. I have crossed the line so I cry out the magic words: "I am a rat, Momma!" I try to kiss Mamma's hand after that, but she won't allow it. She pushes me away. She treats me mean. If we've already eaten, we wait until the next day to make things right, but if we haven't eaten yet, we do it now. Momma loads the rat trap with a piece of cheese. She lowers it into the aquarium. When a rat comes up for a nibble, down the bar slams, crushing its neck and making blood come out of its mouth. Mama pulls the struggling rat out of the aquarium and when it finally dies she pries open the trap and drops the rat onto a plate. She stabs the rat with a fork like you would a russet potato, this so that it doesn't explode while it cooks in the microwave. As the microwave hums, Momma heats up a can of cream of mushroom soup, without mixing in the milk. She pours this gravy over the rat, and I am not allowed to get up from the table until I have eaten the bulk of it, its legs, its tail, its eyeballs, all of its insides. The only things I don't have to eat are its bones and its teeth. Mama uses a nutcracker to bust open the head for me to eat out the brains. If I throw up while I am eating it, I have to eat that up too. When I'm finished, Momma says, "Now you're a good boy."

* * *

The world is home to a full variety of crazy folks, I know, but in Chattahoochee, we house five types: the Pigeons, the Nose-Pickers, the Seers, the Brainers and the Stovepipes. The Pigeons, they rock back and forth all day long on the benches jabbering. The Nose-Pickers pick their noses all day long or masturbate in front of people, not distinguishing the act from normal behavior. The Seers, as we call them, they see things that nobody else can see, like elephants walking down the sidewalk. The Brainers just seem like total geniuses but are in reality schizophrenic crackpots. The Stovepipes, last but not least, are the criminally dangerous ones, the incurable. Stovepipes are good at hiding their crazinesses. That's why we call them stovepipes, because when you look at a stovepipe what else can you see but a stovepipe? It is my opinion that Momma was a Stovepipe.

* * *

My daughters, God bless them, bounce into the store like two thin sticks of joyful butter. I lift them into the air, one by one, and hug them. Penelope is nine, Jurisprudence eleven. They are the loveliest little girls you ever laid eyes on, hands down. Good workers, too. After the hugs, I hand Jurisprudence the pricing gun. Penelope on the step ladder dices garlic cloves. "I'm going to go find that man," I tell Dee, my beloved, and she holds onto my arm tight.

She says, "Jim, you're not planning nothing, are you?"

"Course not," I say. "I just want to talk to him."

"Promise me you're not going to do anything to him. I still can't believe you lifted that plate up like that. What was going through my man's brain?"

"I promise," I say. I say, "If he really is my father, it's not his fault. I'm just something that Myrna stole from him."

"Jim, you're beginning to scare me."

"Don't worry your pretty little head," I tell Dee and kiss her and head through the doors into the sunshine raining down. Across the highway, the institution is lit up like a rectangle caterpillar. All them windows. All them crazy people with eyes that see. They look though their windows at the world out here. I wonder what the world looks like through their eyes. Does it have special colors that normal people like me can't see? Is the air swelled up with God's heartbeat? Can they see its pulse, hypersensitive as they are, the air shifting back and forth, grainy, pulling and blowing, blowing and shifting? That'd be enough to drive a man or woman crazy. My heart goes out to the people in that place. I cannot gaze at the institution without that my heart softens. What those poor bastards must go through every day of the week wins my sympathy.

I walk along Main Street, looking for my supposed daddy, thinking I bet he's gone down to the river. I walk that direction—it's the direction he turned when he left Health Nuts—and when I get there, sure enough, there he is, standing against the concrete edge of the dam, propped against it and looking over at the scenery, his back turned to me. Now he's got a backpack with him, and it's on the ground at his feet. He is smoking a cigar and has no idea that I am behind him. I say, "Daddy?" and he turns. "Son," he says. We look at each other a moment. He sees that I am not here to hurt him, so he holds out his arms. We embrace. After a moment we let each other go, and he says, "I was looking at that black snake, a water moccasin, I guess. Big ass sucker."

I look over at the sludge below. A huge cottonmouth lies over some sticks, but not so huge as to be extraordinary. "He's a fat one,"

I say.

"I sure would hate to get bit by him."

"You'd survive."

"Listen," he says.

I say, "I should apologize."

He says, "There was nobody to report her to."

"Don't worry," I say.

"I couldn't stop tripping. I checked myself in on my own."

"You were a seer?" I say.

"I reported her after I was out," my daddy says. "I know they got a file in there somewhere that says everything I said. All I wanted was to stop tripping, but when the trip eased off, I had all this other shit I was dealing with. Your ma was a complete crazy woman. I was at her disposal." My daddy's body trembles, jerks. He begins to cry a little and is sniffling, remembering those awful times.

"She was a very intelligent woman," I say.

"I'm not proud of it."

"She said you were a rat," I say. "She said that you killed an old lady and stole off with her ovaries. Is that true? Did you pour epoxy over them and try to make golf balls? She said you had it in mind to make a fortune off selling goveries."

"I saw dinosaurs. I was completely mad. I was living in prehistoric America. The shit I saw would knock your socks off, Son, but Myrna, I'll give her this, she made me understand that I was delusional. She was a talented nurse. Other people I have told this story to say it's cool, that I should be happy to have fucked a—wait, I'm sorry, I don't mean to be talking bad about your ma or nothing, but I don't think she should have done that to me, not while I was restrained."

"I'm fine with it. Go ahead."

"She used the situation to cure me. She was a genius and a maniac both at the same time. I bet that's why you're a successful man," Daddy says and laughs, and I laugh.

"Did you love her?" I ask him.

"Fiercely."

"Don't that suck?"

"Enormous."

I grab my daddy in my arms and hug him tight. Then I begin the telling. I tell of his grandchildren Penelope and Jurisprudence, and of Dee, how I started that crazy health food store with what Dee and I saved up from doing so much plumbing and secretarying. The woman who'd stolen his seed, my mother, had had her boobs removed during that last year of her life. When she died, my wife and I became about as high on the hog as we could ever hope to be, having inherited all her savings. I even have a boat now, I tell my daddy, and his face brightens because he loves to fish. We got a steady flow of cash coming in, I tell him, and say that we have a shed in our backyard that could easily be turned into a little bedroom if he wants to stay with us.

"I wouldn't want to put you out," he says.

"It won't be any trouble at all," I say, and I say, "I need me somebody to watch football with on the weekends and somebody to babysit the girls now and then. You do love football, don't you?"

"Aw, shit yeah. Bobby Bowden has got it going on, baby."

"You love little girls?"

"Aw, shit yeah," Daddy says.

"Bobby is a great coach," I say and can just hardly believe that I am standing here talking to my flesh-and-blood daddy about Bobby Bowden and the Florida State Seminoles.

"Listen," my daddy says, "I've been married twice since I knew your mother."

"I don't care about any of that," I say.

"I look like a bum, don't I?"

"Yes, you do," I say.

Daddy laughs. "Thanks for being honest," he says, and he says, "I've sort of been meaning to get me a new wife, you know what I'm saying? I've noticed there to be quite a few pretty gals in Chatta-hoochee."

"Oh, they're all crazy," I warn him.

"Only a crazy woman could love me," Daddy says.

* * *

Daddy moves in. He's here all the way from California, and I am touched. Daddy eats with us at the supper table, us the big happy family, and he works at the store with us and takes the girls on drives and is a great personality. A great many stories Daddy tells, and Dee loves him, loves even his snose, it has grown on us, and it seems absolute craziness that this man could ever have been declared a loony tune. His name is Dan. Dan Hornstein. I'm a Glover, based on Mamma's, what they call, maiden's name. Dan Hornstein and Jim Glover, that's us. It is nice having him around, makes us feel more like a family. That's what happens with people. They get together, next thing you know they're taking delight in each other, just being a family. A real family. A perfect family. A real perfect family.

We are out on the water in my boat, fishing, just me and Daddy.

I tell Daddy that Momma told me that my rat's blood would find me one day, but in reality it found me long ago, I say. My heartfelt prayer, that she kick the bucket, it was answered. Momma sucked a nut down her windpipe and suffocated.

"Damn. What kind of nut was it?"

"I don't reckon I ever found out."

"Well," Daddy says, "I prayed the same thing against her. I bet lots of people prayed for Myrna to die, so don't take it to heart, Son. Me, I'm pretty sure I'm up for the chopping block myself. I got a cancer in my brain, I can feel it."

I think Daddy's bullshitting me, trying to manipulate me into feeling sympathy for him, into being more generous to him and more all-around lenient. Of late, he has been dating Crazy Jeanne from Floor One, who is part Nose-picker, part Pigeon, if you know what I mean. They have been spending time together in the shed in my backyard. I'm pretty sure that's against the rules of the institution and that Jeanne could get in trouble. I have expressed my disapproval to Daddy because Jeanne is one skinny chickadee who has had an awful time of it, just so many people have taken advantage of her— and besides, Jeanne, at least through my eyes, seems way too young for Daddy. Daddy says he just wants to protect her, that he likes her as a friend, that he would never dream of trying to impregnate her. He says they just play checkers together, and acts offended that I would suggest such a thing about his intentions. Really, I should be ashamed of my cynical mind always being at work, but I can't help it. When Daddy says this thing about a cancer on his brain, I play along with it, even though I have my suspicions, and tell him I'm sorry. He asks what for? I tell him I don't want him to die, that he's my true blood father and I'm so happy that he's come back into my life.

"I just want to be a good boy," I say, and finally confess what I've never told a body before, the secret, how Momma would feed me up the most disgusting dishes. It wasn't just rats, neither. I had to eat raw frogs and other creatures both vile and harmless: lizards, garden snakes. She once brought home a fresh dead infant bulldog, put it on a plate, stabbed it with a fork, microwaved it up, and poured butter sauce over it. That was the worst ever. It took me half the night to get it down. My favorite though, what I wished was the only thing Momma ever fed me, was a yellow butterfly. She fed it to me off the tip of her finger, and I'll never forget the way it grabbed the tip of my tongue with its legs, very gentle, as if it understood that this was not my idea. I love that butterfly still, whenever I think of it, and that is why, on our menu at Health Nuts, we have Butterfly Brains, which is a butterfly-shaped omelet filled with garlic and sweet corn.

"That is the most amazing story I ever heard," Daddy says and is looking at me like, Is it possible to eat a baby bulldog?

"I swear to God it's true," I say, and Daddy stands up, causing the boat to wobble. He wants to embrace, which is a thing we've been doing a lot of lately.

"You poor thing," Daddy says, and we are hugging out here in the middle of the lake. "I'm sorry I wasn't there for you, Son," he says, and I believe him. We both shed a few tears and when we sit back down and cast our lines back out, I feel so much better, I do. In fact, I cannot remember ever feeling quite so good as this.

Later, we are in his shed. Instead of saying beer-thirty, like people do, Daddy says, "Peanut-thirty," and brings out the huge plastic screw-can of organic nuts he's got, all the nuts of the rainbow. He bought the damn thing from Sam's Warehouse in Tallahassee, using my card, of course, and we reach in and fill our guts with all the finely salted nuts. I think I see a pair of black panties shoved under Daddy's bed, but don't say a thing. Instead, I agree with him that all that salt on the nuts is a great thing. Dan says they might even put more salt on the nuts. I agree, like father like son. Dan though, he only eats the almonds from the mix. He says, "I'm screwing up the nut ratio," and we laugh. It's just so delicious and so tasty, what else can one say? I reach in, grab a handful and slosh them back and get to crunching. "Pure protein," Daddy says, and we crunch on, just the two of us, crunching the nuts.

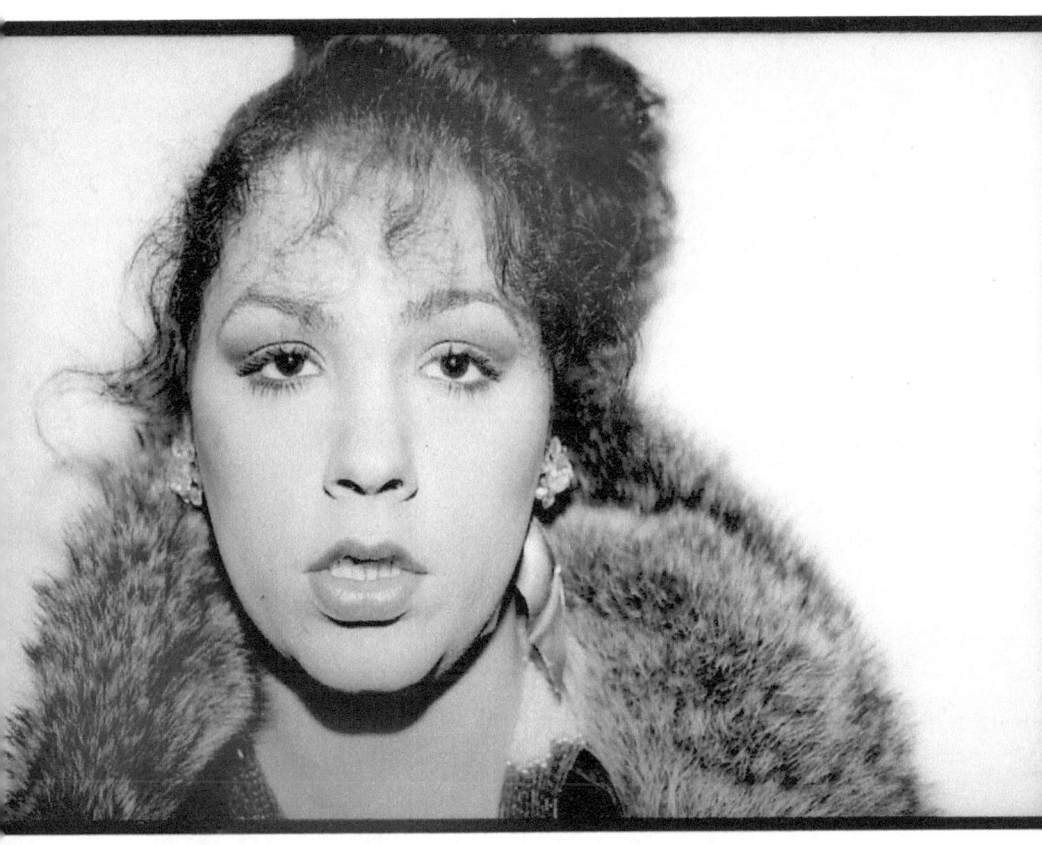

ARBUS

We are at the Met, and we are looking, Bull French and I, at *A young man in curlers at home on West 20th Street*, taken in 1966, twenty years before I was born. Every flaw in the man's face, every pore, every pimple and piece of shaved hair growing back, it all is revealed. This man who wishes he was a woman is not ashamed. Even though his eyes and lips are painted up, he wears no mask and would never kill himself because he thought he wasn't beautiful.

This is what people mean when they say grotesque, Bull goes, and he goes, Look at his ridiculous fingernails.

Oh yes, he missed a spot, I go.

How do you think I would look in curlers? Bull French goes.

I laugh.

What? Don't you think I would look good in curlers?

Oh yes, I do, I go. I would love to see you in curlers, Bull. It would make me very happy, but you would never do that. You could never go against the image you have of yourself.

Bull laughs out loud, too loud.

Shh, I go.

And Bull goes, so loud that people can hear it, I see the image of me, I am stuffing you like a turkey.

I am sorry that I said anything. Sometimes I forget how sensitive Bull is, how it is never a good idea to tease him or go against him too strongly. Poor Bull. I am afraid he has a dark secret that he keeps from himself. Maybe that is why he likes to pretend to hurt me. It is a fantasy, and he likes to have witnesses. When he jostles me in public, when he pushes me and curses, he is returning a bad favor to some woman, or maybe even a man, who hurt him long ago. Whatever happened to Bull, the scar went deep. That, I think, is why Bull is so macho. He works out every day. He is muscular and hairy and he drinks whiskey and he smokes expensive cigars and wears a Rolex. Oh, look at this, Bull goes about another picture, and he reads the title. Puerto Rican woman with a beauty mark. This is another example of grotesque, he goes.

Yes, I go, she too has painted her lips too big, trying for her face to have a different look than what it truly looks like.

She looks disgusted, Bull goes.

She is afraid.

She reminds me of my mother, Bull goes, and he goes, Come on, let's go, Nora. We can stop at the greengrocer. I'll buy you a cucumber, what say? Bull reaches down my back and grabs my hip. A little girl has seen him do this. I try not to show any emotion, but I can tell, the girl has seen me wince, and is appalled.

Wait, what's this? I go, and we enter a room where many of Diane's things are, the things she left after she climbed into the bathtub with all her clothes on and slit her wrists. There are old notebooks and collages and newspaper clippings and things, and I think of my mother, who worked as a seamstress for thirty-five years. She always said that if she lost her beauty she would take sleeping pills. We did not believe her, my brother and I, but she did it. The neighbors called the cops when the smell became unbearable. They took her body away to bury it, but left all her things.

And here is Diane's enlarger, what she used to project images onto light sensitive paper. Here is Diane's passport and here is Diane's camera. What a special camera. I stare at it, thinking how so many people were sucked through that lens, how strange it is, things passing through glass, through eyes. I stand on my toes to look at her camera, her lover, more closely. The space I am in grows small and quiet and intimate. I feel that I am alone. What a magnetic quality the metal has, and peering over the top of the lens, where there is a little dent, I see a finely engraved number, so small and elegant. It is like a secret. I am reading it, yes, it is a serial number, the mark which identifies this camera as Diane's. Under my breath I am reading this number out loud, soft and slow. Three zero one three, I go. And I go, Thirty thirteen nine five. It is a beautiful number, and the number symbol on her camera looks like music, №, so solid and true. I am admiring it when my skirt flies up and Bull gooses me.

I bark out a little scream, because I was not prepared.

Bull laughs very loud.

I start crying and walk away fast.

This is just what Bull French loves. He comes after me, his fancy heels clipping along behind at a trot. What am I smelling? he goes, and catches up to me and yanks my arm. He wants me to fight him, here in the museum hall, but I won't do it. I go limp and he backs me against the wall and kisses me and wipes away my tears with his thumb. What would you do if I ripped off your dress and left you here? Bull goes.

I don't answer.

Then everybody would see how beautiful you are naked. You would have nothing to hide and so there would be no reason to hide it. You would be free, what say? he goes, grabbing my dress at the throat and acting like he will rip it straight down and tear it away and leave me here.

Please don't, Bull, I go.

Are you going to stop being a baby? he goes.

Yes, yes, I am sorry.

Sorry for what?

For being so bitchy, I go, knowing that in reality Bull is upset over my curler comment. No, I don't think Bull would ever put on curlers, or dress like a woman.

Nora, Bull goes, you are one of a kind, truly one of a kind. Not only are you beautiful and a great swim, but smart. I never met a woman so smart as you.

That is because I took philosophy and psychology in college, I go, but I am thinking how in reality I am stupid. I should have stayed in school, at least got my B.S. degree, but instead I floundered out, let myself go. I married. So much for those crazy girl dreams. Destiny? What is that for a girl? Nothing but a pipe dream.

Bull eyes me strangely and with suspicion. I think he is trying to decide if he should rip off my dress for real, let me know that behind his fake abuse of me there is a raging desire to hurt me, a desire that, should it break the surface of his unconscious, would be indifferent to any consequences that might result from being cruel. To rip off a woman's dress in a museum? Bull would try turning it into a work of art. He is a smart man. Bull has *his* degree. Bull would charm the authorities. Look, Bull would go, are there not a hundred paintings in this building that are all about raped women? Why yes, they would go. Bull would look to me. We were doing a performance piece, weren't we? There I am, Nora, nodding her head yes.

I am good at nodding my head yes.

The strange look on Bull's face, in seeing it I cringe. So harsh it is, like he could really do this, rip off my dress and then run off with it, leaving me here. I am afraid, but then he smiles at me tenderly, with admiration and surprise. He even lets go of my dress and smooths out the wrinkles over my breastbone. That's wonderful, Bull goes, and he goes, I never knew you had any formalized schooling, Nora, good for you.

I went to Saint John's University for a year and a half, I go. That's where I met my husband, I go, sort of reminding Bull that if he gets too crazy on me he might one day have to answer to Dominique. You don't know me as well as you think, I go, not without a small measure of pride, I admit it. I like that I have a little bit of power over Bull, that I am a mystery to Bull in some ways, that I am not a complete empty bucket to Bull, even though Bull sometimes treats me like I am.

Now Bull treats me like a lady, a royal queen, holding my hand and playing the part of a gentleman. He takes me daintily through the rooms of classical paintings, commenting on the Vermeers, the da Vincis and Caravaggios. The repetition of the crucifixion is emblematic of man's irredeemably burnt soul, Bull goes, and I giggle.

Soon we are in the modern wing, and I see marvelous colors on the wall, a flower going deeper, sucking your eye down into it like a whirlpool of exciting calm. I want to stand here and stare, but Bull goes, Georgia O'Keeffe was a bull dyke. Instead of putting lipstick on her own face, she painted these paintings, isn't that sad?

I guess it could be, I go, and Bull gives my hand a tender squeeze, and pulls me along. I am thinking about woman's irredeemably burnt soul. I dare not mention this to Bull.

This new room has paintings everywhere hanging heavy and crazy and berserk and full of angst, like animals in a butcher shop, I think, a display of severed muscles and bones, but here is a softer one. Bull goes, This man had a thing about adolescent girls. They were his passion. Look at how he has turned this little no-count nothing of a girl into a god. A man without passion is like an eagle without wings. My own passion, as you know, is doing what I got to do to make myself filthy rich. You wait and see, Nora. One day I will be able to buy that painting, though I would never stoop so low as to buy a painting like that. Look what it says here. It was painted on cardboard of all things.

A syllogism, I go. You said a syllogism, Bull, I go.

I know what a syllogism is, Bull goes.

A man without passion can't fly, I go, daring to paraphrase Bull, which I know he doesn't like. I am a man with passion, I go. There-fore I fly, I go.

Every girl is fucked, Bull goes. You are a girl. Therefore you are fucked.

This is true, I go, and giggle.

Bull calms down. He too giggles, seeing how two young Orien-tal women and a family of Germans have cleared out at the sound of his vulgarity. We are alone now but for the security guard's eyes, the video eyes, and the many painted eyes looking out at us from two-dimensional surfaces. Every girl has nipples that beg, Bull goes in the sexy voice he saves for when we are alone. You are a girl, he goes. Therefore your nipples beg.

Bull fondles me.

No, Bull, I go.

Open your mouth, Bull goes.

What?

Bull presses down with his fingers, pinching me, and he pulls me close to him.

I open my mouth.

The most beautiful mouth in the world, Bull goes, and lets me go.

And I feel rejected, like I have done something wrong. I am ashamed of myself. I want to make up with Bull. Bull, I'm sorry, Bull, I go.

John Oliver Hodges

Sorry for what?

For being so bitchy, I go, and I go, Please, Bull.

Shh, Bull goes. Not so loud, Nora, Bull goes. Somebody might hear you, he goes, and he goes, Oh, look at this.

I giggle.

They saved his palette, Bull goes, excited.

Yes, I go, it has a lot of gray on it.

The palette of Balthus, Bull marvels.

Do you think it's worth a lot of money? I go, and I go, What about his other things? His old shoes and his whatnots? What about his coffee cup?

Worthless, I'm sure, Bull goes, and he goes, In order to make value in certain items, all the other items need to be destroyed. Otherwise you have a competition of items. That will never do.

Oh, I know exactly what you're talking about, Bull, I go, and begin telling Bull of my special dancing pig, what I took from Mamma's apartment, how because all her other things are gone forever, that pig is worth so much more to me. My brother sold the apartment with everything in it, and the people just threw it all away. I did not know he would do this, otherwise I would have taken more things. It is very sad, I think. My momma worked for thirty-five years making people look beautiful, but nobody kept anything.

I don't care about your fucking momma, Bull goes.

My feelings are hurt, but I don't care. I giggle. Bull takes me through the chain mail exhibition and then we are outside. Bull hails a taxi. Flushing, Bull goes to the driver, and my heart sinks. Bull is taking me home. My eyes water, I can't help it. Roosevelt and Main, Bull goes to the driver. These words hurt me so much, more than I can tell. They are like blades, these words, each word a knife blade stabbing me. Bull is wiping himself clean of me. I have performed poorly today for Bull. I am not perfect. I weep.

When Bull sees the state I am in, he runs his fingers through my hair, pitying me, and I feel so close to him. I just wish Bull would fold me up like a love letter and push me down deeply into his warm pocket, never to emerge but to receive his kisses and caresses.

Oh Nora, Bull goes, melting my heart.

I don't want to go home, I go, and grab Bull's arm and pull him close and bite his shoulder through his suit jacket. This is my way of protesting being treated unkindly, and Bull eats it up. Unlike Dominique, Bull enjoys when I pout. Bull takes my pouting as a symbol of worship. In being affected by him, I am enslaved to him, which Bull enjoys the sight of.

I already miss you, Bull, I go, and pull my hand up between Bull's legs.

Bull French does not mind this. He likes to see me desperate for him, for his love and acceptance, here while he is rejecting me, throwing me away.

With Dominique, when he rejects me, I only feel persecuted, ugly, like an ungainly stupid klutz incapable of the simplest human dignities. I kiss his hand, Dom thinks I'm messing with him. I smile, Dom thinks I'm being flippant about something he said, and then refuses to talk to me for days. Nearly everything I do is wrong. I make too much noise. I touch him funny. I wear stupid clothes. Bargain clothes, Dom calls my clothes. Anybody who sees you is going to think you're poor, Dom goes. You should wear something flashy and modern, Dom goes, something to make other men jealous of me. A real pair of jeans would be nice, a cute skirt, maybe worn with pink flip-flops. You have beautiful ankles, Dom goes, but you never show them off. As it is, you look like a goddamn street woman. But worse, Dom goes. You look like a street woman without any style at all. At least street women sometimes have style. You, you're like a dried out dishrag or something. It's not like we don't got money, Nora. And what about that fancy moisturizing lotion I bought for you. I still don't understand why you don't wear it, Nora. You embarrass me, goddammit. How do you think I feel when we go out together and you look like that?

No. Bull French is different. With Bull I never feel self-pity, only sorrow and regret for not being what Bull wishes I was completely. All for him. I want to be his. Completely.

Is this true love?

It must be, because it sucks me into it, that's how strong it is. It makes me a different woman than I normally am. I lose track of who I am supposed to be, and the funny thing is, I don't even care anymore about that person people know as Nora. Nora? Who is that? I go to myself. Nobody, nothing to concern myself with. I don't know her and so how can I care about her? All I know is that I feel something with Bull. I am real. I am alive. I am giving Bull pleasure.

Hey, Bull goes. You crazy thing. What are you trying to do?

I don't want to let Bull go, I am humming with Bull, and even if I did let Bull go, it would be so undignified to speak now, no, I won't do it. His fingers in my hair. Bull, I go in my mind. Don't call it off, please.

Okay, Bull goes, hearing my thought, and he gives to me what he has been storing inside him, just for me, I think, and feel proud because I have given Bull great pleasure. Bull giggles, then reaches both hands under my face and gently pulls me up, my heart leaping because I have made him happy. I am worth something to him. I look out the window as he puts himself away, and see Flushing Noodle.

The driver turns onto Main, and drives us past a store selling homemade Italian ices, a family foot specialist and a Mandarin bakery. There is Chandrigah Fashion, Choopan Kabab, and Kabul Kabab.

Stop here, Bull goes to the driver.

The driver stops beside the Queens Botanical Gardens, and Bull pays him as if he is rich, which he might be for all I know. Bull is never short for cash, all those bills always spilling out of his wallet. Dinners, hotel rooms, taxis. I don't know what Bull does to make such money, he won't tell me, but I like not knowing. In not knowing there is mystery. The mystery compels me. In the mystery of not knowing Bull completely there is hope.

We take a stroll into the Queens Botanical Gardens, where there is a wedding going on. In the middle of a small green field surrounded by flowering bushes a Chinese bride, dressed in a beautiful white gown, poses with her man. The photographer snaps away, getting new angles. "Beautiful," he says, and I hug Bull close, taking refuge in the irony, this watching a new pair in the world, their promises. They do not know what they are getting into, I think, and Bull pulls me along through a maze of red roses where a small boy, the rose bushes dwarfing his littleness, smiles for the camera of his parents.

Hand-in-hand we stroll the winding walkway until Bull pulls me up a hill into a small woods. This is new for us. We never tried anything like this before, not outside like this. Bull takes off my dress, and then he pushes me down on my knees. He pushes me forward so that I am like an animal, a dog, and he plays with my boob so that I feel fat. Why is he not loving me now? What is wrong, I go to myself, and that is when I hear something crack behind me. Bull has broken a stick in two over his knee. The sharp edge of the stick presses against my tender place. I crawl forward to get away, but Bull grabs my shoulder and pulls me back.

Bull, I go.

Shh, Bull goes, and he teases me with what he could do. If I protest, no telling, you know how Bull is, so I try to play along like I don't care. This is your lipstick, Nora, Bull goes, poking so that it hurts. You know that, don't you, Nora, Bull goes.

Bull, I go.

You like this, don't you? Bull goes.

Yes, I go.

You love it, don't you? he goes.

I giggle. I pretend like I like it, making a sound here and there of what it sounds like when a woman is in pleasure, but Bull is not playing this game fairly.

Bull, I go.

You love it, Bull goes. You know you love it.

Yes, Bull, I go, but it hurts, please.

Goddammit! Bull goes, and I want to scream. I bite my lip, holding back my natural sounds. I don't care what he is doing, let him. I look at the ground, the earth black in places, green in others. I am spreading out into the world, growing, getting bigger, fatter.

Bull goes, Oh shit, Nora, you are bleeding.

I giggle.

It's just a little cut, Bull goes, and steps back to look at me. He goes, Oh, man, where is Diane Arbus when you need her? This is a picture that would be loved for years and years.

Bull, I go.

What a beautiful picture, Bull goes, and I look back at Bull and see he is putting me in an imaginary frame, making a square with his hands and looking through it at me, as if I am a picture. "Girl with stick, Queens Botanical Gardens," he says, and I don't even know what I should do. I do not even know. I am so confused, but I must look adorable to Bull, in my confusion, because he laughs.

Okay, Bull goes, and he goes, I'm sorry Nora, and I think that now Bull will take me to dinner, but instead he leans over and, in the sexy voice he saves for when we are alone in our usual getaway, I love you.

Oh, to hear the words. Everything is better, but then I hear the terrifying sound of my lover moving away through the leaves. I see him galloping down the hill with my dress. Bull, oh Bull, please, I beg in my mind, but he doesn't even look back to see what he has left. Oh Bull, I go, and am clutching the stick, and I cry out and push my face and my whole body into the earth.

I wait now, I am waiting, simply and with love, the smell of the dirt in my face. He will come back to collect me, I go in my mind. I know he will come back to collect me, I go, and open my eyes. He is not there, but looking through the trees and down the hill I see the Chinese bride walking with her newly wedded man. The photographer is walking backwards in front of them, snapping his camera, going, "Beautiful! Beautiful!"

TROUTSKY'S
PARADE

Brian is Jewish by blood, but goes to Asheville in Lisa's black Lexus, with Lisa, his roommate, a blond-haired Aryan beauty whose family is in jewelry. In Asheville Brian drives the Lexus down a downtown alley to where Lisa's friend, Deziray, currently lives in a spacious state-of-the-art music studio identified by the Xeroxed grenade pasted to the door, an easy find. Lisa knocks. Deziray opens, says, "Hey hey!" and, looking Brian over, says, "Oh, you cut off your beard."

"For that smooth feeling," Brian says.

"I just had my hair cut today, see?" Deziray says. "You like it?" she says, and bounces her curls and plays with her bangs. Deziray opens a bottle of organic blackberry wine and pours three glasses. The toast is to friendship.

Deziray is quite the drinker. The month before, Deziray passed through Tallahassee, and the three of them drank an enormous amount at Posey's Raw Oyster Bar on the gulf. Once back at the shotgun shack, Lisa passed out and Brian and Deziray rolled in the grass by the bonfire, hugging and kissing. Brian loved her smell, and her happy face, and was charmed by her style. She wore a knit sweater with sleeves down to her fingers, and Brian loved that she piled firewood logs into her arms without considering the dead bark and dirt that got all over her—and she wore a knee-length pleated skirt above leg warmers. Sort of a big-bones girl, Deziray, pale and giggly and somewhat squeaky. Brian ran his hands up and down her thighs and stuck his fingers into her leg warmers. It was beautiful by the fire, but they went into his room where the clothes came off, all but for Deziray's leg warmers, there she was, on the bed, beneath him, her legs wide apart. She removed her tampon as though giving Brian permission to fuck her, or perhaps eat her out, but you never know these days. Casual sex with strangers, no matter how pure and beautiful they might look, no matter how charming, how soft, how special and whatnot, is not the best idea. Deziray's tampon left a stain on Brian's sheet, which happened to be pink, it was a pink sheet.

Deziray does not know this, or maybe she does know this, but Brian cut off his beard in order to, should the chance again occur, eat her pussy out with great feeling, none of that crazy beard hair to mess things up.

Deziray takes her visitors to a nearby bar, buys them massive Pabst Blue Ribbon cans, what are called oil cans. At the bar Deziray talks on about her boyfriends. By the way Deziray talks, she must have ten boyfriends. Deziray's last steady boyfriend just broke up with her, and Deziray wants to get "super-drunk" tonight to celebrate. The bartender does not seem to like Deziray very much, even though she dumps a ton of bills into her jar after buying Brian and Lisa double shots of Lord Calvert.

From the bar Deziray and Brian and Lisa walk a dozen blocks to see a hardcore show at a fancy neighborhood house packed with punks and hair-heads. The band plays loud and fast, but with a working man's quirk to it; it sounds to Brian like a cross between Jody Foster's Army and Huey Lewis and the News—there's even a saxophonist. But the house isn't made to have so many people in it. The whole floor bounces, feels as if it will break any second now. Brian pictures everybody falling down into the basement, the splintered floorboards digging into stomachs and piercing drumheads and speakers. It might feel kind of nice, he thinks, having all those people piled on top of him. In any event, he can barely see the band, so squashes in closer through the jungle of sweaty arms, and sees the singer's face and part of his shirt. The singer is a midget, Brian thinks, then realizes that the singer is also the drummer.

* * *

So this is Asheville! What a place! What a scene! In the kitchen, cases of found food stack halfway up the wall, and many of the punks and hair-heads walk around with black books in which their observations and musings are jotted. Brian sees how important they feel. They are tattooed, and involved in a great cause. NO WAR! FUCK BUSH! Solidarity is in the air. The fliers and posters, what Brian has seen on walls and stapled to posts since he and Lisa arrived, are political, take-a-stand type stuff. And Asheville produces what is claimed to be the country's only Leftist newspaper, the *Asheville Global Report*, in which Mad America and His policies are exposed and denigrated. The AGR is released all throughout the city every Thursday.

The AGR is sponsoring a benefit tonight, Deziray says, so from the show they pile into a car with a bunch of punks and hair-heads and head downtown to the Asheville Community Resource Center, this huge bottom floor of a building used for giving out free bicycles, for yoga classes, talk groups, classes in homeopathic healing, and for teaching women how to defend themselves.

The outside doors must be twenty feet tall, and are studded with rivets, and Brian feels grand walking through them into the huge open space where all these people stand around or sit by the stage from which a young woman poet delivers her message of NO WAR! and FUCK BUSH!

Brian is tired, though, has not slept for thirty hours. A cozy chair in the corner is empty, so what the hell. Brian plops himself down in it in relaxed watching and watches one poet after another take the stage to lambaste Bush and the approaching war. Everybody gets a turn. Some speeches are made in which the local government is ridiculed, and a collection bag is passed around. A man strums guitar, singing of how great marijuana is. And there are rappers, first several white rappers, then some Puerto Rican rappers. All of them mention the catchphrase: NO WAR!

Brian's been to some readings, he's seen poets and writers, Poet Laureates and Pulitzer Prize winners. What these people are doing is better. There is more expression, more feeling, more aggression in what they do. But then some guy, one of the leaders, it seems, for he is older and dressed more professionally than the others, gets on stage and sings yearnfully and hopeful of the day when "democracy" is true and rules. The song makes Brian nervous, just hearing that word, "democracy." FUCK democracy! Brian thinks. And he's thinking, since democracy is a fiction, why not burn a few cop cars? These people should spray-paint the walls, bust out the windows of food chains and department stores. Those here gathered seem ready for action against the state, yet their leaders speak dreamily of "democracy" as though quite in love with, not only the myth, but the word.

* * *

Lisa donates three dollars to democracy, comes over with a large cup of red wine for Brian, compliments of the organizers. Plenty of wine for everybody. The creative juices here flow freely, and Brian and Lisa just love the woman who reads a poem about how fat she is, her woe over the shape her body has come to inhabit. Her poem highlights the image of a sharpened knife entering her vagina. "I want you all to know that I was sexually abused as a child," she says. A burst of feedback eggs her on, and she says that Feminism taught her to be strong and proud of her body. At this, Brian's eyes water up, and he nearly sheds a tear.

Tired as he is, Brian is caught up in the communal spirit, so what the hell—as the last stragglers take the stage, Brian puts his name on the list. He is called. He steps up onto the platform. His voice comes out cracked, unsure and soft at first. He says, "I heard this guy talking about democracy." He clears his throat. "Democracy," he says, "claims to represent the interests of the people. But the term 'people' is so abstract that it includes everybody, and there is no such thing as the representation of the interests of everybody." All is quiet but for Brian's voice. He has an audience. "Besides being a total fraud," he says, "democracy mobilizes large masses for wars, more so than any other form of government. It was after democracies appeared that World War One appeared, followed by World War Two, mass holocausts, the greatest horrors. What is worse than exploitation? DEATH! All in the name of the people!"

"That's what I'm talking about!" somebody shouts.

Another person yells, "Hell yeah!"

"In the past," Brian says, "prior to the appearance of democracies, it was clear to most people that there was an exploited underclass, but the underclass, at least, was not mobilized for war. Since the French Revolution the underclass has been mobilized for war. So you get the worst of two possible worlds, an underclass used as cannon fodder. If it isn't exploitation that democracies provide a justification for, it's murder, death, massacres."

"Fuck that," some guy with a goatee says. The guy looks a bit like a young Trotsky, tell the truth, and the guy says, "This man is talking fascism!"

"Fascism schmashism," Brian says. He says, "No need to have an intellectual debate here. All I'm saying is that what we need in the good ole U.S. of A., right now, is Anarchy with a capital A. We need to take back America! Anarchy Anarchy Anarchy!" Brian says, pushing his brotherly fist through the air.

They eat it up like piglets sucking milk out of the mother sow. "Anarchy Anarchy!" they cry, and push their brotherly fists with Brian. Brian enjoys the support, and suddenly he is no longer tired. When the people stop shouting Anarchy, this to hear what Brian says next, he clears his throat. "All this fear," he says, "of the American public and the American government in the year two thousand three about weapons of mass destruction and the need to fight a war in order to eliminate them? That's fucking bullshit, man! There were no instruments of mass destruction prior to 'the people' appearing on the scene and becoming the supposed focus of political power. In the name of the people anything is justified!"

"You come from a different people, dude," the Trotskyite says. "Why don't you tell us what planet you're from? You need to get down to earth with the rest of us."

"Okay," Brian says, "go ahead. Sacrifice your life in the name of freedom. Give all your support to Jesse Helms. Isn't old Jesse your hero in Asheville? Isn't he all about Freedom? Democracy? Don't you feel satisfied and exalted when you raise your bird-blasters to splatter whom? Why, your own brothers and civilian sisters."

"Oh, he's getting beatnik on us now," the Trotskyite says.

"The failure of democracy is the failure of capitalism," Brian says, "because capitalism is supposed to be the economic form of democracy. I've been listening to you tonight, and I've noticed that many of you speak out against buying and selling, yet in the same breath you laud democracy. Am I mistaken in thinking I've been listening to a gaggle of hypocrites?"

"Beware of the wolf in sheep's clothing," Brian's esteemed heckler announces.

"Listen," Brian says, "the greatest tyrant in world history was Abraham Lincoln, your apparent hero. He was responsible for a war that took a million fucking lives in defense of a democratic government. Do you think of old Linc's assassin as a hero? As someone who eliminated a tyrant responsible for the greatest war machine in world history? Of course not. You're a Demo-Trotskyite, by the looks of you."

A lot of the people out there laugh at Brian's little joke. They clap hands and his goateed heckler looks quite ridiculous now. Brian sees his face squash up with doubt, and feels sorry for him. Brian is a compassionate guy, all for the people, so pities the poor ignorant fool.

Nevertheless, lifted up by the support of the majority, Brian rags him out further. "Listen," he says, "if the Confederacy had survived, it's very unlikely that there would be plans for a war on Iraq!" With mock-disgust Brian leaves the mike and joins the people who, sorely confused over this last statement, give him nods of approval. He can tell, they want to join his party, whatever it is. Somebody hands him a DIY beer in a bottle, and the beer is very good, as only homemade beers can be, with all the hops and yeast, no stinting. Rich and full.

* * *

Deziray Boot steps up, hands Brian a big cup of red wine. She says, "That was Harold, my new boyfriend you just trashed."

"Whoops," Brian says, and wants to say something about her taste in men, but *Let's not be cruel*, he decides.

"Harold edits *The Red Trout*," Deziray informs him.

"Doesn't surprise me."

"It's a communist rag."

"Obviously."

"You're such a crab," Deziray says, "but you're bad-ass, I admit it. That was a great speech. You're so awesome."

Harold Trout, or Troutsky, whoever he is, comes up with one of his sidekicks, and he says, "I think you're one of us. What's your name, compadre?"

"Adolf," Brian says. Harold's whiskey breath blasts all over the place, a strong one, him.

"That's good," Harold says, and says, "I agreed with all that you said, just so you know. I was giving you a backboard, right? We've got to work together in these times," but Brian's thinking Anarchy will never, never, never in a million years happen in the United States. The "people" are under the influence of beer. What need to fight, except in the social aspect of getting together to pretend to share a cause? That does nothing. It's beer and tobacco, that's what's important. And tattoos. The folks are serfs to the capitalist regime, deceived into believing they are cognizant enough to want to over-throw the state. Only what is want without action? It's like faith and good works, the one qualifying the other, all that silly shit from the bible. What matters is that Anarchy in America is a lifestyle only. As a political force it's passive, impotent, useless as a noose made of sweet spaghetti. There will be no guerrilla warfare in the U.S. The U.S., that is to say, US, will go to war. We will fuck ourselves in the ass again.

A party is to be held at The Grenade, a party Deziray, Brian and Lisa's eloquent and generous host, is hosting. The man who owns The Grenade has told poor Deziray that she must move out in two days, but no matter. She's got enough money, moolah, cash, greenbacks and what have you, to rent her own place. Deziray is a sandwich-maker. Sure. Today's daughters of the American elite work menial jobs as waitresses, cashiers, even mechanics, as though making up for the crimes of their parents. Even Lisa, whose last name is Jewel, works in a teeth-making factory. Her parents think her mighty weird. It's a low-paying job, making teeth, a redundant job. Lisa Jewel of Jewel's Jewels arrives, not without embarrassment, at the teeth factory in her sleek black Lexus, but who cares what people say? Brian and Lisa hit the Tallahassee dumpsters regularly, pulling out cantaloupes and Hostess cupcakes when she gets off work, packing boxes of veggies into the trunk of the Lexus. And meat, so many sausages and porterhouse steaks, hot dogs and packs of ground burger that they then distribute to the poor hippies on the east side of town, and the dumb rednecks on the south side of town. Lisa is a great friend, a Lutheran and, like Brian, a vegetable-eater. Everybody should have a friend like Lisa.

At The Grenade, Deziray puts on some *Godspeed You! Black Emperor*. She quickly realizes that this won't do the trick, so switches them out for some *This Bike Is A Pipe Bomb*, which gets the party started. The anarchists dance, drink whiskey, and beer, and talk. A couple of homosexuals dance a dance that can only be called "The Buttfuck," and then Harold Troutsky comes in with his entourage of bearded followers. He gives Deziray a kiss on the cheek and whispers in her ear. Deziray lilts to the stereo, cuts off the music. "We came to tell everybody about a No War parade we're having," Troutsky says to the bunch. "Tomorrow we meet at the ACRC at noon with banners and signs. We're going to march seven miles through Asheville."

"Yes," Brian says, "but you've got to do something to piss off the police. You've got to get the police to fire their guns at you."

"Aw, man, now what're you rambling on about?" Troutsky says, and looks around at everybody. "This here is Adolf," he announces.

"You've got to get the cops to fire at you, kill some of you," Brian explains. "That's the best way right now to begin to imagine stopping the war. What America needs is an internal massacre."

"Kent State never accomplished anything," Troutsky says, and says, "You still haven't told us what planet you're from."

"You've got to make it better than Kent State. You've got to justify rising up and taking arms. Why are you all so lame here in Asheville? I don't understand it. Cynically I see why, but damn if you people aren't just like a church, just like any social institution. It's all about social exchange, communality, that's where it ends. A No War parade without a secret agenda is like pissing in your face. If it was only innocuous, just a powerless display of brotherhood, it would be forgivable, but in reality it supports the enemy because it makes you look like idiots."

"Pure wisdom," Troutsky says, and says, "Does anybody here want to volunteer as a martyr?"

"He's obviously a violent sort," a Troutsky sidekick says.

"The mind of a terrorist," Troutsky says.

Even though it seems like a lost cause at this point, Brian goes ahead and says it: "Force is the only way to achieve revolution. Even a fool can see that in the case of the United States, the means of taking up arms and killing people will justify the collapse of your hoodwinkage. The trick is to get the people you aspire to be like to throw the first punch. Make them massacre you!" Brian says, and slings up his brotherly fist. "Make them massacre you!" he repeats, hoping to draw the piglets back to the sow, but nobody joins him. So much for fundamentals. Brian feels defeated, but then some smart person, the handy Lutheran, it turns out, Ms. Lisa Jewel of Jewel's Jewels, puts forth: "Like Jesus."

Lisa Lisa Lisa!

"Do you think Jesus was completely naked on the cross?" Deziray wonders aloud.

Some of our budding revolutionaries laugh at this obscene comment. But one must not blame others for being callow or sheepish or insensitive to the sufferings of the Jesus. One can blame others only for the degree of denial they possess in relation to their knowledge and intelligence.

"I think Adolf could be a Malcolm-X-ist," a Troutsky sidekick posits.

"Look," Brian says. "I thought Lisa's comment said it. Like Jesus. Jesus made them kill him, but in Asheville nobody cares. In Asheville they make hot air for the sake of it. Hot air on a hot day. Here we are, going to war, possibly to some final method of annihilation, and everybody is just too afraid to jack up somebody's shit!"

"There isn't going to be a massacre," Troutsky says.

"Not here," Lisa says.

"It's our children that will be coming home in body bags," an older man with a soothingly deep voice remarks. The older man, baldish and bold of chin, but too fat to resemble Lenin, says, "I'll be in the parade. Perhaps I'll bring a potato cannon and shoot off some frozen taters."

"Not in my parade," Troutsky, that pacifist, pitiful but not pitiable, says.

"Then get the fuck out of here!" Brian says. He can be mean, sure. He gets sick of people, of their indefatigable fears, and of their obedience and lack of self-loathing. That's why he avoids people two days out of the week, at least, or anyway finds himself alone a lot of the time. He's a tall guy, Brian, carries a lot of anger around with him everywhere he goes, under the surface. His mother disappeared when he was a baby, which he considers to be a meaningless fact, but his father was, is, a Communist intellectual, an important contributor to anarchist theory (right up there alongside Bakunin and Magón!) but a horrible—was, is—dad. It just gets into him. As if to drive his point home, Brian throws his bottle at the brick wall. It blows apart into smithereens, and the Troutskyists, unnerved by Brian's childish display, leave. The anarchist homosexuals leave. The women in black skirts leave. Even the old man of the potato cannon leaves. The Grenade has cleared out.

* * *

"Thanks for crashing my party," Deziray Boot says, and smiles, laughs, does her quirky dance of jerks. Deziray is about drunk as a skunk, super-drunk, but insists that Brian and Lisa go with her to this nearby party. Soon the three of them are standing in a dark alley that smells like cleaning solvents. Brian looks around for the source of the smell, but doesn't see anything. When Deziray bangs on the door, a sad guy opens, revealing a hall where three more doors are lined up. The door at the right end of the hall is open wide, light falling through it. Deziray tells Brian and Lisa to go in there, that she will join them shortly. Brian and Lisa obey. They go in there where some bearded, rather morose, vacuous-looking men play mandolins. A bunch of other equally stoned-looking people hang around doing nothing, unless listening to the mandolins is doing something. Brian and Lisa don't know any of them. They try making conversation. The guy who opened the door for them, Brian thinks, looks a bit like Bill Clinton might have looked in his younger days, only depressed. "Do you play the saxophone?" Brian asks him, but the guy pretends not to have heard. They drink a few beers. A huge aquarium with fish in it bubbles below a large framed black and white photograph of New York City.

"Please let's get out of here," Brian says to Lisa.

But where's Deziray? They've been waiting around here forever for her. She must have gone back to The Grenade, they decide, so back to The Grenade they go, but The Grenade is locked. Brian bangs on the door. Nobody home. It has dropped down into the twenties, and is pretty fucking cold out, so Brian and Lisa get in the Lexus and run the heater, sharing the thin sleeping bag they brought along, and sharing a beer from the Styrofoam cooler. An hour later, when Deziray still is not back, Brian says, "So Deziray just disappeared, huh?"

"Yeah, man, I can't believe she ditched us."

"Is this normal behavior for her?"

"I don't know, why? Do you think something happened?"

"Happened?"

"Yeah, like maybe something bad?"

"She's probably with one of her boyfriends," Brian says.

But it doesn't make sense. Deziray is always referring to Lisa as her best friend. It doesn't make sense that Deziray would suddenly disappear. Brian and Lisa try getting some zees, but Brian's mood is bad. Some guys might be manhandling Deziray. He pictures her surrounded by Troutskyists, one of them with a video camera—they are making a movie to support their efforts against the war—and Brian sees himself cutting in to save her, dragging her barefooted and naked out into the freezing weather. After more time goes by, he says, "She still isn't back."

"Oh really?" Lisa says. "So you think something happened? Maybe we should look for her?"

"The last place we saw her was at that stupid party."

So Brian and Lisa go back down that other alley and Brian bangs on the door. It's late, after three. The young Bill Clinton opens and Brian is nice first off, simply asking the dude if he knows where Deziray is. "No," he says in his robe and slippers. He is tired, starts to close the door, but Brian inserts his foot. Raising his voice, he says, "What about those other doors? She came in here with us and then disappeared! Could you knock on those other doors please?"

Somebody calls from somewhere, presumably one of the mandolin guys in bed: "What's going on out there?"

"Hey, sorry for bothering you!" Lisa says.

Brian says, "Can't you at least tell me that she's not somewhere in this building? What's behind those other doors?" The doors look sinister to Brian, flat gray. The whole place is stale, too secure, and reeks of abject cleanliness.

"There's nothing I can tell you," Bill says.

"Sorry for waking you up," Lisa says.

"Deziray!" Brian shouts.

"Goddammit, what the fuck is going on out there!" cries the voice from within the lair.

"Okay, whatever, fuck it," Brian says, and lets the fool close the door. Brian and Lisa, freezing, hurry back to the Lexus through the fresh-falling snow. They check The Grenade again but it's locked still. Brian starts the Lexus, runs the heater. But how stupid to run the engine all night to run the heater. Brian kills the engine. He tries to sleep. He shivers and worries, holds his warmth to himself. It gets light out. Then Brian hears something, sounds like a car letting somebody out, but he doesn't lift his head. If it's Deziray, he doesn't want to know. Somebody else ate her pussy, sure. Brian just wishes he was asleep now. He is glad she is safe.

Finally Lisa leaves the Lexus to find a place to pee, and checks The Grenade. It's open. Brian and Lisa check Deziray's room, and there she is, sound asleep in her cozy bed. Brian goes to the kitchen, pours the leftover coffee back through the machine, and reads the B. Traven novel he brought along, finding out after a few pages that he doesn't much care for B. Traven. The book has a political agenda that is plain as day (what kind of novel is that!), but B. Traven did, after all, write *Treasure of the Sierra Madre*, which must be the greatest movie ever made.

Oh, what Brian wanted very much to do while here was eat Deziray Boot's pussy. Brian had been remembering their night together ever since they'd spent it.

Yes, the bonfire, the grass, and then later, in his bed, the pink sparsely-haired squiggle between her legs, the elegance of her posture, the slight turn of her head and the tension in her neck, a hint of shyness when he spread her legs farther apart to marvel over it, admire it—but now tired, nervy, zoned-out, Brian smokes, reading B. Traven until the phone rings.

It's Deziray's boss calling to say, on the answering machine that is turned up full blast: "Dez, it's ten thirty. There's no cashier at the Green Blouse." The Green Blouse is a homey food type place for Asheville's punks and hair-heads, a meeting spot for democratic-conversations-under-the-guise-of-Anarchy. Deziray passes Brian on her way to the bathroom, emerging later ready for work, the smell of a lit match lingering in the air. And is gone. Brian, on the couch, thinks he'll sleep now, but can't. He paces The Grenade then looks in on Lisa, who is asleep, lucky girl, on Deziray's futon, one bare foot sticking out from under the comforter.

Brian slips off his shoes and crawls under the comforter with her, and Lisa wakes up a little, and makes room for Brian to crawl in closer. She inches back against Brian so that they are two S's side by side, a Secret Service icon of compromised angles, none of that dagger-like business, that business of lightning bolts to frighten one. Brian drapes his arm over his roommate and draws her close, her body warm, his face in her hair. She is not like Brian's roommate now. They are not in the shotgun shack that they are used to, and they could be anybody, not friends, but complete strangers, or what if they were in Iraq and were just regular civilians? What if they were in Iraq, just living their lives, a man and his wife, and here come the Americans, invading their home?

Brian can't sleep so parts her hair and licks the back of her neck. The Aryan responds favorably. Brian pulls her close. He hasn't slept for what? Forty-five hours? That ought to be nothing, but what with all the partying Brian has done he feels unhinged, his brain off the hook. His body floats through space and is falling right along with all the snow falling outside. Colors break and merge on the inside screens of his lids, colorful blobs blobbing around as the warmth of his roommate draws him nearer, his hands fitting down through her shirt and clutching her. In all of the falling his hooked Jewish nose enters her body. It's the most natural thing in the world, drinking from a woman. Brian laps at the German as if she is a salt lick, and she trembles. She pulls Brian up onto her, tugs at his belt, but "We're roommates," Brian says.

Brian drives Lisa through Asheville in her sleek black Lexus, all around Asheville on down to the river where so many abandoned buildings, the leftovers from past industries, crumble slowly into the future. They smoke beside the current, then Brian drives them to the Green Blouse. Deziray brings them their plates. She apologizes for locking them out of The Grenade during the freezing weather last night. "Where were you? What happened to you?

Where did you go?" Brian asks.

"I don't remember," Deziray says, and laughs her laugh, dances her jerky dance, knowing, as she must, whether or not somebody fucked her while she was passed out.

"We damn near to froze to death," Brian says.

"I'm sorry," Deziray says. "I completely let you guys down. I heard that you went to Rick's last night at like three in the morning and threatened to beat him up. Is that true?"

"He was worried about you, Dezzy," Lisa says.

Deziray laughs way too loud, a sudden burst that quickly dies. It's the laughter of a crazy woman, a woman who uses laughter to hide things from herself. The girl is crazy, Brian thinks.

And they are out of there. Goodbye Asheville, but leaving, they see Troutsky's parade, the punks and punk-hippy-hybrids walking the downtown sidewalks with signs that say the usual: NO WAR and FUCK BUSH.

"They ought to have a sign that says RAW ON," Brian says, noticing the potato-cannon guy, potato-cannonless with a cardboard plaque on his bulging stomach that reads: "MASSACRE ME!"

A *wise-guy*, Brian thinks, and drives Lisa to Atlanta, and drives around Atlanta, also known as the Pearl of Dixie, in the black Lexus, looking at things. Brian shows Lisa the cinder block building where he and his old girlfriend once lived, back when he, the exploited, worked in a bottling factory, and then a potato chips factory. Now Brian is a student, hooray! Brian drives Lisa through Cabbage Town, looking for the inbred Appalachians known to be living there, and from the Lexus windows they see a few sitting up on their porch, or perch. The inbreeds rise up and scream at them as they pass them by. That's when Brian realizes he's driving the wrong way down a one way street.

TOOTHPICK

Toothpick stole the fridge, not our fridge, the fridge left in the house vacated by the woman who shook her baby and ran. The woman had me break into her house once because she locked herself out, but that's all I knew of her. Two years they lived behind us. She left the baby in the living room, on a blanket, called the cops from a pay phone in Atlanta to let them know. Thing is—and I get this from Gabe who is a dispatcher—the rats feasted on it. There wasn't much left of it, Gabe told me.

I told Toothpick. He smiled, rolled the toothpick around in his mouth and spat, said, "Shake the baby and run." Next thing, I hear wheels out there squeaking beside the house, rolling over the rocks. Toothpick's got the danged fridge on a dolly and is taking his sweet time. A few days later the cops are knocking on everybody's doors, asking have they seen anything suspicious going on around Smokey Hollow because the landlord who's trying to rent the house where the tragedy took place has come up with a missing fridge.

I don't like to lie. Plus, I suck at it, but I lied for Toothpick. I said no, nothing suspicious, officer. I don't think the orange-haired rookie believed me, but I kept up with my story, thinking geez, he just drove by Toothpick's place where Toothpick's old fridge is lying there in the trash pile. I even looked down the street from where we were standing on my porch, sorta giving the guy a hint, but he didn't take it. I watched him drive back down the street. He didn't even turn his head when he passed the tossed fridge.

Now Toothpick, you gotta laugh. I don't know him that well, but he strikes me as the kind of guy who can slip out of anything. He lives in the shotgun shack five over with one big mama. That woman must have eight kids and seven grandkids, and she's not even all that old. I don't mean to sound off-color, but she really takes the cake on being a big black mama. She's just what you think about when you think about big black mamas. More often than not she's got pink curlers in her hair, and is wearing furry slippers. When you see her standing up there on her porch, she's always got her arms crossed and is looking down imperiously at her children gadding about in the dirt yard, which I have on occasion seen her sweeping. Toothpick took up being with her after the last guy was hauled off by the cops for stealing cars.

Toothpick has no steady job, though I know he does on occasion offer his services at the Labor Force. That's not a way to build up collateral, as everybody knows, but if you work all day in the hot sun, you do come home with forty dollars. Toothpick just loves taking it easy, nothing bothers him. I think if I told Toothpick that a bomb had been dropped in Atlanta and that the poison gas, the fallout, the nuclear rip-your-skin-off stuff was on its way down south, here to arrive at any moment, he would just smile, chuckle to himself, and lean over and spit, not disrespectfully, but off to the side. Now and then I hear the big black mama ragging his skinny ass out, but all that woman gets in return is silence.

Toothpick seems like he's got everything figured out. He doesn't say much. What's there to say? He just does what he does, plays Game Boy a bit, works on his jalopy, and lives in the world. When the baby died, that's one of the few times Toothpick spoke up all on his own. "Shake the baby and run," he said, and the very next day, right after the cops cleared out, that's when I heard the squeaking wheels of his dolly.

A few days later I hear the squeaking wheels again. This time Toothpick has got the bedsprings on his dolly, and is having some trouble with it. When the dolly wheel hits a root the bedsprings shift suddenly to the left and Toothpick has to catch it. I'm just peeking out the window, you know, but I see Toothpick is sweating up enough perspiration to create a summer rain with. He's still got the toothpick in his mouth, and I'm giggling to myself each time he has a little trouble, till finally, just when I think Toothpick is about to snap and fly off the handle and get mad at the bedsprings, he just lets it fall on the dirt road. He doesn't look perturbed at all. I'm a little disappointed. Toothpick leans the dolly against the dogwood like he's got all the time in the world. He considers the bedsprings, looks at it appraisingly, then in one sudden decision leans over and hefts that sucker up on his back and clears the corner with it and runs it down the street to his big black mama's shotgun shack.

Next evening the carrot-haired rookie is back. Again he wants to know have I heard anything suspicious. No, I tell him, and look down the street at Toothpick's trash pile. Now, in addition to the fridge, there is an old worn out mattress, along with its partner, the bedsprings. I'm not worried this time that I might be in trouble. I think I'm learning a few things from Toothpick, from his come-what-mayness. I wish I could walk around with a toothpick in my mouth instead of worrying over silly things like being seen by people when I walk around in the world. It's a messed-up fear, but I really hate the fact that people can see me. If I was like Toothpick, I know I wouldn't worry about it. I told the red-haired rookie not a thing suspicious had entered my ears in years. "Not even a squeak," I told him, and watched him drive away, not even slowing down as he passed Toothpick's place.

I went in and made a peanut butter and jelly sandwich, and sat on the couch and was chewing it. I was thinking of all the stuff going on in Smokey Hollow lately, that baby that wouldn't even grow up to reach its potential. I guess she shook it too hard, eh? Maybe it cried, would not shut up, close his aching mouth begging for a worm like you see in pictures of birds. How mama birds feed their babies worms is one of the first lessons we learn as children. That poor woman must've been terrified when her baby stopped crying, when his mouth stopped wiggling and drooling. Who knows what she went through. I hope the cops don't find her. Maybe she'll find some romance in her new life as an outlaw. I'm staring off into space, I guess, a bit dreamily because when Mary comes in through the front, she drops her purse on the floor. "What are you doing?" she says.

"I'm eating," I say.

"What's wrong with you? Why are you looking like somebody is pushing a fork into you?"

"I am?"

"If you could see you, you'd know what I mean."

"I was wondering why Toothpick never seems to be afraid of anything. He just does what he does. He leaves plenty of evidence of all his crimes, but nobody cares. It's like because Toothpick doesn't care, nobody else cares. Nobody sees Toothpick except for me. Why is that?"

"That is really something," Mary says, and goes to the bathroom, slamming the door behind her. I've offended her. Maybe she didn't like the way I was chewing? I've stopped trying to guess what upsets her. I don't know why she hates me, but I wish nobody in the world could see me when she lets it be known how much I disgust her. I know she does this for something, that she can't help it, but forgetting it all has turned out to be the best solution. The woman who shook the baby has the same build as Mary. I sometimes think people come in builds, that if you're broad-shouldered, like Mary and the woman who shook the baby are, then maybe you're also bent on arguing. Me, I'm sort of narrow like Toothpick, but for some reason I don't have that wonderful indifference he exhibits at all hours of the night and day.

The next day there's a knock. I open. It's a white guy with a beard, holding a cell phone. "I am pissed," is the first thing he says to me, and I'd like to disappear. "Somebody has been breaking into my house every goddamn night and nobody in this neighborhood seems to know a thing about it."

"I haven't heard a thing," I said.

"Somebody's holding out on me," he said.

"I'm sorry," I said.

"What the hell are you sorry for?" he said, and he reminded me of Mary, his inflections. It was like, if I didn't say the right words he might try to strangle me. I sometimes thank my lucky stars that we don't have any babies. We've never used birth control. But the horror of what that would be like is beyond my capacity to imagine. When people go off like that, I wish I never was, and when I get to thinking like this, I don't feel sorry for the baby that got shook. The mother did her baby a favor, I think, and see it in my mind, there it is, in the middle of the living room floor, no longer alive, all those rats chewing on it. The rats in Smokey Hollow are fairly abundant, but our house is well sealed against them, who knows why.

"Do me a favor and keep a eye out," the pissed-off man said. "All you got to do is look out your back window now and then. If you see anything going on out there, I want you to give me a call. Here," he said, and handed me his card.

I read it: *Harold Vauss, Rents and Repairs.*

"Do you rent lots of houses?" I asked.

Harold Vauss looked me up and down, looked like he'd spit if it wasn't so rude, like he'd just put down a plate of sour lima beans. Instead of spitting he said, "Just call me," and I watched him get in his huge truck. I took his card inside and stuck it on the fridge with a Q magnet. Mary works with kids, and sometimes brings home learning devices from the school. We got a whole alphabet of magnets stuck to the fridge.

That night when I heard the squeak, I got out of bed and peeked through the blinds. It was a full moon night, and Toothpick looked like Toothpick, just going about business as usual. The toothpick projecting from his rather large-lipped mouth was even lit up, that sliver of wood a delicate paintbrush stroke of moonlight. I had a slight impulse to run off and call Harold, and I wanted to go do it, I did, I wanted to make an end of this, but the moment washed away in my admiration of this big man who could pass over pebbles barefoot with a squeaking dolly, and who just didn't seem to have a worry in the world. Toothpick hypnotized me. His easiness in the world could be counted on, like tomorrow, it always came, and tomorrow, I knew, I would see the old microwave discarded on his trash pile.

ZOOGANROUX

Edward says now's a good a time as any, so I sit in the wet grass and pull the laces on my shoes. I take everything off and stuff it into my Winnie the Pooh knapsack, what I picked up for a quarter at the Salvation Army in Juneau, and we walk through the muskeg, Edward snapping pictures, saying he wants me to act like a wood sprite. It feels ridiculous, but I flail my arms and hop about amongst the flowers, trying to be flighty and free, a disciple of Bacchus, only where's the wine? Where're the girls with pine-cone wands? Where's Pan? The earth squishes through my toes.

Now Edward wants me to be Narcissus. I crouch onto my knees and lean my face over a dark puddle. I'm not pleased with how my breasts hang down, I wish they were smaller, but I wait for my image to appear. Edward isn't convinced. "You don't appear to love yourself at all," he complains. "Open your mouth a little, like you simply can't believe how beautiful you are." I try that, but truth is, I don't much care for the way I look. Love has always been a problem for me. The water smells like sulfur.

Edward switches out rolls, then photographs me dressing, as I brush wet pieces of the earth off the bottoms of my feet. It's disconcerting a little, but I need the money.

We head back into the forest and climb. About an hour later we break through the trees into the alpine, and we cross through patches of snow and climb up to where the ridge begins. It's beautiful up here, the best day we've had in months. Juneau weather is the pits. It'll rain for sixty days straight, so it's a good, rare, marvelous thing when you get sunshine. The mountains light up. When the rain stops, people go berserk with happiness, forget things, crash their cars. People get the feeling that The New Jerusalem has landed, but a day later, when the clouds come back, when the fog returns, the endless rain, the beautiful promise is crushed.

At the top of Thunder Mountain we have a decision to make. We can walk up the ridge to the crest, which involves a few tricky maneuvers, or we can cut to the left and head peacefully through the alpine flowers in the direction of the Mendenhall Glacier. This is the direction that Edward, who is just beside himself with the splendor all around us, wants to go. But first he takes a few pictures of the heavenly vista. He wants me to take off my clothes again. It's no big deal. I strip naked and lie down in the flowers overlooking the airport and Auke Bay and, beyond that, the Chilkat mountain range.

It's before six in the morning, there isn't a soul in sight. Edward carries my Winnie the Pooh knapsack, and photographs me walking along the little trail cutting through the tundra. Now and then he instructs me on how he wants me to pose. He tells me to lie down, to make like I'm sleeping, and he tells me to step into a pool of melted snow.

"Is it cold?" Edward wants to know.

"Melted snow usually is," I say.

Edward laughs. "Is it too cold to act like Ophelia in?"

"It's pretty cold," I say, but slip below the surface and stare through the water's membrane, skyward at an eagle passing over me. I am secluded beyond all reckoning, isolated in ice, buried within this mountain, I am nothing.

But I rise, coughing out the little water drops, Edward laughing and snapping pictures. "That was great," he says, and wants me to roll around in the grass. I'm already wet, so sure. The air is warm, and I guess by now I'm used to being on display for him. So I roll, crawl, slither. I'm part human, part animal, part other-worldly something or other, a creature of dilutions, yes, these impurities please me.

Something screams. I lift my head to see a little animal, a marmot. It's hopping up the hill with my shoe. I'm suddenly human again with two legs and a brain, and I'm running after the marmot, looking around as I run for something to pick up to throw at it. I shout, "Stop!" and the marmot hops along faster. I see the hole in the ground it is headed for, and you can imagine my relief when, just before diving into the hole, it lets go of my shoe.

Edward thinks that was real hilarious, and we continue along eating peanut butter sandwiches. It's weird, being naked and walking along with somebody who has all his clothes on, but I agreed to do this last night at the Alaskan. I need gas for my van, which I've been sleeping in for three months now. Cigarettes, and a bag of dope would be nice, some weed by which to while away the hours in scattered dreaming. Apparently Mr. Edward Ghorbanpour can afford it. He's a contract resource inventory guy. He's come to Alaska from Oregon to study the marbled murlet, which, Edward told me last night, is a near-shore marine water bird about the size of a robin.

The Mendenhall Glacier falls into view. It's a beautiful but weird seeping body of ice, a side winding thing of knives that draws the eyes and holds them, cradles them. You can't look away for fear that it might rise up and strike you down. God's glory is in it. It's an uncomfortable sight for me, but we stand here, taking it in. Edward asks have I seen that Andrew Wyeth painting called "Christina's World."

"Yes, everybody has."

"This will be my homage to Wyeth," Edward says. "Instead of a house in the background it'll be a glacier. I want you to be Christina. Instead of Christina's World, we'll call this Marion's World."

"I don't know if I want you to use my name in any of this," I say, and say, "What were you planning on doing with all these pictures, anyway?"

"Exposing them to the world."

"I feel strange for some reason."

"Don't worry about it," Edward says, and I strike the pose that I think he's after.

"Yearn for the glacier," Edward commands, frustrated over my poor portrayal of Christina, and I try. I yearn for the glacier, but I don't feel any great love for it. The glacier scares me. I'm so small. I look back at Edward. "I'm sorry," I say.

Edward laughs. "You're doing great," he says, and just seems to have an endless supply of ideas. We walk back up the hill, and he takes pictures of me trying to look like Zeus holding a lightning bolt. He photographs me looking like I have indigestion, looking like I am overblown with joy, and looking like I am retarded. I just do what he says, and he laughs all the while, and now he wants me to act like I've committed murder on somebody, that I have blood all over my hands, that I feel guilty about what I've done.

"Serious?"

"Just do it," Edward commands, and motions with his arm that I should stop stalling and get to work. I am being paid, after all, so I drop to my knees and look at my hands, and see the blood of my lover. All she did was invite somebody else to live in the house where all I did in it for a full decade was produce art. I painted, was a painter, and then she bought the house when it came up for sale. I refused to be diluted by her poisonous friend. I had too much integrity. She could invite anybody to live with her that she wanted — the house was hers — and I'm afraid to look back at Edward now. I don't want him knowing what is happening to me, how weak I am, how I am guilty of once having taken myself seriously. When Edward says, "Suck your stomach in and try to look pitiful," I do it, and imagine her standing behind me, hitting me with a sharpened broomstick, and then stabbing it through my back, all the way through so that the sharpened end pierces the earth below me and holds me firm, my arms dangling lifeless at my sides.

Edward says, "Hey, what's up?"

"Nothing," I say, but I'm a bag of mush, a dolt, this shouldn't happen, Jesus, I'll be turning thirty next month, yet look at me. "I'm sorry," I say, and wipe my eyes, and Edward tells me what I suffer from. He says, "You suffer from zooganroux."

"What?"

"Zooganroux," Edward says, "defines the behavior of migratory restlessness."

"You mean like with birds?"

"To put it simply," Edward says, "whatever brought you here has lost its magnetic hold, I see it all over you — you're not here because you're supposed to be. The time for that has gone. You were supposed to head out one evening, but stayed. What does that make you?"

"A jerk?"

"When you fight the circadian rhythm, you go against nature, lose your sense of identity, become nobody, which can have its therapeutic effects, but in the long run self-effaces you. Something is calling you, Marion, talking to you, yet you close up your ears, refuse to listen. I won't call you a spoiled brat, but I've known your type. You think you are selfless, that you are beyond pride and vanity. In truth you are so full of yourself that you deny the beauty of others. Narcissus is you."

"Well, thanks," I say.

"Whatever you did, whatever happened to you, the what you tell yourself you can't get over, that you can't forget or forgive, it doesn't matter now. You are helpless in the pull and release of Nature's migratory rhythms, an anomaly. Flotsam is an appropriate metaphor for what you've become."

"I'm garbage," I say.

"Self-deprecation is just another form of denial, Marion. Aren't you tired of being miserable?"

"Yes."

Edward pats me on the back. "You've been in a time warp for years, I can tell, but it's never too late." I'm about to ask him how he knows so much, but he's thinking pictures again. Edward takes numerous pictures of me. Am I beautiful? Am I garbage? Am I impervious to the pull and release of Nature, an exile of the world, without a home, without a country, without a planet, without a lover? At one point, fetal yet mortally constricted, I'm reminded of a picture I once saw of a disinterred, half-mummified prehistoric man. I could be that man, I am thinking. And I think of the friends I once had, those people that I thought were my friends, who I loved with all my heart before they betrayed me.

"Let's walk," Edward says, but my old dream rushes in and fills me, and I remember how wonderful it was when I was painting every day, my life a revolving palette of infinite color and promise, a canvas of the world as I saw it, as I wanted it to be, an ocean where I could breathe under water and defy the laws of gravity. I've heard it said that people come to Alaska to find themselves, but it's pretty damn clear that I came here to forget. "While you were out to lunch," Edward says, "an army walked through and burned everything. Welcome to paradise," and damn if he hasn't used up all his film, all but for one picture. Even though we have a long way to go before we get back to the car, he wants to take it now. He never was one for saving stuff up for later. It's best to get rid of it all at once and move on. "Just be yourself," he says, and I hug my legs as if I love them.

THREE

JINXED

In Funland we play Asteroids and Space Invaders. We walk polished floors, steal dimes, pennies from the fountain. See ourselves in store windows. A gang in reflection. Benny with hair down his back, me bald with razor cuts and a nail that juts up from my widow's peak, Larry with big brown curls. That's us. And the jinx.

Back at the Impala we spleef out, drink more Crown. Led Zeppelin blows through the JVCs, and when the tape ends Benny says, "I bet you're tight, huh?"

April up front between Benny and Larry goes, "Um," then giggles.

"Hell, yeah you are," Benny says, and pulls April's face close, sticks his tongue in.

Then Larry kisses April. Then it's my turn.

"Go on," Benny says.

April's face above the seat watches me, and her mouth opens a little for my tongue.

"Hurry up!" Benny says. Tired of waiting, he grabs April's neck, kisses her more. His hand up her shirt. When Benny lets go, April says, "My mom's gonna freak."

Benny unbuckles April's belt and reaches down her jeans. "You won't remember this tomorrow, doofus."

"She's got these threats," April says. "She's saving up her stamps to send me to China."

"Look how drunk she is," Benny says. Pulls his hand out, smells his fingers, offers them to Larry to smell. To me. "She's not as tight as I was hoping."

"Proves she's a slut," Larry says.

"She'll wake up tomorrow wondering why her pussy's so sore," Benny says, and ruffles April's hair.

"She likes to play the flute," Larry says.

April starts to cry.

Benny starts the Impala, shoots woodward through the parking lot. Down into the woods behind Montgomery Wards Benny drives, shouts Indian war screams out the window. Larry's hand takes a turn under April's shirt.

I want to hit Larry, but can't be sure about anything. I'm trashed. I'm nervous. Don't like this. I say, "Man, I've got to get home."

Nobody hears me. I say it louder.

"Calm down," Benny says. "Your house ain't gonna sprout legs and hide behind a tree."

"I'm supposed to cook dinner for my mom," I say, and picture Mom. Last night at the table, as we ate, she saw the tiny swastika penned in blue ink on the hem of my shirt. "We had relatives in concentration camps," she said. "They had their heads shaved against their will, had numbers tattooed on their bodies. Were treated like dogs." She kept getting madder, could hardly bear to look at me, so I told her it was nothing, I just like the way swastikas look. "Go wash it off!" I forked peas. "Now!" she screamed and grabbed my shirt by the neck, green peas flying. She might not have meant for it to rip, but once it did, she just ripped the whole thing off me. She threw my shirt in the garbage bag under the sink.

Benny parks in a nook in the trees. Pulls out a sack of the same good shit Larry's got. I'm thinking oh, god, we're gonna smoke another joint. If this goes on much longer I'll be screwed. I'll have to wait hours for my buzz to fizzle, but worst is Larry, I can't believe him, what he is doing. I keep hoping April will try to stop him, but she just sits there crying about her stupid mom. "I ruined our family," she says.

"That's because she's a jinx," Larry says.

"All I do is destroy things," April says. "I feel so sorry for you guys."

Larry pulls April's shirt up, and it paralyzes me. This isn't fair, I'm such a moron. I look out the window at the trees, then look back at April, and at Larry's hands.

"That's all superstitious bullshit," Benny says.

"You'll see," April says, "you'll see, you'll see, you'll see."

"Why don't you shut up?" Benny says.

"These are nice-ass tits, don't you think?" Larry says.

"Bouncy bouncy," Benny says.

"Earlier," Larry says, "when my mom was passed out in the lawn chair, April threw grass on her."

"Damn, Larry," Benny says. "Somebody threw grass on my mama I'd beat the fuckin crap out of her."

April knocks Larry's hands away and pulls her shirt down. I feel some relief, only now she leans over Benny's lap, trying to press the button of his special horn. "Make it sing Dixie," she says.

Benny pushes her face against his crotch. "Suck me off, bitch," he says.

April breaks free. "You guys got to stop fucking with my head," she says, and looks back here at me, smiles, and climbs over the seat. "Hey neighbor," she says, and clutches my arm.

"Hi."

April starts laughing. Benny and Larry laugh. I laugh. We all of us laugh. Us, the gang.

Finally Benny says, "Let's hotbox it, baby," and we roll up the windows. Smoke more spleefs. The Impala's cab grows thick with smoke, with our sweat, our breath. April blinks her eyes, rolls them around goofily. I notice freckles she has, a beauty mark that looks like a tiny Africa on her neck. Then it's down for the windows. Fresh air sweeps in, along with a motorbike sound. I remember the sound from earlier today. When I skipped school and walked home through the woods. What a freak that guy was, driving his motorbike up to me, killing the engine, going do I have any drugs. I told him no, and he goes, Are you sure? And gave me the hairy eyeball, looking me over and twitching. You know where I can get some coke? he said, and told me he saw me in the mall the other day. Said I was fucked-up, and he knew I had some drugs, and he said that I was lying to him. I tell Benny about it. Benny says, "Not to worry my Snollie."

The guy rides up. He looks through the window, sees me, gives me this knowing look.

"Fuck you," I say softly.

April looks at me like I'm a big shot.

April lives right next door to me, but I only know her a little. Now that we are becoming friends, we can sneak out late nights, get stoned, swim in the pool. I'll teach her how to play guitar, and who knows, maybe we'll start a band. I think I'd love to hold April's hand, walk through the woods while holding her hand. Whenever she speaks I always hear how nice her voice is. I love her voice. Just the other day I was on my roof, checking my reefer plant, and saw her in her yard, pulling weeds and dropping them into a bucket. She wore cutoff shorts and a yellow T-shirt and was barefoot and seemed like she was pissed off, like she was being punished by her mom. At one point she cupped her hands around her mouth and shouted, "Don't blame me if I get mono!" at her house. As I went to sleep I kept hearing her voice. "Don't blame me if I get mono!"

"Something I can do for you, mister?" Benny says extra nice.

"Hey man," the twitchy guy says. "What's up?"

"You mean besides the sky where heaven is and all the angels live?"

"I'm trying to get me some weed," the guy says. "I'm not a cop."

"I see," Benny says.

"Well?" the guy says.

"Oh yeah," Benny says, very nice. "We got all kinds of herbs man, and you know what? We got cocaine. We got acid and pussy and all kinds of shit, man."

"I'd like to buy some," the guy says, and really reminds me of the jocks from school. He is what they will grow up to look like and be.

"I tell you what," Benny says. "Give me a couple teeth, I'll give you a sacky." Benny holds up his four-finger sack of juicy green bud, bounces it in front of the guy's face.

The guy's expression brightens. "What are teeth?" he says.

Benny lives for this.

"What the fuck you mean? Don't you know what a goddamn tooth is?"

Benny gets out of the Impala. The guy sees where Benny's coming from. Tries kick-starting his Kawasaki. Benny pushes him down.

April leans across me to see out the window. I put my hand on her back. Together we watch Benny kick the guy in the stomach. Benny kicks the guy in the chest and legs with his cowboy boots. The guy heaves and cries out. I'm getting revenge on the jocks who fuck with me all the time at school, but I don't like this. I wish Benny would stop it, but Larry's out there going, "Fuck him up, Benny! Fuck him up!" Benny looks like a crazy executioner with his long brown hair flapping up wild. "I told you I want them teeth, you motherfucker! Cough'em up!"

There is blood.

April turns her face at me, sighs as if she is bored, then rolls over, the back of her head in my lap now. I smell her. I'm worried that she's going to feel that I am hard.

"April," I say. "Let's run through the woods together. We can walk off our buzzes on the way home."

April's eyes open up, she focuses.

But Larry and Benny Lovely get back in.

"Cripes," Benny says. "I step out to take a leak and the Jew-boy gets himself a piece."

"Where's the bottle?" April slurs. She sits back up.

Benny hands April the Crown. April swallows a bunch of the nasty stuff, hands it to me, and I swallow some. April says she has to take a "you know," steps out, stumbles over the twitchy guy's Kawasaki, walks down the road a ways, staggering.

"I gave her a lude," Benny says. "Looks like it's hitting her."

I swallow again, hand Larry the Crown.

Benny pumps his pistol pellet gun, scoots his head out the window, aims. "Watch this," he says, and pulls the trigger. There's a whiz, a pop. April collapses.

I laugh.

It was funny, April falling down like that, acting like Benny killed her. Larry's laughing. Benny too is laughing, pumps the gun again, fires at the little mound of her in the sandy road. April sorta looks like roadkill.

Then Larry fires. There's the whiz, the pop sound of the pellet smacking April.

Benny lights a new spleef. We smoke, take turns pumping the gun, firing at April's butt, which pretty much faces us the way she's fallen.

But Larry's going, "Oh shit, man, look! She's pissing!"

I'm aiming.

A dark shape spreads out from between April's legs. I don't like this. I toss the gun and we hear it clink against the Kawasaki.

Benny looks at me like I've lost it, like he's thinking of knocking my lights out.

"Why are we shooting her?" I say.

"Snollie the humanist!" Benny cries, throws up his hands.

"I am not!" I protest.

"He's a Jew," Larry says.

Benny rolls his eyes, presses the button for the special horn. Dixie plays into the trees. When Dixie ends we get out. Benny gets the gun. Pumps it. Shoots April as we walk up to her, and Benny says he's fixing to get some, kneels down beside her, peels her shirt up along her back. It grosses me out, all those places where the pellets dug in. I didn't know they did all that.

Benny's going, "Come on girl" and shakes her. He pulls her over, her head flops back in the sand. Her eyes are open. Her eyes aren't even looking at anything. "Let's go, Ape," Benny says. He tells her to go ahead and barf, to let it out, but then he says he can't feel any air coming out of her mouth.

"Stop fucking with us, Benny," Larry says.

"No," Benny says. "I'm serious." He's trying to take her pulse, the woods are quiet.

Larry's going, "Fuck!"

I'm ready to wake up now, I want to open my eyes, please, and I try to open my eyes, but my eyes are open all the way.

"Does April's mother know where she's at?" Benny says.

"Don't say that," Larry says. "Please don't say that."

"Maybe they'll pin it on that guy?" Benny says, and pulls off his shirt, spits on it, wipes April's nose with it. He's afraid his finger-prints might get left on her skin, he says, and brushes his spit along her arms, wipes her hands.

"You know, I just thought of something," Larry says. "All you're doing is putting your DNA on her, Benny."

"Fuck!" Benny shouts, and Benny's back muscles flex. He stands up and kicks the sand and starts to walk away. "I can't believe this shit!" he screams, and then April coughs.

I am so relieved, God, so happy. I'm thinking this is over now, we can go home, forget it, everything will be fine. Only Benny is pissed. "She made me think I was going to prison," he says. He squats down beside April and puts his hand on her forehead as if checking to see if she has a fever. Then with one hand yanks her shirt off and throws it in the same motion. He looks around, scanning his eyes through the woods, then undoes April's jeans. Benny pulls them down her legs, inside out. They snag at the ankles. Benny drags April backwards through the sand till her sneakers let go, taking her socks along with them. April crawls off a ways. She seems to be realizing what is happening. She manages to stand, but Benny grabs her arm. With his other hand he pulls her panties up from behind, giving her a wedgie. "Hey," April says.

"Benny," I say.

April struggles to get away, so Benny pushes her into the sand. He yanks off her panties and spreads her legs.

"Damn," Larry says.

"See what I told you about?" Benny says.

April kicks.

"Cut it out!" Benny shouts, and balls his fist up in front of her face.

"No!" April says.

"Benny," I say.

"Damn, Benny," Larry says.

I look at Larry, thinking we should do something, but Larry only shakes his head as if Benny is such a trip, isn't he?

In a little girl's voice, Benny says, "My mother says that I'm a jinx and that anybody who touches me gets jinxed but y'all all know

I'm just a slut piece-a-shit."

"Stop it," April mumbles.

Benny hefts her up over his shoulder and carries her down the path and flips her onto the old mattress. He pulls his jeans down just enough to start having sex with her.

"He's got it in," Larry says.

"Benny," I say, and feel so sick inside, and wish somebody would help, please.

I light a cigarette, drag deep. I'm trying to be all cool about things, but get dizzy, and then April is vomiting, and I guess I drop down into the ashes of an old fire, and the world spins below me. There is laughter, I hear scratching in the leaves. Then, "He's turning green," I hear. They are talking about me. With effort I open a eye to see them walking up the trail. There's Larry. And Benny. There's April, naked and white up on tiptoes, following them like she is one of them, like they are great friends who have bonded and grown close. I want them to look back, hope they will not leave me. But hear the Impala start. I close my eyes, hear the engine fade into the trees, and sleep until somebody shakes me. It's that guy in the almost dark. I'm naked. His pants are opened, I'm wet. A rope is around my neck. He yanks it so that I have to grab onto it not to choke. In his other hand is a crowbar.

EARTH SHOES

We ate in the kitchen, and all through dinner Mom kept bringing me out presents and making me open them even though I prefer to open my presents on Christmas morning, the right way. It was a lot of the usual stuff, lots of new panties and bras. I don't mind about the panties but we've talked the bras to death. She kept saying "Oh Cindy, they're just bras, don't get excited. They're good for you."

"But I told you, I'm not going to wear them."

"Oh Cindy," and she would laugh, and I had a lot of good reason to be pissed. I was still pissed over the deodorant she left in my room for me, two different kinds of deodorant on my dresser, it's the coolest dresser, I painted it blue and black when I was in elementary, with yellow stars and moons on it and comets.

Then we went to church where Mom played the bells. Four wide screen TVs in the foyer, the lobby or whatever. The pastor wears a headset, it's so retarded. They're trading all the windows out. Doing web-cast. Pastor Bender. He's into folksy Christian goof-ball, super weird. That headset thing. Saying hi to everybody, always going, "Hi Cindy, how are you?" What a spaceman. You try to be nice. I videoed Mom. She was real cute, kinda. Hard bells. Two notes. Dong dong. Dong dong. Four ladies standing up there donging their bells. Mom was the best donger, hands down out of Breezer and Tina in their strapless prom gowns. Breezy even wore a G-string. Mom wore black pants and a white shirt and wedge heels. I'm videoing, and Dad's like, "I don't feel like greeting everyone," and was looking around like he was trying to be incognito. Miss Smith walked up. Howard came by. My parents know so many people. This other guy who was like ninety came up and jived with my dad. Dad laughed to be polite. "How are you, buddy?" Dad said, hardy har har. The old man sat with us, and was in on the when-is-Cindy-going-to-get-married bit. "She's choosy," Dad said. Then Mom did the Silent Night thing where she wore a pashmina shawl and the crowd sang along, and a little girl dressed like a shepherdess played a flute.

Other people came over and tried to talk, and of course all the talk centered on me because nobody had seen me since last year, and everybody was wondering. At the first chance Dad ran for the car. He took me aside and said, "Get your mom, I'm in the car." I looked around for Mom but couldn't find her, but when I went back to the car she was there. We drove home, passing the Lighty House, blow-up Santas, icicles on the house, Rudolphs over the top. A ton of traffic in the neighborhood because of the Lighty House. "This damn Lighty House traffic, stupid ass, they should contain it," Dad said.

We pulled into the drive, went inside and Dad went to bed and

Mom tried to have a little talky-talk with me. She made us two cups of Sleepy Time tea and we sat at the kitchen table and she said, "So, any boys in your life?" I said, "Boys rhymes with noise, I just noticed that." Mom said, "Oh Cindy," and laughed, but it wasn't natural, her laugh. It was a pained laugh. She kept trying to talk about it, but I changed the subject. I talked about Dad's shoes, and how he ought to have much better luck with the earth shoes that I bought him for Christmas because the toes are higher than the heel. That should work out some of the tension in his feet. Mom got tired of listening to me and went up to bed, and I watched some TV in the living room. I turned it off with the remote. I hit the lights, went upstairs to the bathroom and brushed my teeth. Then I was in my room, where I lived from ten to eighteen. My room. They painted the walls, but my bed was glow-in-the-dark. Cool metal tubes on my awesome bed. Swirly. You turn off the light, it glows, and some tables in the room too, and my cool dresser.

I put on my new pajamas. Mom gives me new ones every year. These are pink with white hearts. I turned off the lights.

I didn't pray unless it's in a way. I thought of the mooing, my dad, when he called the cows earlier in the day. "Gif! Gif!" he said, and the cows came running. I looked at him and was full of admiration. My dad. Over fifty cows and some of them babies. His oldest cow might be ten, but most of them are really young. I didn't pray. I just thought of the mooing. Cows have long vocal chords. That's how they hit you the way they do. Cows force a bunch of air through the chords and there it is. When Mom donged the bells, she smiled. I did not say, "Now I lay me down to sleep." I just laid there until I noticed that I didn't like the smell of my new pajamas. I couldn't stand the smell, so I took them off.

HOW I SUPPORTED MY HABIT OF COLLECTING SCABS

When I'm out collecting scabs I feel empowered, confident. I have an excuse to socialize. When asked what I'm doing, what I want a person's scab for, I say I want the scab for the people yet to live. The scab is my gift to the future. When the future-people see the scab, they will conjure the image of the person who provided it. The future-people will fill in the space of that person no longer here. The future-people will want to know how the scab was grown, and the mystery will give them pleasure. "Nice," my people say when I fill them in, for they know the truth when they hear it. They give me permission to examine their scabs. With some picking and pulling, I peel scabs away from their bodies.

I am very selective. If I like you, I will make the effort to acquire your scab. Take this girl I saw through the windshield of my car. I simply had to have her scab, so later that day I ambled down Ponce De Leon to the spot I saw her leap barefoot onto the hot asphalt, her legs crissing and crossing tiptoe style, a kitty cat patter to lessen the sting. As she crossed in front of the traffic of which I was a part of, I knew my life could only embarrass me should I live it without doing my duty. I simply had to have her scab.

So I scaled the bank up to the tracks and walked down a ways to where this tent made of bed sheets and sticks was. I said, "Anybody home?"

A raggedy man poked his head out. He said, "What you want?"

"I was wondering if I could have a scab," I said.

"A scab?"

"You know," I said, "so people in the future can look at it and be pleased."

"Sure," the man said. "Take all the scabs you like." He came out and handed me a can of Hamms. I took a little drink then peeled a scab from his leg—it was the largest of all of his scabs—and put it in a plastic egg and marked it. I noted the incident through which he obtained his fine scab, and took a picture of the spot where his scab had been, pink and raw, with a disposable camera. The man, Toby, said his life had been fine up until he'd come home to find his wife stabbed in their bed, her own panties from Victoria's Secret stuffed in her mouth. That was up on Linwood Ave., he said, which happened to be the Ave. Linda and I lived on. These were my scab notes.

"That sucks," I said.

Linda has told me I should become a priest because people love confessing stuff to me. Toby, apart from going into detail about his murdered wife, and the condition he found her in, had three children somewhere in the world, and one of these days, he knew it, these children were going to die before he got the chance to tell them sorry. His sob story roiled my guts, so I thanked him for the Hamms and started going, but there she was, the girl. She wore the same shorts and shirt I'd seen her in before—and at this distance I saw she had a slight harelip. Her smell preceded her. Cheese, and mixed up with the cheese I guess I'd say I smelled the tingly ferment of her privates. She stepped through the weeds with her elbows up, as if chest-deep in water and trying to keep her arms dry, but they were just tall weeds. She had Neanderthal features, high cheekbones and a mandible generously padded with muscle. When she got up closer she said, "Look is not here." I saw she had freckles.

"Look?" I said.

"You're that reporter, ain't you?" she said.

"He ain't lookin' for no Look," Toby said.

"Well in case he didn't know," she said, "I was telling him Look ain't me. He's got a camera don't he?"

"That he do," Toby said. "Come over here and get your picture took with me. He's cool. He ain't no goddamn cop."

"What does he want my picture for? Tell him it'll cost him. I don't take pictures for free."

"Why do I have to tell him?" Toby said.

"You're supposed to be my friend!"

"Shut your mouth up. I ain't your goddamn protector."

"I'm no reporter," I said, and repeated what I'd told Toby. I was a preserver, I collected scabs of all the best people I saw in the world everywhere, and the reason I took pictures was so people knew whose scab they were looking at. I added that with all the new DNA science and technologies yet to be developed, a scab could be used to make the person whose body the scab came from live again. The pictures could be used for fine tuning.

"Well, I got some scabs," Look said, and sat on a bucket. I peeled a

Florida-shaped scab from her knee and put it in a plastic egg. She said she couldn't remember how she got it. There's no need to be delicate. She was a prostitute, that's how she made her money in life, got on her knees and bobbed her head up and down. Her other knee had scabs too. When I saw her jump out in front of traffic like that, that wasn't the first time I saw her. The first time I saw her was while I was getting gas. She was in the passenger side of another car, running a brush through her sandy hair. A guy got out to pump the gas. I did not want his scab at all. He wore fancy slacks and had a neatly trimmed mustache, and I guessed he was a businessman.

I gave Look a twenty for her scab. About this she was pleased. I took some pictures of her on the upturned bucket. When she smiled for the camera, she held her lips shut tight. That made her harelip less pronounced, but I liked her the other way, when she wasn't trying to hide anything. I asked her not to smile. She smiled. I went into the tent with her where she wanted me to take pictures of her boobs. I said no. When she tried to show them I stopped her from doing it. She called me mean. She begged me not to leave her, her harelip lifting up in her desperation. Beyond it a white valentine of chalky teeth was. It was freaky, but I liked it. I don't know why she liked me. She said we could be a team and was tender and altogether crazy. "I can make us money," she told me.

Look walked with me all the way to Kentucky Fried Chicken. Again Look latched onto me. I had to push her to get away and she fell onto the concrete sidewalk, plunked down on her ass and bounced—I think she did that on purpose. Made me about think real highly of myself. Then Look got up and ran as though should I change my mind the opportunity had been withdrawn. "Look!" I called out after her, but she did not look back.

I stopped at Kroger to buy a paper to see what other jobs were going on around Atlanta. I was tired of what I did for Curry Brothers, making freezer dividers and shelf covers. While at Kroger I checked my handiwork in the long sunken freezer, the Minute Maid and Tater

Tot freezer dividers with ventilation holes punched by yours truly.

I was home then after that. Linda mopped on, was mopping when I stepped in, still, just as she'd been mopping when I'd stepped out in my search for better scabs. Linda was losing it. When Linda saw me, I think she wanted to cry. Linda knows that when I'm on my "long walks," I'm out collecting scabs. I have asked Linda to collect scabs with me, to share this part of myself, this quest, but she will not understand. Linda has implied that I seek professional help.

I just wish Linda saw how what I do is unique, all about the sanctity of life, and how talent is involved, deserving of care. I have never collected the scab of a person whose presence in the world I found annoying.

That night Linda cried herself to sleep. In the morning I made her buttermilk pancakes. By the time Linda came out of the shower her pancakes were cold. Linda did not want my cold pancakes. Linda sat in the spaceship couch looking at the help section of the *Atlanta Constitution*. Then she looked like Linda with a sudden idea.

"Oh neat," she said.

I sat down beside her and we looked at the ad. It said, Come work in the largest haunted house in the world, make BIG BUCKS on your evenings. A temporary job. The ad said they were auditioning that night.

I drove us to the audition. While driving us out to the audition, Linda told me of a long-ago Halloween. She crawled into a thing her neighbor built, a cardboard thing with four small rooms in it. Each room had a fright, and the fright, Linda said, that scared her most, was the bowl of brains. It was just baked beans in there, but it was dark, and she'd been made to put her hand in the bowl. "I think the experience scarred me permanently," Linda said.

"Is that why you quit school in Baltimore?" I said.

"Are you being funny?"

"I'm just saying, there could be a connection," I said.

"That's a asshole thing to say," Linda said, and maybe Linda was right, maybe I was being a asshole, but Linda had quit art school four times in four different cities, and each time she quit art school it was while she was on scholarship. That just seemed like a lot of waste to me. The last time she quit art school was in Baltimore, and the reason she gave me was that she didn't like the way some girl's calves jiggled as she mounted the steps that led to the entrance of the building where all the classes were held.

I had a job and everything. It didn't pay a ton, but it was enough to help support my habit of collecting scabs. I was on a roll, but I get home from work after the first day of classes, and there's Linda, sobbing on the futon. "I'm sorry," she cried, but the girl's calves, no, that just wasn't a very good reason to quit anything.

Not that I didn't understand it, or sympathize. "I'm glad you quit," I said. "If you didn't quit, we never would've come to Atlanta. I like Atlanta."

The world's largest haunted house shifted into view, a temporary affair of sudden carpentry under a massive circus tent. I parked. We got out. We followed people through the entrance where a bald dude told everybody to line up against the wall. A gorilla with a large stick ran in through the door. The gorilla raised the stick as if he would slam it across our faces. Quite a few of us screamed. It scared the bejesus out of me.

"The thrill of the dance," the bald dude said.

"That was not necessary," I heard Linda say.

"Our object," the bald dude said, "is to scare both children and adults."

Linda and I were first to audition. We followed the bald dude and the gorilla into a room that smelled like cedar. There were cedar chips beneath us on the floor. The floor shone like so much gold, all these gold coins scattered everywhere. "You've crawled out of graves," the bald dude said. "You have no souls. You want back what you've been forcefully deprived of, that precious elixir."

Linda and I stuck out our arms. We lumbered forth haltingly, wiggling our bodies, our hands, our fingers, trying our damnedest to look like scary zombies.

The bald dude laughed. The gorilla followed suit. I saw us there how they saw us there. The bald dude clapped inside of the laughing he was laughing, and the gorilla did same, though when the gorilla clapped, the clap was of rubber gorilla hands clapping, not real hands clapping.

"You two are natural zombies," the bald dude said, clearly excited by our performance. We had the job. We were to meet for rehearsal tomorrow at noon.

In the car Linda said she'd never felt so humiliated. "What a bunch of ridiculous craphole stupidity," she said, and said she did not appreciate being made the fool. "They were laughing at us," she said. "You can degrade yourself if you want to, William, but I'm not going back there again, not ever. Nothing is worth doing that."

"Okay, no problem," I said.

"What? Are you making fun of me?"

"I've got to take the job because my art is important to me," I said.

"Oh, that's right, your scabs. That is the grossest fucking thing in the world and you call it an art? How did this happen to me?"

"We must be in love," I mused.

"Natural zombies!" Linda cried out, and she said, "That bald man has got it coming to him. One of these days somebody is going to mess him up and he won't have anybody in the world to blame but himself. The thrill of the dance is right. He'll be dancing to the tune of a prison door closing and all he ever gets to eat is lima beans and some nasty watery soup."

"You mean baked beans?" I ventured.

"What?"

"Baked beans, you know? Isn't that what's all behind this?"

"You just amaze me, William."

"I'm serious. I mean, who knows what all kind of repercussions you sticking your hand into the brains bowl could have had? All we are is what has happened to us in the past, isn't that a reasonable statement?"

"Uh, no, I don't think there's anything reasonable in it at all. I think you're a sonofabitch is what I think. In fact, that's all you've ever been as long as I've known you is a sonofabitch. You were a sonofabitch then, and you're a sonofabitch now. That's all you're going to be in the future, is a sonofabitch."

"I just have to wonder," I said, "why it doesn't bother me in the slightest when you call me a sonofabitch. All I feel like is that you are stating the obvious. I wish I could get mad and upset about this. What I do wonder about, though, is why you like my mother so much if she is such a bitch."

Linda was a silent body of calm water after that. She just sat there fuming as I drove, her arms crossed and her lips pursed tightly together. Whenever I asked her questions, she said nothing. I felt pretty riled up inside, myself, to tell the truth. The whole thing upset me more than I was willing to admit. I know it, because the next day I hardened my heart bigtime.

I'd lived with Linda for three years. I'd put up with Linda's bigtime fashion magazines all over the fucking apartment, her zombified appreciation of designer jeans and all things mass-produced—*Vogue, Elle, Lucky*, those were her icons—and her jealousy over bigtime actors such as Wynona Ryder and Gwyneth Paltrow, especially Gwyneth Paltrow because Gwyneth Paltrow had attended the same university that she had before she'd quit it to go somewhere else. Etcetera and etcetera. Linda was just all hopped up on diamonds and jewelry and the personal business of celebrities. Like my mother, that was all she seemed to care about.

I was tired of Linda. Linda was not pregnant. We were not married. Linda was too lost in her world of wishful gastronomy and beauty products that didn't do a thing for her beauty at all. Such beauty products were not only useless, I thought, but in the short- and long-run produced the opposite effect: a punctuated ugliness. When night came along, I waited for Linda to be sleeping. As Linda snored soft, I packed my duffel bag, and then left the apartment with my Hefty Cinch Sack filled with plastic eggs of scabs. I also had, of course, pictures of my donors, neatly catalogued, and the corresponding notes. The letter I left for Linda said, "Maybe we'll do like we talked about and get back together way in the future, like when we are thirty-five or something crazy like that."

I found Look. Look still smelled like a festering vagina, but was thrilled to see me. I collected her up and drove to Daytona Beach, where I had met and sorta fell in love with Linda. On the drive down Look told me all about herself, including the bit about how she thought that I was a reporter the first time we met. She had filled out a police report on a guy, see? It so turned out it was the guy whose car I saw her in that day when I was getting gas. I was right about him being a businessman. He was the CEO of a manikin factory. After having sex with Look he wouldn't let her go. He beat her up with a plastic arm and locked her naked in a second-story room. Look escaped by hanging from the window ledge and dropping into the grass. Of course, she wouldn't have reported had somebody not seen her scrabbling through the trash looking for clothes. When the cops arrived, she had fashioned a sort of diaper out of a plastic grocery sack. The cops hounded Look for information, so she told them, and then they locked her in jail. That's what Look told me. I rented us an apartment on Oleander Street not but five blocks from the Atlantic.

Look, of course, knew how to make money without my help, but I drove her to the Washarama on Ridgewood on the weekends. We pretended to be doing laundry, and Look would mosey down to the curb and strike cool poses in her shorts, cowboy boots, and see-through top. In this way our souls grew into each other. It took only minutes for a car to pull over. Look would look my way. I'd give her the nod and she would climb into the guy's car. Many a time I watched her head grow smaller as the car rolled away. That is how I supported my habit of collecting scabs.

BOXWOODS

Our boxwoods are God knows how old. They are the healthiest, greenest, lushest boxwoods you ever saw, and are put together in the finest hedge. Our boxwoods run the edges of the whole house, making of it one fine southern lady come out from the old times, prim and proper, sort of like Mama when she was a young girl, a real Georgia Peach. I'm always out there cutting her skirt, shaving off each little twig that would make her untidy. I am talking perfection. Our boxwoods have no curves to them, none of that round boxwood business you see. In the quiet of the twilight I scan the flat surfaces and plane them with my shears, little Mickey Mouse ears hopping up from the blades. It's my time of peace and tranquility, and if Bill looks at me through his window from across the street, what he will see is the best friend he could ever have had gone up in smoke. I'm not like Bill. I happen to be loyal.

Now Mama takes to bed come eight. I lock myself in my room, take me a double hit of white, put on the headphones and let it roll. This girl's all right. All white but Japanese and the only three words she knows in English are "Fuck my ass!" Over and over she says it, and the four superstar studs—they are Americans—oblige her.

Next afternoon I'm microwaving our dinners when Mama says, "Flat, come in here quick!"

I pop in from the kitchen and looky here, here comes Connie flying across the street like Oh Boy, I can't wait to take me a shit in the yard that has the greenest grass in the neighborhood. Connie doesn't even slow down. She plows into our yard, takes the shit stance, and down it falls, plops for me to have to go clean up. Connie then runs back to Bill's, claws the front door. A crack is made for Connie, and Connie wiggles through, her Irish setter tail the last thing to see.

"That's it," I say.

"No, Flat, no."

"I already told Bill that he was to control that dog from now on," I say, and push outside, get the spade from the shed. I scoop up the Irish setter shit and march over there with it. I fling the turds at Bill's front door, the turds hitting it and falling to the door mat. I am so pissed. I run up and hit the doorbell and when Bill opens, acting like he doesn't know what the hell is going on, I say, "If your dog shits in my Mama's yard one more time I'll cut your head off with this shovel."

Then I walk home, Mama trying to talk to me when I come inside, going, "Flat, Flat," but Mama can't talk. Mama runs her mouth too much about me, runs it on the phone going, "Flat's done did landscaping up. Once you done quit working for all the companies, you got to try you another field, I'm guessing."

"Shut up!" I tell her.

"What did you say to him, Flat?"

"Didn't I tell you to shut up!" I scream, and I notice that I'm still holding the spade. I open the back door and throw it into the yard. I go to my room, slam the door behind me and lock it, put in some Black Flag to bust Mama's eardrums. I had wanted to go to the ballgame tonight, but I'm too upset. I put on the headphones and watch Mokie, that is her name, take it up the ass. The guys are going at her all at once. It looks like more than she can handle, but I can still hear Mama in my head, running her mouth about me. What I'd like to tell her is "What the motherfuck have you been doing in the last goddamn thirty something years that you've been in this house doing nothing but sitting on your goddamn ass? Tell me, go ahead and tell me, Mama? If I recollect, you've been doing nothing but sitting on your ass!"

That's no way for a man to talk to his mother.

I need to get me another forty rock, what the hell, I'm pissed, but the door is banging. I can hear it through the headphones, through Mokie screaming "Fuck my ass!" and Henry Rollins going apeshit wild through my speakers. "Leave me alone!" I shout, but the banging goes on till I just yank off my headphones and shut the world down, turn the world off. I open my door, thinking I'm going to rip Mama a new asshole, but it's the cops. You can't threaten to cut off a man's head with a shovel, they tell me, and next thing I know I'm resisting arrest. They get me down to the station and book me, and if that ain't embarrassing enough, a few weeks later I stand before a judge and go, "Yes your honor, I did throw dog shit at Bill's door."

They give me a hundred and twenty hours of community service to do, and I'm just pissed off as all getup. To think that Bill and I used to be friends, it don't compute. Come to think of it, my only friends in the world are Mama and Mokie. How did this happen to me? I don't know, but somebody's got to keep after the boxwoods. If I don't do it, nobody will.

OVEN

Caroline knows that when her belly growls, Larry knows that his knobs will be fingered, that he will grow hot inside, that a pepperoni pizza or crème brulèe, maybe even a late night meatloaf, will be produced with his help. The growl is what Larry most loves to hear, Caroline thinks, and squats beside him close and intimate. "Hear it?" she says. Caroline fingers Larry's racks, turns him on. As she stuffs him full of Idaho potatoes, she sings to Larry.

Caroline eats her baked potatoes while watching the Monday Night Movie, just an awful movie. Her potatoes are drenched with butter, and very delicious, but when she finishes eating, she feels sick. She should not have eaten so much. Why does this always hap-pen? Caroline doesn't know. She needs to put smaller portions on her plate.

Caroline needs help. She isn't obese, but still. She decides to do something about it, so goes to Overeaters Anonymous. "My name is Caroline," Caroline says, "and I am an overeater." She tells these people that she speaks to her oven, that she calls him Larry and that his knobs are shiny and black and that she doesn't clean his glass because the burn marks around his corners give him character.

"Get rid of him at once," the great large huge man says. His name is Gary and Gary is from Vermont originally. Gary says, "I have a truck and I'm sure my son Kent will help us load the oven. We'll drive the sonofabitch to the landfill this weekend."

"Oh, I would never dream of it," Caroline says.

The enormous woman beside her puts a hand on Caroline's arm. "It's okay, dear."

"No," Caroline says. "I'm not getting rid of Larry."

"She said she wanted to stop overeating," Gary says, looking to Evelyn, who is the leader of O.A.

Evelyn says, "Caroline, the fact that you find your oven cute is proof enough. Ovens are not cute and you should never talk to an oven. You're going to have to kill this absurd fantasy of yours. We are your friends, Caroline. We care about you."

Later that night, Caroline watches a movie on TV, just an awful movie. She has not eaten a thing since dinner, and when her tummy growls, she cries out, "Did you hear that, Larry?"

Caroline turns her head to the side. She lifts a hand to hold off the sound from the TV, and listens. When Larry does not speak, she stomps to the kitchen, flips on the light, and stares at Larry's burn-ers. "You heard it, didn't you?"

Larry just sits there.

"Say something," Caroline says, but Larry is too good to say any-thing. Larry has all the character, the spirals of his burners more lovely than lace, their texture so fine, sensual to the touch. Caroline likes to watch them change color, come alive, becoming dangerous with their exquisite fire. Caroline would like to take things to the next step with Larry, make him her lover, but one does not take an oven to bed. She'd rather make love to Larry though than Gary. It is their last night together. Caroline undresses in the bathroom, showers, puts on lipstick, then makes love to the oven.

Next day Gary comes over with his son Kent. Kent, a muscular young man with a crew cut, is on the football team at Ole Miss. The young man's thick neck reminds Caroline of the biscuits that would grow inside Larry, the plump rising of them, golden, and she would like to touch the young man's neck, but she is not crazy. Caroline is a normal thirty-five-year-old woman with a normal nine-to-five job. She was married once. Her husband left her for a thinner woman, but that is neither here nor there.

"Nice blouse," Gary says, and Caroline notices afresh how large and huge and big Gary is. Massive. Gary is like the blob in the movie *The Blob*, but Caroline curtsies. She is a genteel Southern woman. She says, "Why thank you, Gary."

Out from the duplex comes Kent, tugging Larry along on the dolly, bouncing Larry down the steps. Caroline just doesn't want to see it. Earlier, as Kent unhooked Larry from the wall, Caroline noticed some lipstick smears that she had neglected to wipe from Larry's smooth steel body. It was shameful. She'd blushed and was feeling nauseous, so left the house. Now she tries not to look at Larry at all—it's true, only a strange person could feel emotion for an oven—but her head snaps Larry's way and she just feels awful. What kind of cruel person would do such a thing? It's like looking the other way while your children are sold into lives of slavery.

"You're doing the right thing," Gary says, and he says, "I'll keep you company while Kent does the honors. When Kent is done he'll come back for me."

Caroline looks at Gary standing in the yard in the full sun and wishes the ground would open up and swallow him. "No, please, I've got a ton of paperwork to do," Caroline says.

"I see," Gary says.

"It's nothing personal," Caroline says.

"Well, if you start to overeat, you know who to call," Gary says, and leaves with Kent. Caroline watches them drive off, Larry in the back of the truck, his bits of chrome flashing in the sunshine. Goodbye Larry. Goodbye Larry.

Caroline goes inside and pretends to feel fine, but she is thirsty. When she enters the kitchen for a glass of water, there is the empty space where Larry once was. Caroline breaks into tears. She runs to the bathroom, holds her face over the commode, and heaves, but nothing comes. She sniffles. Her tears fall into the water, breaking her reflection. The porcelain is very kind, she notices. "I am a miserable woman," she says, and hears a little sound down deep in the pipes. She holds her breath and listens.

REFUSE

He was a carpenter.

He lit one first thing out, and we rowed along the shore, and we rowed up a little river thing into a swamp and parked the canoe under some cypress trees. He wanted to show me The Cathedral, he said, which was this long stretch of secret land, nothing in it but tall palms, no undergrowth. It sounded cool. It was February, but warm, no mosquitoes or snakes out yet. Now and then, as we walked, he set his arm across my shoulder and sort of hugged me in. He was a big man, a carpenter with a big head and big gray eyes. He'd been hitting this bottle, and whenever he held the bottle to my lips, I drank. He ruffled my hair. When we entered The Cathedral, everything became so quiet and peaceful. I had lived in Florida for thirteen years, but this was a first for me. We walked through to where the shade left off, giving way to a broad expanse of saw-grass that stretched out under the bright sky, all the way to the Gulf of Mexico where I saw the dark water shimmering as if sprinkled over with crushed glass. We sat down on a fallen palm tree. He said, "Damn."

"What?" I said.

"Why don't you take off your clothes?"

"What?"

"If you want to," he said.

"I don't know."

"There ain't nobody here. Ain't no reason not to that I can tell."

We were side by side on that fallen tree, and he like started lifting my shirt up. I raised my arms, what else to do, and he pulled it off, and he rubbed his hand down my back and said, "That's better, ain't it? Why don't you loosen up a little bit? Go ahead."

He kept talking at me that way until I did what he said. I was naked beside him, the two of us sitting on the log, and he kept rubbing me and he kissed my neck and was feeling me all over and he turned me over the log. He bit me a bunch then, and like chewed on my rear end, I guess, and he fucked it with his fingers then screwed me for about twenty minutes until he ejaculated.

It made him happy.

Later, after we'd paddled back to his place, he fried me a steak up, despite that I'd told him I don't eat meat. I hadn't eaten it in over ten years. I wanted to go, but each time I tried he frowned, so I hung around and ate the damn steak. It sickened me to have the stuff in my mouth, to bite into it, that flesh, and chew it, it was so freaky. He'd gone to all that trouble, though, so I ate it. He asked me to come back tomorrow night. I didn't have the heart to say no.

I came over tomorrow. He had cleaned his house up and had

bought candles. Each room was lit by candles. After dinner, this time pasta shells with a creamy tofu sauce, he started in on me again. I did what he said. He took me to his bed, and he wanted me to sleep the whole night with him, but I told him, I said, "My wife will be worried sick if I don't come home."

"Screw your wife," he said.

"That's not very nice," I said.

"Depends how you look at it," he said, and smothered me in kisses. When I pulled away from him he slapped me. "I love you," he said.

"I got to go," I told him, peeling his huge arms off me. I stood up and he started hemming and hawing and looking at me like I'd broken his heart.

"You'll be fine," I said.

"I need you," he said.

"Shush," I said.

"I hate you," he said, and I made for the door, but he pulled me down and stripped me and messed with me. After that he was embarrassed, as was I. I put my clothes on. I was leaving, but he pressed me to the wall. He wanted to know would I come back later.

"My wife's leaving for the Keys," I said.

"The Keys?"

"This Friday, it's her vacation."

"What's in the Keys?"

"She has a friend there."

"Is it a guy?"

"No."

"I'd think she'd want to spend her vacation with you," he said.

"We already spend every day together. On vacations you're supposed to do something different."

He cleared his throat. "Well, how long will she be gone for?"

"Two weeks."

"That's fourteen days!"

He was what, twenty years older? More than that. We met at a job-site. After work, everybody stoned and drinking beer and all that, somebody pulled a guitar out and I played it and sang these songs that I wrote. After that, somebody else took up the guitar, but my new friend here kept going, for just me to hear, "Mmm mm mmm," and said it over and over, like he would give anything to have me alone with him.

I was like:

In olive green shorts, and wore black Rockports with worn down heels. I had old man socks on, the nylon thin kind, a dark red the color of bright red wine, what I inherited from my grandfather who came to America as a Hungarian immigrant escaping Hitler. Other than that, I wore a shirt that, in the screwball sewing of its hem, provided great ventilation that was good for bicycle riding. The shirt was lifted up on one side, an overturned U arched against my ribcage. On the front of the shirt was an iron-on photo of children shoulder-to-shoulder, their faces turned toward a wall as though they were about to be executed. VOTE BUSH was the slogan below the children. I'd made the shirt myself, easy. He had commented on how neat that shirt was, and he invited me to go canoeing. Knowing he had liked my shirt, I wore it the day we visited The Cathedral together, all those children turned toward the wall, as if they were about to get their brains blown out one by one.

So my wife went south for her vacation. At the time I didn't have a job, because I had finished grad school and was floating. When she was gone, I worked on my stories for about a week, then rode my ten-speed the twenty and something miles to his place. He lived way out beyond Pine Flats in a ranch house set back from the woods against the St. Mark's River. When I arrived, he was pissed that I hadn't come over sooner. He made me a purposely disgusting dinner of caramelized onions over burnt rice, then again started telling me how beautiful I was. He asked questions about my wife, and finally said that I should divorce her. He was buzzing pretty good at this point, and wanted me to wash the dishes naked. "Will that make you happy?" I said, and he nodded his head, so I took off my clothes. I was going to wash the dishes, but he said wait, and got some toilet paper. He ripped a bunch off the roll and handed me the wad. He said, "Pretend like you wiped your ass but forgot to pull away the paper."

"What?"

"Like maybe you were wiping your ass when the telephone rang. You got up to answer it, but the toilet paper stuck to your asshole."

"Forget it," I said.

"No, seriously," he said. "Go to the bathroom and come out that way and wash the dishes."

"Okay, whatever," I said, and did like he said.

He was a carpenter. This toilet paper thing was him getting me back for the day I first met him. He had come out from the Portalet at the job-site with toilet paper stuck to the back of his jeans. Everybody laughed, him not knowing what was going on, and me, like a fool, I walked up there and snatched it away and threw it onto the refuse pile. I was the refuse boy, the person responsible for sweeping out sawdust and piling up wood scraps and basically doing whatever the carpenters wanted me to do. It had seemed appropriate at the time.

"Come over here," he said.

"I'm still washing the dishes."

"Goddammit!" he shouted.

So I walked over there with my hands soapy. He grabbed my wrists. He pulled me onto his lap and kissed me, sticking his tongue into my mouth. When I pulled my face back from his face he like pulled my ass apart. He held it open that way, and I said, "You happy?" He said, "Stop looking so fucking intelligent," and ran his finger up in it. He was hurting me, so I tried looking stupid, like maybe I'd had a lobotomy like in The Planet of the Apes. But I wanted him to stop it, so I leaned over and kissed his neck and stroked his hair.

He was a carpenter. He'd been married for seventeen years, but had divorced after he came to find out there were seven Steves. "There were seven Steves," he said that day we'd gone out in the canoe.

"I'm sorry," I said.

He was a carpenter. His fingers were in my ass.

"Are you happy?" I said.

"You're the craziest motherfucker I ever come across," he said. "What's the matter with you?"

"Ow," I said, and lifted onto my toes.

"Open your mouth," he said.

I opened it.

"Keep it open," he said, and was tugging on me, and he said, "That's right," and I opened my mouth until it was like all the way open, and was straining to be more open.

He laughed. He liked this. I felt totally gross and I knew how stupid I looked. In my mind I was thinking, Are you happy?

He was a carpenter. With his wife he'd had three boys. When he pulled his fingers out, he saw the pained expression on my face and then slapped it. I deserved it, that's what the slap felt like, like I deserved it. He told me to finish washing the dishes in an ugly voice, and I did. When I finished washing the dishes, he was in the living room watching a movie he had rented, and I went out there. I said, "Where'd you put my stuff, David?" He said, "Your wife's been gone seven days and you didn't even pop in to see me. Do you have any idea what's been going through my head?"

"I'm sorry," I said, and he motioned for me to get on my knees. I did to him what my wife does to me, and held on tighter when it began to go, pulling down on it and swallowing. When it stopped, I was afraid to raise my eyes, but did, and he slapped me off him so that I fell back onto the floor.

"You make me sick!" he said.

"I'm sorry," I said.

He motioned with his fingers for me to sit on the couch beside him. He was a carpenter. He searched out blackheads on my back and squeezed them out, saying, "You obviously got some serious shit wrong with you, but I guess I shouldn't complain. Let me ask you though, would you let anybody do this to you?"

This was a question with a right answer. I'm no idiot. I know when somebody's trying to play me. I'm not very good though when it comes to delivering right answers that are lies. Ask my wife, she'll tell you.

"My wife sometimes does what you're doing," I said.

"Mmmm, you're so soft and smooth," he said. "Does your wife make you wash the dishes?" he said, and chuckled.

"Not like you did," I said, doing my voice to make it seem like he was the big cheese.

"Would you let anybody do what I do to you?" he repeated. Before I could answer he said, "You know damn well what I'm talking about. Don't evade it."

I sighed.

"What? What's the matter?"

"I don't know," I said.

"You can tell me," he said.

"I can't stand to see anybody unhappy. If somebody wants me to do something I usually do it."

"Anything at all?"

"I reckon," I said.

"You make me sick," he said.

"I can't help it."

"Don't you even have any feelings or anything?"

"Of course I do," I said.

He started laughing again. "I swear to God, you are the craziest sonofabitch," he said, and I laughed with him.

"What're you laughing at?" he said, no longer laughing.

I stopped laughing.

He balled his fist up and shook it in my face.

I kissed his fist, then looked up at him. "I don't like to be hurt," I said.

"Neither do I," he said, "but I want you to act like Donna. When your wife comes home from the Keys, you can be you again, but until then you're gonna be Donna."

"You want me to stay here with you for seven days?"

"Don't fuck with me, Donna!" he said.

"I'm sorry," I said, and he proceeded to beat me up. He's a big man. For the next week he got his fill of Donna. I wore Donna's old clothes, her cutoff shorts and print dresses and skirts and tops. He ripped them off me and fucked me with Michelob bottles and sticks and his cock and about whatever he could think up or find: old forks, a can-opener, a crescent wrench, a spoon. He stuffed me with pennies and sprayed me down with hose water and stepped on me in mud and blackened my eyes and burned me and shoved a carrot up my ass and called me Donna, Donna, Donna. He made Donna do all sorts of stupid things, like flip burgers with corn husks stuffed in her mouth. He made Donna clean his house, sort his tools, feed the animals, his chickens, the rabbits, and the two Vietnamese potbelly pigs fenced against his property line. He made Donna get down with the pigs on several occasions to eat the feed out of the dirt, all without using her hands. Donna's fear that the pigs could attack her made him laugh. He kicked her, especially when she whimpered. Her body was colorful with bruises. He made Donna say thank you whenever he penetrated her, and act like she liked it, pain be damned. Donna was not allowed to refuse. If she did, if she wiggled her shoulders like maybe this really didn't feel all that great, or if she forgot to smile, he retaliated, searched out new stuff to put in her. He tied her hands together with a rope and sent its end over the great magnolia bough, raised her onto her toes and tied it off and left her that way for hours. When he returned, Donna's hands were blue and cold. She had pissed herself. The urine had soaked her panties and streamed down the insides of both of her legs, all the way to her ankles, her legs freshly shaved because he didn't like seeing hair on Donna's legs. When he cut the rope and eased her down, she collapsed onto a magnolia root, and he dumped out the rest of his beer on her, the swill, the warm stuff that's left at the bottom after you've drunk the best part.

Other times he was nice to Donna. He fried Donna bacon. He washed Donna with vanilla soap. He ran a comb through Donna's long hair, rubbed lotion into her skin, and pulled splinters from her feet, put Band-Aids on her when she needed them, and plucked her eyebrows, kissed her and stroked her and caused her to have orgasms. Whenever this happened, he laughed. He called her slut and whore, two of his favorite words, and smeared her juice over her face, and made her eat it off his fingers. At night, when they fell asleep in each other's arms, his cock in her ass, he held her close to his heart and whispered her name, over and over, into her ear, wetting her neck with kisses and tears.

One morning, after Donna finished the breakfast he'd cooked her, a stack of pancakes sloshed over with too much butter and maple syrup and walnuts, plus two eggs over easy and sausage links, he said, "I want you to paint the shed, bitch," and we walked out back. I had on Donna's yellow string bikini, and he stood over me as I stirred the white paint. Round and round I stirred, the paint becoming creamier, and as I stirred he talked on soft about his life with me, going over great memories, such as the time we drove to California to see the Grateful Dead. "Didn't we have fun?" he said. I nodded. As he spoke, he smoked, now and then leaning over to put the cigarette in my mouth so as I could puff too. Finally he said, "Donna, I'm really sorry, baby, but the day has come. I'm going to have to dump your sorry ass, but first I want you to paint my shed. When I see that white paint I'm going to remember all the good things about you. That white paint you're looking at is a symbol of my forgiveness you fucking whore piece of shit. You cum-burping sonofabitch! You goddamn whore! You cock-sucking piece of shit!"

"Thank you," I said, and meant it. I was afraid. All week I'd tried to please him. I wanted him to feel proud of himself, good in his life from every angle, but he was unhappy, I could tell, and it was all because of Donna.

"You think I won't stomp on your head and crack your skull so bad that you won't know what hit you? Huh? Answer me you cock-sucking piece of shit whore!"

Donna started crying. On her knees, the can of white paint between her legs, she looked up at his huge gray eyes staring down bulbously and meanly at her, each eye like a whole egg, and said, "Why won't you forgive me?" I grabbed his legs and hugged them. He reached down, put fingers in my hair. "What's done's done," he said, calmer now, "but I want you to paint the shed. Think of the shed as a bunch of Steves. I want you to paint over all the Steves."

I did as he said, painting the Steves while he watched from his hammock on the porch, drinking from his Michelob, now and then cocking his air gun. Each time a pellet hit me I said, "Thank you," loud enough for him to hear, and I counted back in my mind and figured out that today was the seventh day. My wife would be home tomorrow. Having grown much closer to this man in the last few days, I knew his word to be good. When he'd said he was getting rid of me, my heart pulled some awful thing into it. The food he'd cooked turned sour in my stomach, but I painted his shed the best I could. A pellet slapped my neck painfully. "Thank you!" I shouted. Inside the shed sat the canoe, what he'd bought to float Donna to The Cathedral in, him thinking they'd marvel over Florida's natural beauty all along the way, a shared hobby here going on and everything, oh, look at the river weeds fluttering below us like so many celestial ribbons, check out the vines drooling from the trees along the shore over there, like a jungle, right? And oh hey, look at that eagle so peaceful against the sky's huge blue slate.

Down, finally, from the porch he came, the rope from earlier not so long as it was before. He'd cut it in half and had made a noose that he looped around my neck and cinched. At first it cut off my air, but then he loosened it and I said thank you, and I hoped he would drag me into the house now. He said, "Fuck you, bitch," and told me to drag the canoe down to the river.

I did that. He got in it. I pushed the canoe out and climbed into it and took up the paddle and carried us downstream. We passed a small boat with a family of three in it, them no doubt wondering what I was doing with a rope around my neck. I'm sure I was quite the sight with a yellow bikini top on and two black eyes.

I paddled us into the swamp, pulled the canoe up onto the cypress bank. Into the forest we walked, and whenever I tried to say something he kicked me and said shut up. He pulled a disposable camera from his vest and snapped pictures of me. He directed me into poses, like smiling like I'd won the Florida lottery, and up on one leg, acting like a flamingo. He asked me to hit myself, and photographed me doing it. Then tugged me along farther through The Cathedral. When we got to the fallen palm tree where we'd had our first intimate experience, he laughed. "I sure put one over on you," he said, and said, "I hope you've learned something from this."

"No, I'm Donna," I said.

"Shut up," he said. He said, "There's nothing worse in this world than a guy who will take it up the ass."

"But you kept asking me to take off my clothes," I said.

"You could have refused," he said.

"I wanted you to be happy."

"Oh, you felt sorry for me?"

"I did."

"You feel sorry for everybody?"

"I do."

"That's what's so fucking crazy about you. Why don't you feel sorry for yourself?"

"I don't count," I said.

"Look at you," he said, and grabbed my arm and shook me and let go. "Why aren't you ashamed?" he said.

"Maybe I am."

"You don't look it."

"I told you, I don't count."

"Why not?"

"I just don't."

"Now we're getting somewhere," he said.

"All I want is for you to be happy," I said.

"You're a goddamn faggot is what you are," he said, and told me to lie down on the palm tree. I did. He took pictures. "Pretend like I'm fucking you," he said, and I did that.

He was a carpenter.

I tried making him happy. I tried. I did what I could to please him. I'd had my successes throughout the week, but these victories were temporary, I knew, and I wanted his happiness to last, stick, so grabbed a palm branch up and gouged at my stomach, trying to open up a hole for him to peer into to see that I was in league with him, on his side. I would reach into the cut and pull myself open as far as I could for him to see, all that was in me, that was my desire, but he laughed at me stabbing myself, and took pictures of me bleeding. At least I'm worth a picture, I thought, but when I asked him what he would do with these shots, he said he would never even develop the roll.

FOUR

HURRY

I painted the board with Gesso. When the Gesso on the board was dry I unscrewed the cap on the bottle of boiled linseed oil. I unscrewed the caps on the tubes of pigments, those pigs, the Sap Green. There was Ultramarine Blue and King's Crown. There were crimson pigs, Vermilions and Alizarins, and there was ocher and black and yellow and Vandyke Brown.

I mixed them around on glass, the oil and the pigs. Each pig had its own little spot. I set the easel by the mirror and painted what I saw, me shirtless in the mirror, my face not nice, dark circles under my eyes. I was alone in the house while she, Miss Gorgeous, was off picking peaches with Sid, wonderful hot exploding peaches. I know about those peaches. Those peaches explode in your mouth when you bite into them.

I painted myself shirtless and sad, pathetic, ultra-skinny. It was a true rendition of what I looked like in the mirror, and I got the knife, the buck knife. I clutched the buck knife and stabbed the board. The blade stuck into my ribs, and I painted the gash with blood pigs. I painted the gash, the wound, painted the blade of the buck knife too.

Miss Gorgeous came home for cream, for fucking cream! Not so she could be with me for the rest of the day, but for cream, so that she and Sid could go to Sid's house and eat their freshly picked hot peaches from a bowl of cream. I saw it all, the bowl, the clay bowl Sid made, the wonderful artist, the wonderful great artist, Sid. I saw the bowl on Sid's futon between them, filled with fresh hot peaches drowned in cream. I saw them reaching their pretty fingers into the clay bowl at the same time. His fingers, you should see Sid's fingers, the fingers of a great artist and musician. You should see Sid's living room, Sid with his tall walls and cobwebs and musical instruments and paintings. When she saw my painting, of sad me with no shirt on, the buck knife stuck in my ribs, she said, "What's that?"

"What's it look like?"

"Like you're trying to be a martyr."

"It's a voodoo painting."

"I'm still waiting for you to grow up."

Then she was gone, again. I was alone, again, alone in the house while she, Miss Gorgeous, was with Sid.

Miss Gorgeous did not come home that night. What happened that night is not hard to imagine. Imagine the woman you love on a futon, her legs, her ankles, her feet held aloft by the talented hands of Sid, who has already touched her face with his genius hands that know how to paint a painting. Sid's talented hands have taken special delight in the shape of her clavicles. Now Sid's hands hold her feet. Sid's fingers are curled around her insteps. Sid's stomach brush-

John Oliver Hodges

es her stomach. He was your best friend. You took him into your bosom and Miss Gorgeous took him into hers. In the woods one day, their palms stained with blackberry juice, they fell in love. You saw it, it!

A week later the painting stares over her boxes of packed things. She has ten or eleven boxes, maybe twelve boxes. All of her things are packed up in the boxes, her candles, dresses, her plates, silverware, her bone collection, her marbles, her record albums and sewing supplies and real bee earrings. She'll be off in the morning, off to Sid. They can live happily ever after. Miss Gorgeous can really have at it forever with Sid.

"I painted the painting for you," I say. "The painting is yours."

She doesn't want the painting. I sure don't want the painting. Neither of us wants the painting. It isn't what you hang on your wall, the painting. It isn't the sort of thing you care to look at, the painting. I suggest she pull the buck knife out of the painting, use the unpainted side of the painting as a cutting board. The cutting board was a gift from her mother, after all. The board is hers. There is nothing wrong with the board. She can cut garlic on the board. She can sculpt clay on the board. She can sculpt a clay face of Sid on the motherfucking cutting board.

"Oh yes. Ha ha ha," she says.

Which is how we come to put the painting in the trunk, Miss Gorgeous putting up with me one last time. It's our last outing together. We must find a place to hang the painting, so I drive south, south for the woods. In the woods is where we picked blackberries with Sid that day. I can still see it, them, Miss Gorgeous and the genius artist, there they are, under the sun squashing up blackberries in their hands, staining their palms black and blue with drupelet juice.

Rage is what I'm choked up with as I drive us, a quiet rage, secret, the rage of grown-ups. Not a rage to share, this rage. It is a rage to keep inside, keep stuffed down. That night of the peaches, when she stayed with Sid, I ran myself headlong into a solid wall of bricks. It hurts when you run yourself headlong into a solid wall of bricks. I was choked up with rage then. I am choked up with rage now. As I drive, all choked up with rage, I feel the taste of the peaches on my tongue, the taste of the peaches all in my mouth.

Miss Gorgeous takes off her shoes. Miss Gorgeous takes off her shoes and she takes off her socks. There is her foot. There is her other foot, both feet, her feet that Sid has touched. She sticks her left foot up on the dash, her damp toes smudging the windshield glass, the light coming in flickering, oh.

Do I want to lose my mind? I don't think anybody wants to lose their mind. I don't think anybody wants to lose their mind ever, not ever, never ever in a million years.

I pull the car onto the shoulder of the road. I park the car on the shoulder of the road where the trees begin, where the blackberries grow. I take off my shoes. I take off my socks. Here we are, in the same place she and Sid made themselves have something in common that day. But it is just us today, the two of us, us with no shoes, us with no socks on our feet.

I pop the trunk.

I give her the nails.

I give her the hammer.

I pull the painting from the trunk.

We walk.

It has been sticky, a miserable, hot day, but the day changes quickly. Clouds slide in thickly under the sun, and are dark up there now, the clouds twisting around in mad bands.

We see a red turtle in the sand.

We leave the trail.

We walk down a hill through the trees and find a good tree to hammer the painting of me all sad into. I want the painting of me all sad hammered up high so that if somebody is walking through the woods and sees me, some rednecks maybe, they won't be able to rip me down. Maybe the rednecks will blast me with a shotgun, a pistol, use me for target practice, which is fine by me.

I get this log and prop it against the tree, and I balance myself up there on the log, and she gives me the painting, the buck knife still stuck in my ribs. The oily pigs haven't dried yet. The oily pigs rub off on my hands and arms and some gets on my face.

She gives me the nails. I put the nails in my mouth, tasting rust, and I notice the wind has picked up, it is really going, the wind. She gives me the hammer, and it is really blowing, the wind, so that my hair keeps flapping in my eyes. I hold the hammer back, and when I slam the hammer onto the nail, at the very instant of contact, metal on metal, the world flashes bright yellow and explodes, KABLAM! This flash, this bang, it about scares me off my log. A tree somewhere has cracked in half.

"Hurry," she says.

I finish hammering quick. I hammer me in there good into the tree, and jump down from the log and we stand here, transfixed, looking up the hill at this violence that has erupted around us. The trees have gone crazy, are thrashing back and forth, waving their branches thick in the sky, and bending way down, their tubular trunks creaking, stressing. It starts raining. The rain comes down sparsely at first, in thick capsulate drops that are heavy and cold, and explode into many little droplets when the drops slam against us. We run up the hill through all of the blowing trees, and the twigs and branches and leaves falling down, and the rain that is falling down crazy now. All the way up the hill we run, up to Big Dismal.

At Big Dismal there is a deck, a newly erected observation deck made of wood, and we scramble down the rough slope of eroded earth, the roots curving out handy for maneuvering, and duck below it where a lot of mud is. The mud under the deck is deep and hot. It's like the ground has a heater in it. The mud sucks up around our ankles and shins, quicksandy, the mud, silty and sucky and warm, the mud.

In the mud, soaking wet, we hear another tree falling, hitting other branches as it falls. It is scary. The tree is falling close to us, a massive tree that will squash us and kill us to death if it lands on the observation deck and causes it to collapse. It is the sort of sound to make you want to grab the nearest person and hug her close. But we don't hug. We are at odds, as they say, at odds. She is in love with Sid now. She doesn't want to have anything to do with me now. She's told me plenty, it is Sid she now loves. I am the poison, she's told me. The pollutant. It is her duty to think highly enough of herself to rid herself of me.

The sound of the rain grows louder, slamming against the earth harder in the thunder, drubbing the earth as the rain pours in through the slats above us cold and dribbling, the rain, falling down in cold dribbling sheets of rain.

I shove the hammer-handle into my pocket, and reach out with both hands. I unbutton her shirt from the top down. I spread her shirt apart to see the russet freckles that I know so well, her breasts white and glowy and freckled. In the shadowy pulses of cloud-choked light, in the turbulence of impending death—for that is what it feels like, like our lives are in danger—I touch her, ever so lightly, my fingertips drops of rain, nothing more. That's when she takes her shirt off the rest of the way off. She takes her shirt off and hangs it on a splinter in the boards above our wet heads.

Then I see pity. Through pity she has done this. Through pity she has let me touch her. Through pity, oh pitiable me. In pitying me she grabs my head and kisses my mouth. She takes off her skirt, tosses it onto a fern. Turning her back to me, she lowers her knees into the mud. She leans over the mud and puts her hands into the mud and sinks down into all that hot heated mud.

Watching her, my torture, looking down at the long wet stretch of her in the choked light, I pull the hammer from my pocket. You hear about this. Such thinking happens in the minds of men. But I don't. I throw the hammer instead. The hammer falls down through

the rain and hits the water of Big Dismal far below, breaking its surface. Down through the throat of the hole the hammer I threw rolls.
I take off my shorts.

Her back and hips together form the shape of a guitar. She is a
woman that is a guitar, her body warped by rain, her curved spine a
wet fingerboard.

I say her name.

She stays like she is, waits there.

This is not the normal her way.

This is a new sort of her way, a way she's picked up off Sid, the
talented genius who knows how to paint a painting. Sid is all about
spontaneity. Sid has given her this. She worships Sid. She belongs to
Sid. I put my hands on Sid's hips. In the rain coming down against
our spines I play Sid's guitar.

I'm not the sort to bawl or cry—I'm a holder-insider, a slam-
my-head-against-the-waller—but I cry. The loveliness does it, the
delicate wavering movements of her scapula, those panels meant to
guard what's precious against the assaults of picks. Her neck reaches down from between her shoulders, her golden locks flowing like
broken strings over the dark mud. It's insane, so I push her forward.
Her breasts press down into the mud. She pushes herself back up
and the mud sucks at them. If the mud was chocolate, her boobs
would be chocolate-dipped now in the way of Dairy Queen. She is a
pale guitar with chocolate-dipped tits that are Sid's.

The storm blows over. Sunlight falls down around us, and the
leaves of the ferns sparkle. Everything sparkles. When she gets up
out of the mud she sparkles. She is covered all over with mud, a mud
woman—we both are mud-covered—but she sparkles, and her eyes
of blue. She dives into the hole sparkling and I dive down after her.
In the cold dark waters I see the blur that is her, and kick her way
and grab her body. She struggles at first, trying to get away from the
poison that is me, but I find her hand and she relents. She is mine.
We are sinking, together, and I'm thinking of the hammer way down

there at the bottom where electric eels live. I see the eels in the murk, swishing around this iron thing that has invaded their space, but she makes for the surface. Her leg, then her foot, slips through my fingers.

We climb out of the hole and put on our wet clothes.

Walking back to the car we do not speak. We see things in the woods, the fallen trees, and the ferns getting lighter, perkier as they drip. A silky mist wanders through the needles of the trees. We do not speak on the drive home.

But it isn't home.

It is a rented apartment, an apartment we've rented for three years, the Christmas lights always on, our little home.

She does not wait for tomorrow to leave. She packs her boxes into her van. She drives off with her bone collection, with her sassafras incense and real bee earrings. As she passes by the window in her bright blue van, I hear her scream, "You stupid fuck!" That's her screaming at herself. She is driving off to Sid, already spoiled. They can pick peaches all they like now. They can take their time.

WHERE THE BODY WON'T FOLLOW

Tina played Edward Weston's Charis in the South Daytona dunes, her body kinked at the waist, legs run out like an opened scissors. Tina played Man Ray's Kiki with f holes Sharpied to her back, played the Nagasaki Girl on the rooftop of the Ormond Hotel, and played Thérèse, the nine-year-old neighbor of Balthus. Thérèse would slip through the forest and enter the painter's castle where he would pose her in wicker chairs like with panties showing, or on the floor on elbows and knees, face hovering over an opened book. I photographed Tina playing Thérèse in our living room at Palm Place. The book she's reading from is about the Agony Tree, where Jesus prayed the night before his body was destroyed.

What sucks is printing when I'm in the darkroom at school trying to get stuff done. People in there always want to see what you're doing. I was printing my new shots. After soaking Tina in fix five minutes, then washing her some, I put her on a red cafeteria tray, took her to the squeegee room to check her tones under the fluorescent tube. I thought I'd burn the marble cat, dodge Tina's left ankle veiled in shadow. This picture would be better if Tina had socks on, I thought, and espadrilles like Thérèse in the Balthus painting. I was about to head back to the darkroom, but somebody behind me went, "Gosh, Jesse, how'd you get Tina to strike that pose?"

It was James.

"My girlfriend would never do that. What's your secret, dude?"

Steve came in. "Holy shit," he said.

James said, "What a great model. Do you have any beaver shots of Tina?"

"Cut it out," I said.

"Does it go side to side?" James asked.

"Fuck you."

Steve said, "I always liked your pictures, Jesse, all those homeless people and weirdos, but most people will think you're trying to copy Diane Arbus. With this you got something cool and original going on. Look at the tones in this shot. What a vibrant picture."

"She's got a killer ass," James said, and Tina stepped in from the hall with some cookbooks she'd checked out from the library, all this fun stuff on cakes and brownies because she had it in mind to bake something special for our landlady, Miss Libby, who shared the duplex with us. When Tina saw us watching her on her elbows and knees, her skirt hiked up above her hips, her eyes blinked a bunch of times real fast.

"We were just admiring the porcelain quality of your skin," Steve said.

"Yes, and Jesse's brilliant compositional eye," James said.

Tina looked at me.

"Wait," I said.

Tina left the squeegee room and I chased her down the hall on outside where a full moon floated above the parking lot. I ran up and put my hand on her neck. She turned and faced me.

"I've got to print somewhere," I said.

"Maybe you should stick to bag ladies."

"Tina."

She dropped her books, peeled the wet print off my tray, ripped it in half and threw the pieces onto the asphalt. She stepped on them with her sneakers and ground them into the asphalt.

I said, "Jesus."

"My body's not a book for anybody to open and look at."

"Then why did I photograph it?"

"Because I'm stupid."

"So I'm not supposed to show my pictures of you to anybody, ever?"

"Once I'm dead I won't care."

"Tina."

"You were showing me off, Jesse. I saw your face."

"You saw wrong," I said. "But I don't like hiding my pictures of you. It makes me feel creepy."

"Okay then, show them to whoever the fuck you like."

"But you just said—"

"Who cares what I said?" she said. "They're your pictures. If you want to parade my body in front of Steve and James and every other asshole, who am I to stop you? I would never try and get in the way of your artistic vision, you know that."

"That makes sense. You just destroyed my picture. Should I stop photographing you?"

"Stop it, Jesse," Tina said, and hugged me. After we hugged for a while she said that as a photographer herself she knew she was going to feel shitty about this later. And she said maybe, she wasn't sure about this but maybe, just maybe she was annoyed by how our teacher always raved on about how great my pictures are. Ever since we moved to Palm Place she hadn't felt inspired to photograph stuff. Her only class right now was Studio, it met once a week, and she hated it, was thinking of quitting. Then she said she was here for me, that she wanted to be my Emmet Gowin's Edith. I could use her body however I wanted. She'd rather I photograph it, she said, than all those crazy people I dig up. She said, "I have this fear that one of those guys will stab you. Those bikers are dangerous. I heard that in some gangs they won't let you be a member unless you first have sex with a child."

That sounded so stupid and like it couldn't possibly be true, but we stayed out there hugging under the lamp in the parking lot. Our discussion left us feeling closer to each other. We laughed at ourselves, we bonded. Tina showed me a picture of the blueberry pie she planned to bake for Miss Libby, who lately had been moping around the backyard a lot. Her husband was ill, and Tina wanted to cheer her up. We looked at more pictures of desserts, then walked back to the darkroom where I reprinted Tina playing the Balthus Girl. I squeegeed my prints and put them in my blotter book then drove us toward the river on my Kawasaki. Once back at Palm Place we made love on the couch, the moon a soft blur on the jalousies. The doorknob rattled, but we didn't catch on until Miss Libby was in the living room with us, her beehive hairdo silhouetted against the moonlight coursing through the palm fronds beyond the door.

Tina fell off the couch. Her face in Miss Libby's flashlight beam looked wild like some animal's, her lips curled inward against her teeth, her outgrown canine dripping clear spit. She reached for her jeans, grabbed them, and scuttled backwards so that her back was against the wall. She was trying to cover herself with her jeans, clutching them to her chest.

"It's Miss Libby," I said.

"Get out!" Tina screamed.

Miss Libby cleared her throat. "This is my house. I think you should take your whore's bath now because Jesse and I have stuff we need to discuss." Miss Libby gestured with her long white fingers that Tina was excused, that she could run along.

"Jesse, tell her to leave!" Tina shouted.

"Oh Jesse, you ought not let her speak that way to you. She hasn't a single right."

"Go to bed, Miss Libby," I said.

"But you were knocking on the wall, Jesse. What did you want?"

"Nothing, we're fine, go to bed."

"Were you enjoying her like I told you to, Jesse?"

"Get out!" Tina screamed.

"He's never going to marry you," Miss Libby said, and stepped Tina's way. She leaned over, raising the flashlight as if she intended to smack Tina over the head with it. Tina lifted her arms to fend off the blow.

"Miss Libby!" I shouted.

Miss Libby froze, a halo of light on the ceiling above her head. Thank God she caught herself and did not go through with it. When Miss Libby unfroze, she shined the beam in my face, ran it down my body then turned and left us, closing the door behind her.

Tina jumped up and locked it. We put on clothes and hugged in the shag. We didn't speak. I think Tina was genuinely traumatized. I felt her heart pounding hard against me. I cradled her skull and stroked her hair. Her body relaxed. We fell asleep and dreamed. Later in the night we woke at the same time, and made for our bed, holding hands as we bumbled down the hall. Again I fell into the place people go to when sleep happens, and Tina followed me there. I photographed her in a field of purple and white and red flowers where she stood naked and bronze, and above her a storm boiled, and there were yellow flowers too, and the petals brushed against Tina's ankles and calves, caressing them and reaching up for her in all of their marvelous hallucinogenic color and velvety smoothness. Though it wasn't raining yet, lightning bolts flickered in my lover's hair, faraway flashes that promised a heavy downpour. I began to fear for my film, but then Tina's alarm beeped, releasing me from that familiar anxiety. It was five a.m., dark outside, and as Tina dressed for her job at the International House of Pancakes, I lamented the fact that those pictures hadn't been—they had never happened. It was upsetting, but once Tina had left the house, I drifted back to sleep.

* * *

Midmorning a fist hits the jalousies. I wake. "Jesse, I know you're in there."

I yank wide the door.

"Jesse, you look miserable," Miss Libby says, and comes in. Who am I to stop her? She owns the place.

Miss Libby sits in her couch, pats the spot beside her.

"Wait," I say, and hop to the bedroom, put a shirt on, then hop back to the living room.

"Oh, Jesse, you didn't have to dress up for me, Honey. Why don't you take it off?"

"I'm fine. What do you want?"

"You're mad."

"I'm not mad."

"You're cute when you're mad, you know that, Jesse? Why don't you tell me what you're mad about?"

"I'm not mad."

"You are mad."

"Okay, I'm mad," I say. "I can't believe you said those things to Tina."

"Phooey, I didn't say a thing to that brown unspeakable that she doesn't already know. I did her a favor, Jesse. I'm a compassionate woman. I feel sorry for her."

I roll my eyes.

"You're very cute when you do that, Jesse."

"Shh," I say.

"Listen, Jesse, there's something you need to know right this minute. Please sit down." She pats the cushion.

I'm thinking, okay, here she goes, but I sit, the better to get this over with.

"We were mad in love," Miss Libby says, and tells the story of her life with Jim, how they met at a bar when she was twenty, back when she still had her "big bubbies." Jim had lost a kidney in Korea, was slightly disabled, but he could sure sweep a woman off her feet. She thought the world of him, but eight years into their marriage a short brown woman appeared at the door with Jim's child. The short brown woman looked like a monkey, Miss Libby said, as did the child. "Since that day I have hated the Tinas of the world," she confides. She says, "They are all scoundrels in my book, just plain verminous creatures if you ask me. They are all born of a communist mentality and their intention is to ruin all white people. I think we're going to stand by and let them do it. Hey, you over there, you want my husband's kidney? Have at it. Take his liver too if you please."

"Gosh, Miss Libby."

"Jesse, in my wisdom of having lived sixty-three years on God's earth, my advice to you is to dump that flat-nosed rat of a woman into the nearest canal. Go ahead, have you some fun on her like I told you, but when you're done, boy, you'd best to clear out. You'll be sorry. I simply hate to see a prostitute take advantage of you in your innocence, because you are a fine child, Jesse. You have got good breeding, I see it all over you. I see the light of Jesus shining in your eyes."

"Tina grew up in Texas, Miss Libby. Only her dad is Korean, and he was a police captain, not just an officer but a captain. Her mother is part Hungarian and part Egyptian. "

"Jesse, listen, the doggone woman worked as a pedicurist at the Daytona Mall? I went over there and she did my feet? I thought we could come to an agreement. I thought that since Jim was paying her money, we could take the little monkey off her hands, free her up. In truth her son did not look half bad, he was about cute as all getup, but we all knew she was doing a lousy job raising it. The boy needed a cozy home like Palm Place to grow up in, not some ramshackle hovel where who knew all what he'd be exposed to, his mama being what she was. That boy needed a woman like me to give him love to thrive by, not some loose goose dishrag sort whose only purpose was to ruin his chances in life. I would have protected him, Jesse, and fed him good food, none of that weird stuff."

"I love egg rolls," I say.

"Honey, I'm not talking about no egg rolls. Jim told me what and such those people in Korea eat. You don't want to know."

"I once ate a turtle," I say.

"Soft shell turtle is a Southern delicacy," Miss Libby says. "When I was coming up in Georgia we hauled them out the lakes. My mother nailed their heads to a tree, and she would rip their backs clean off their bodies. That's where the delicious meat is stored. She cut them into squares, rolled the bits in batter and deep-fried it all up. Honey, you've not ate until you've ate that. But listen," she says, "she wanted Jim's money. I tried to pay her off. I said, give us the boy we'll give you five grand, that's a lot of money, you could buy a new toothbrush with it, but the harlot cut my pinky toe, Jesse. She pretended her scissors slipped. It got infected. Had to see me a doctor. She might've dipped her scissors in dung."

"I'm sorry, Miss Libby."

"Thank you, Jesse," she says, and squeezes my knee. She says, "I hope you never know what it's like to have your world shatter in an instant." After a short pause, she says, "Jesse, I came over last night because I needed a shoulder to cry on."

"Miss Libby, what is it?"

"He was a fine man. He was my man."

"Jim?"

Miss Libby sets her face on my shoulder, her beehive hairdo scratching my neck. Her body begins to jerk, she is crying, and then she sobs, and her tears flow down through my collar. I feel them dribble down my chest, and I pat Miss Libby, comforting her, what else can I do? But I really ought to be getting this, I think. I should think photography at all times. I should be recording Miss Libby's agony. I say, "Miss Libby," but Miss Libby kisses my neck. She sucks it. It hurts. I pull away. Miss Libby wraps her arms around me and squeezes.

"Miss Libby, don't."

"He's dead!" Miss Libby cries out, and laughs now, her tears gone to laughter. She is laughing her pain, hugging me harder. I feel so bad for her. I don't know what to do, so just sit here and after a bit she peels away from me. To be supportive I take her hand in mine and squeeze it soft. Don't want to mash the thick veins all over it. With Miss Libby's other hand she dabs her face with a handkerchief. When she has regained her composure, she says, "Well, I guess I'd best to call the undertaker."

"Undertaker?"

"To come get Jim."

"You mean Jim is in the bed still?"

"Where else might my Jim be?"

"I've never taken a picture of a dead body," I say.

"Oh, Jesse," Miss Libby says, touching her chest delicate, "you know I will do anything to help you in your little photography career."

I grab my Leica M3 and we head next door where Jim's in his bed dead all right. Not breathing. It's a hospital bed. I frame him up, suck his body through my lens. Miss Libby, on the other side of the bed, brings a hand up behind her beehive hairdo. She likes this picture stuff. She feels much better now, so tries looking sexy. I snap one, ask her to kiss Jim if she wants to. It might be her last chance, so she leans over and presses her lips to Jim's forehead. I arrange the frame so that her beehive hairdo doesn't mix in with the poster of a sheepdog on the wall. I snap it. After that, Miss Libby, with sly eyes and a wet smile, pulls Jim's sheet down, slow, and I'm thinking, Miss Libby, don't do that, but she pulls it down over Jim's bald emaciated speckled chest, down farther to where his member pokes out, then emerges pink and swollen and looking like it's filled with air. It looks like a bloated dagger made of human flesh, the handle part on top. I hadn't known a man could get like that when he was dead. It's huge, bigger than it's supposed to be, looks like. Miss Libby pulls the sheet down to Jim's knees, grabs the dagger by the handle and squeezes it, the diamond ring on her finger all a-sparkle. Looks like she is stabbing poor Jim between his legs. "Go ahead, Jesse," she says, and I suck their bodies into my chamber.

* * *

Tina's home from IHOP a little after three. I hug her in the living room, loving her smell of sweat and pancake batter and bacon grease, and I smell her breath and her scalp, then follow her to the bedroom where she peels out of her uniform, her cute blue bow tie, the nylon vest and skirt and hose. While standing beside the vanity table she reaches behind her with both hands, her scapulas rising, to unlatch the strap where it crosses her spine. She drops her bra to the floor then pulls pins out of her hair, the black silk cascading down her back. "They work you hard?" I ask from the bed.

"Don't start, Jesse, I'm very disturbed today."

I grab my Leica from the nightstand, snap Tina reaching for the glass of water on the vanity table. I always fill Tina's glass full to the rim, always all the way up. It tickles me to see her trying not to spill it when she brings it to her mouth. That glass of water is one thing Tina counts on. It's always there for her when she returns from IHOP, filled to the rim.

I say, "Jim died, by the way. That's why Miss Libby barged in on us."

Tina pulls the glass down and looks at me, her big lips wet.

"You know that's not something I'd lie about."

"Jesse, I don't like it here, there's something wrong with this place, I've decided."

I motion for her to come to bed, quick, so I can wrap her in my loving arms and soothe away the troubles of the world.

"No," Tina says. She sets the water down, grabs the brush off the vanity, runs it through her hair.

"If I died after we were married for forty-three years, you'd barge in on somebody too, you know you would."

Tina sets the brush down. She slips into a halter top, steps into her purple Wal-Mart skirt. When the light's right you see her legs through the cheap soft material. I love that skirt, and I love the smell behind Tina's ears, and the way her feet smell when she pulls her socks off, like corn chips when you pop open the bag.

"Hurry," I say, doing my arms.

"This is so depressing."

"A man died behind that wall last night, don't you get it?"

"I only met Jim once. He looked at me like he knew me, but he didn't say a word."

"What if I died, would you care then?"

"I was going to cook Miss Libby a pie, can you believe it?"

"You can bake her cookies instead," I say.

"Sure," Tina says. "Where's that bottle?"

"If you died, I say, I would want to join you."

"Jesse, that's sweet, but doesn't Miss Libby know it's illegal to walk into somebody's house in the middle of the night? She could go to jail for that."

I fetch our bottle, swallow, hand it to her. In a few minutes she's got the Asian flush going on, her cheeks all aglow. She's drinking the stuff too fast, I think, but photograph her stumbling room to room. This is German glass I'm sucking her through, a 28mm Zeiss Icon lens. Tina's details will be crisp. Tri-X developed in HC-110, according to Ansel Adams, is the sharpest combination. Because of the low light I'll have to push-process the film, which will make the prints look extra grainy and rich.

"Next time that bitch comes in here," Tina says, and says, "That woman is such a sneaky *bitch*! I can't *believe* you stick up for her, Jesse. Why does she hate me? What did I ever do to her, I don't understand it, you try to be nice."

"Miss Libby's husband had a baby with an Asian woman," I say, but Tina doesn't seem to hear me now. She turns the bottle up again, and I drop to my knees before her. I could ask her to marry me. Instead I grab her elastic waistband, pull her skirt down mid-thigh. Tina staggers backwards, her face very round and puffy in the air above me, like a moon. I yank her back. "No," she says, "too many germs," but I lick it. I'm like the pet rat we had, Super Supper, how he would stand on his hind legs licking at his water bottle until he was no longer thirsty. That's me, it's just so delicious, but I can't get enough. I have to sweep Tina into the air, her skirt dangling from one foot as I carry her to the bedroom. I toss her onto the bed and she bounces and I jump down there and from her loins drink out the dark flavors of the Orient. Then I am making love to Tina Chang.

I guess my Leica is on the nightstand, so I grab it and snatch Tina's face from the pillow, that's all, but the window is open and in the yard I see Miss Libby, her blind sheepdog quiet beside her and glowing whitely in the sun. She holds a yellow pitcher, leans over. Water streams from the spout, sparkles on the flowers. Her husband was carried away this afternoon by the undertaker. Jim's blood will be sucked out of his veins, if it isn't being sucked out now, all that red syrup replaced with clear liquid.

I have never photographed Tina like this. It feels strange, or wrong, or something, I don't know, but Danny Lyon once aimed his Leica at a mirror that showed his wife Nancy on top of him, connected to him. Our teacher talked about what a great picture that was, how it represented a new kind of journalism, journalism of the self, he had called it, so I snap another one. Tina doesn't mind, so again I snatch her body from the world, saving it. I don't like that I am in the pictures, too, though, so pull out of it and stand back and suck it though again. I stuff it down into the box where I keep what I love. Standing on the bed above her I take more pictures, careful not to include my bony foot in the frame. That's when it occurs to me that with a little bit of adjusting Tina could be playing the My Lai Girl. Maybe later we can do that shoot. I will need a fat boy-doll with no pants on it to put face-down between her legs. Already I know of several dirt roads that are perfect for this. We can use manikins for the other bodies, and I know where to get them. Tina will need to wear a long-sleeved shirt, and I'll have to arrange her hands in the correct manner. Everybody will get the reference. The Nagasaki Girl and the My Lai Girl together will constitute a series that I can then further pursue. I will be hailed a genius.

Only Tina groans, moves her face back and forth as if she could barf. This happened the last time she drank, after which she swore she would never drink again, or at least wait until she was twenty-one so that she wouldn't be mad at the man, in this case our photography teacher, who bought us the bottle.

I hop to the kitchen for the sauce pot. Reentering the bedroom I see that Miss Libby and Boofis have heard our commotion because they are strolling over. Something is coming together here, but I freak. I hop into my shorts, cover Tina over, then think, wait, what am I doing? I'm supposed to think photography, that's the rule that we are taught, so I yank the sheet aside and release it, and take more pictures of the police captain's daughter. By the time Miss Libby arrives at the window, she is like a turtle in the middle of the bed, one with no shell, each nodule of her spine seeming to breathe between the symmetry of her outspreading ribs, all those mouths. As she barfs into the sauce pot, I snap away. Miss Libby steps in closer, and stares down at her through the screen. "That's a good boy, Jesse," she says, and crosses her arms, striking a pose of deliberate disgust.

Tina calls in sick, sips water, gets up from bed to puke, I hear the echo in the toilet bowl, painful-sounding, like her stomach is pushing up through her throat on out of her mouth, a big shiny bubble that she is then forced to suck back inside. I should photograph it. I should, but I'm stupid. Before I started taking pictures of Tina, I was passionate about photographing old men and smelly children with grape jelly smeared across their faces, stuff like that. I have these pictures of Tina now, of her body that at first had been shy. Once I'd managed to peel away its layers, it relented, and I photographed it in the old Negro graveyard making rubbings off the homemade stones, its fingers blackened with charcoal dust, the arched bottoms of its feet blackened, its toes digging into the moist earth. Her feet looked burned in the dusky light, as if she had walked over coals. That was our first shoot. Now I can photograph it however I please, but it has dimmed my love of the homeless, of the wandering preachers, and street children and wayward weirdos.

I scramble eggs for Tina Chang, bring Tina Chang eggs on a plate, but Tina can't eat my eggs so I eat her eggs for her. She sleeps, beautiful and snoring with her high sexy cheekbones, flat forehead and awesome skin tone. In time, Tina Chang will overcome her hangover. It happens to everybody. In time, Tina will be her regular self again.

I ride to my Aesthetics in Photography class. The imitation assignment is due. Our pictures are to be mounted archivally on ragboard, to show that we care, our teacher has told us, but I show nothing. I sit through class as he lectures on "repetition with a difference," and comments on the works of my classmates. Their pictures bore me, so many Van Gogh imitations, flowers dangling over the rims of vases, self-portraits with bandages wrapped around the head. While our teacher summarizes the merits of each image, I think of Tina in the window light of yesterday's afternoon, her left foot drawn up against the window jamb, sort of caressing its painted wood. I took a picture and somewhere high above us a cloud parted or a branch fell. The light dropped upon us like this great force of nature, illuminating every contour and tonal variation of her body.

After class, in the hall, James wants to know why I didn't show my great shot of Tina playing the Balthus Girl. He says I deprived him of the opportunity of impressing our teacher with his photographic acuity. He says, "I've thought a lot about this, Jesse. Would you like to hear my theory about why Edward Weston's photographs don't give me a boner?"

"No thanks," I say, and James asks if I think Tina will model for him. He likes this imitation business, he says, and offers to pay Tina a hundred dollars to pose topless with a split watermelon. "Like one of those Paul Gauguin paintings," he says.

"Tina is not a sex object," I say.

"But you'll ask her for me, won't you?"

* * *

Back at Palm Place Tina is up, has an appetite, so I spread chunky peanut butter over toast for her. She eats half while on the couch, but hasn't bathed. She's got the great smell going on. Rank, they call it. I could push her buttons on this, but we have shit to discuss. I tell Tina that even though I mounted the best picture of her playing the Balthus Girl, I didn't show it to anybody, not even privately to our teacher. "I was afraid."

Tina squeezes my hand.

"It's like a sickness," I say.

"Stop," Tina says.

"I don't understand what's happening to me."

Tina puts my finger in her mouth and gnaws it. It squeaks against her teeth. We sit here listening to the squeaking and the blue jays out there chirp, the squirrels claw the bark of the trees. These wonderful sounds mesmerize me. The palm fronds rustle in the breezes blowing in off the river. As Tina gnaws, I tell her that as I walked up, Miss Libby, who was on her way to the funeral home for the open casket viewing, invited us both to go with.

"Now why would I want to see a dead man in his casket?" Tina wonders aloud, her mouth filled with my finger still so that her words come out garbled.

I say, "You know, I took some pictures of Jim naked while being dead. Maybe that's a sign I should stop photographing you. We could make a rule. No more naked pictures of Tina. I don't like that I photographed you last night. I'm sorry."

Tina pulls my finger out. "Did you really take a dead picture of Jim?"

"He had an erection. Miss Libby grabbed it."

"I don't think so," Tina says.

"I did," I say, and want to feel good about it, for they've got to be different and fresh and original, unseen, which is a word our teacher uses to describe the best pictures, the pictures that matter. I just feel awful, though, like I should have said something, stopped it. I feel worse over what I took of Tina puking, Miss Libby watching over her like some derelict guardian angel. I think maybe I've looked at the world through glass too long. I want to make up for it by taking "decent" pictures of Jim, and am about to beg Tina to go to the funeral home with me so that I can photograph him in his death suit, but a shadow flickers through the room. We look out the window to see a snowy egret land in the backyard. It hops around in the grass and Tina gets excited. With a disposable camera she photographs it through the window, but wants to get closer. We open the back door and head out. Tina snaps a shot of the egret flying away, then turns the camera on me.

"Take off your clothes," she says.

"What?"

"Undress," she says.

I don't like it, but I peel out of my shoes and jeans. I take off my shirt and stand naked in the grass in front of her, the light all over me. I'm embarrassed. Tina snaps and winds, snaps and winds.

"Stop," I say.

"Elbows and knees," Tina says. "I want to shoot you being the Balthus Girl."

"That's crazy. I can't do this outside here like this."

"On your knees, girl," Tina says.

I do it. I'm Thérèse. Tina walks around me, snapping pictures. She says, "Your feet are wrong," repeating the words I once said to her. "The tops are supposed to be flat on the ground. Stop using your toes. Let your stomach hang down loose and low, that's right, like the bottom of a canoe. You're doing it. That's right, that's it. That's a good girl. Good girl."

This is so ridiculous. I'm going to stand now and run to the house, but when I turn my head I see Miss Libby staring through her kitchen window at us. She's just sitting there at her window, looking out at her beautiful backyard.

"Come on over here little girl," Tina says, snapping her fingers.

I want out of here, but feel locked into this. I feel obligated to follow through, and maybe Miss Libby needs to see it, I think, so crawl, elbows and knees, pretending I'm Tina's doggy. I think Tina will teach me tricks now, like how to shake, how to bark, how to roll over. Maybe it'll be fun? I will do whatever Tina says, and Miss Libby will be horrified. We will also be doing Miss Libby a favor, for her mind will be taken away from her grief. That's when I see what Tina has called me over here for.

"Forget it," I say.

Tina laughs. "You like nasty smells. Go on. Stick your tongue out. Pretend like you're going to lick it."

I stick my tongue out. The smell is awful, nothing in the least bit like her body. Her allusion is offensive to me, and the stuff is fresh and piled up hugely, fresh out of Boofis, totally gross.

"Go ahead, little girl. Put your face in it," Tina says, laughing.

"The Balthus Girl was reading a—"

"Shh," Tina says, and pushes down on my spine. "That's right," she says. "You're doing real good, real good, ha ha!"

I know she's bluffing, but I deserve this. I lower my forehead into the wet pile, and think of Tina's body.

"Hey!" Tina shouts.

"What are you waiting for?" I say.

"Jesse, stop!" Tina cries.

"I'm not moving till you take a picture," I say, and close my eyes. I push my face down further into the pile. All Tina has to do is take a picture.

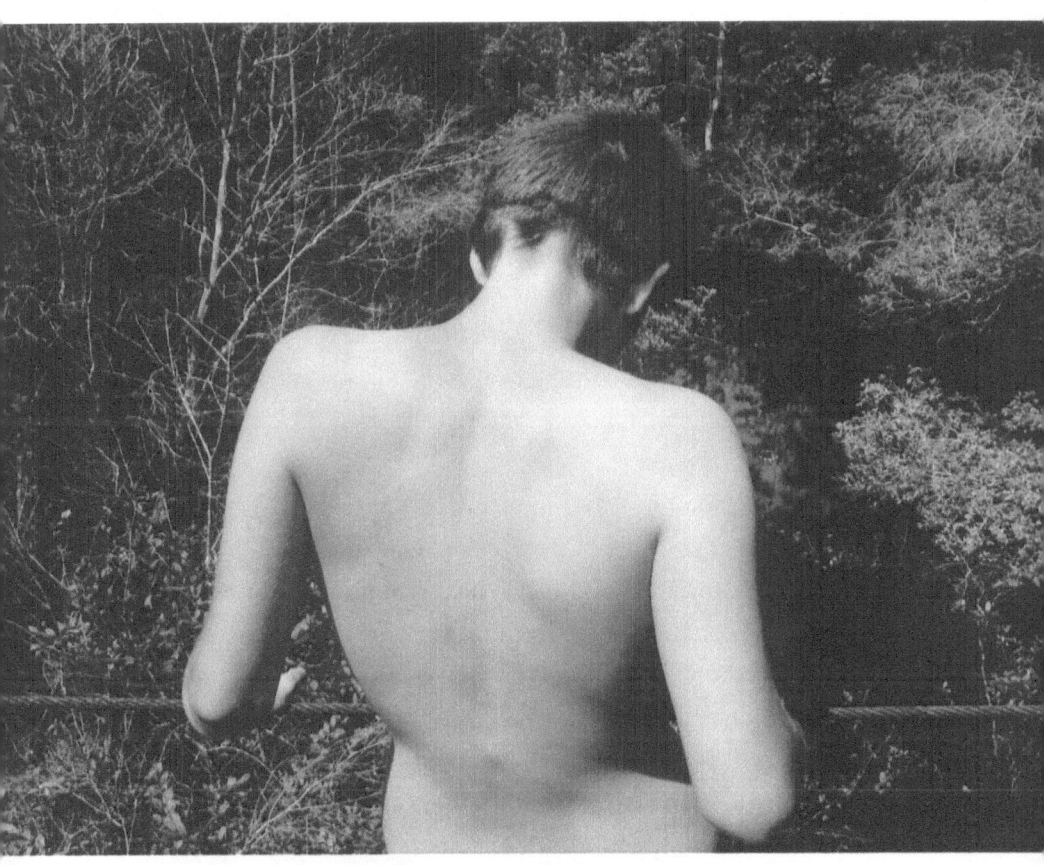

GIVE UP, WOMAN, SURRENDER!

My heart acts tough, like he don't care. Says it'll keep us another month in the doc's basement, but I'd rather be homeless. I think he should listen to me, only the Q44 approaches and I hug him tight. He pushes me away. I understand. By holding him dear I have drawn attention to my disapproval. I'm a stupid that way, a bag of grease or dead baby pigeon, not what you pick off the ground, let alone stuff down in your pocket.

My heart leaves me in the Laser Bleaching building shadow,

the sign up there saying they do implants too. The bus travels down Main, and I follow it with my eyes, already bereaved, or bereft, however you say it. It always happens when he leaves me, but the bus travels past the library. That's why I follow, I tell myself, not because I'm afraid I'll never see him again, but to read books and surf the evil Internet, exercising my will.

The library people know my name. After two months of coming here I am familiar to them, as they are to me, and entering through the glass doors the tall brown boy called Nadir, always politely officious and holding a clipboard importantly, says, "Greta, number three's ready if you want it."

"No, I don't want it," I say, and feel as if I've talked my head off. It's strange to hear my voice pop out unless I'm talking to Danny. My voice grows comfortable inside me. I picture it nudged against a rib like some newborn pup hiding from the light.

I look for a book, something gentle to read for an hour. I browse the shelves. None of it is gentle. It all feels forced and too ready-to-go. Where are the gentle books? The books you don't have to hide from before you even start to read? Where are you? I'm calling in my mind, and find myself in the heatedly Jewish section, all these books on Hitler and the Holocaust, the S.A. and the S.S., the Nazis Goering and Hess. Some of the books seem to say *How could this have happened?* while others say *This is what happened, may we never forget it.* Still others say *Gather round children, let us learn about what they did to us,* and others: *Look how strong what happened has made us.*

The book I find most soothing is a collection of pictures of mass graves, all the bodies piled up haphazardly, half-dressed, naked, all these white limbs tangled up within long stretching rectangles cut cleanly out of the earth. The geometry stills me. It's hard to explain, but I feel tranquilized, sedated, even though it's upsetting, what people do to each other, how compelled we are to mangle and maim and destroy. The open graves stretch on forever, or at least as far as the eye can see. Bosnia, Lithuania, Poland, see how the grass grows clean and even up to the ledges where the people fall in.

A large woman wearing a New York Yankees cap sits down across the table from me, and she snores as she reads, even though her lips are pursed tightly and she is wide awake. I guess I keep looking at her, because she hooks into me with her pale green eyes and says, Goy to Goy, "You got a problem?"

I close the book, put it back on the shelf, leave the library.

Heading back for the doctor's basement I see more dead pigeons. I don't know why there are so many. I cross Main and walk the strip, pass Primo Hatters, the Super Star Nail Salon, a variety item store called Jerusalem, and step into the Ramatali Gana fruit and vegetable market, specialists in Israeli imports. This is where I buy our food because the owner of the store gives me deals on the rotting veggies he keeps in a wax box on the floor. I'm squatting by the box, picking out the best tomatoes and bell peppers, when a voice behind me whispers, "Whore."

I know this word is meant for me, only it has flown from the lips of the owner's wife. I've bought things from her before, no problem. Once, when I was in here getting a pack of Brooklyn-baked pita bread, a fishmonger came in. This man was a giant, stooped and bearded, wore a long white apron from neck to ankle, and smelled strongly of gutted fish. I stood behind him as he pulled out his money clip and fondled his greenbacks, tossed a twenty on the counter as if parting with nothing significant, but you could tell how highly he regarded it. It was hard-earned, valuable to him, yet somehow contemptuous all the same. I felt a strange mix of admiration and loathing, like it wasn't fair that he could pull off such a stunt as that. But the real magical thing was, after the man had left with his huge sack of parsley, while I was getting my pita bread rung up, a woman came in. She was one of those short, beefy, curly-haired, indistinct women of which there seem to be countless millions. In that nasal, high-pitched Queens accent she said, "Oh, I didn't know you sold fish. How long have you been selling fish?" That's when the owner's wife and I looked at each other and smiled. We had shared that.

"Get out," the woman says.

"I'm sorry," I say, and don't know why I'm apologizing. Maybe it's a Jewish holiday, but standing up, I fairly tower over her. I feel like a big ugly bitch, and I leave her store, telling myself I'm never going back, but I want to. I want to even now. I always liked that woman's manner, so quiet and smart. She has this dark beauty, something sorrowful yet willing to enjoy. In her long dark earlobe is a magnificent diamond, and I like how her hands, delicate as they are, are always busy. I once saw a Band-Aid wrapped around her index finger. Unlike me, she is pretty, and I walk through the sun feeling jilted and shamed. To make matters worse, when I'm passing the Seven-Eleven, the sidewalk is empty but for me, the usual trash strewn about, and a man wheeling beer from a refrigerated truck. When the man sees me coming he stops wheeling, and he says, "Hey, I can see your panties," and he says, "Holy shit, are you serious?" I pass him without looking at him. "Hey!" he says. I don't look back. "You cunt!" he says, then gives me a real earful.

I've heard it plenty, only it gets to me. Once down in the doctor's basement I sit on the concrete floor, draw my legs up and hug them, and cry. This morbid depression I do not enjoy, as a number of girls I know do, displaying self-inflicted cuts like trophies on the arm— needle marks—like proof. Those girls are in love with drama. The more drama, the more abuse and trauma they can claim, the more hurt and hate and craziness, the realer they feel. It's crazy, and I feel sad about it, this desperation to be seen. It hurts me. I once felt that need. I took delight in it. I would enter a bar all breathing heavy with my hair messed up, acting like I was in trouble or like somebody was chasing me. I fucked a lot of guys and bragged of assault. I would do anything to be seen, but now I want those feelings in me purged. My mantra is: *I am not important.*

I am on the floor when my heart returns. I did not hear him

stepping down the steps because he is light-footed, a sign that he is, as Nietzsche once wrote somewhere, of God. When the door swings wide, my impulse is to jump up to right myself, make myself look pleasant and self-absorbed in a good way, involved with something useful and creative, like drawing, writing, maybe boiling rice with chopped celery while teaching myself how to sing on key. But it's too late. He has caught me looking unhappy, wet, like a human mop, and already he needs to know what made me this way. Danny has never liked my woe-is-me-ism, and I can't say I blame him.

The big nothing of the day was the nasty beer-wheeler, but it's an easy excuse. It hides what really bothers me, that a woman I admired used that word on me, called me that, even used a nasty whisper to voice her disgust: *Whore!* She hadn't the right, she didn't have any right, but as always, me, I'm supposed to forgive people for their ignorance, for their shortcomings and cruelty and thoughtlessness. That bothers me, not because the woman was intentionally cruel, but that in forgiving her I take pleasure. I hate that pleasure. That, and that I didn't stop my heart from doing what he did today.

I tell him. He's heard it all before. I tell him had I been wearing skintight jeans like most girls in Queens, the man might not've noticed me. I would have blended in like a green pea in a sea of green peas. The man might've even said something nice, but instead I get threatened with sodomy and a bloody mouth.

"That's them," Danny says, not comforting me. Danny is big on the us-them binary. When I told him how I used to call myself a bitch and then slap my face whenever I looked in the mirror, he said no, it wasn't me slapping me. What it was was me trying to agree with *them*.

The doctor's basement is concrete. The walls are concrete, the floor, the ceiling. One small window high on the wall lets light in from the street, and we see legs up there now and then, walking, and there's the constant sound of buses passing. Our place has a stove, a sink, a toilet, and is equipped with a single bulb screwed into the fixture on the ceiling.

We are on the mattress. My heart pulls things from his pockets, a plastic dime, a one-eared bunny, a snapshot of four Asian girls, and a yarmulke to add to his yarmulke collection. This is his fourth yarmulke, and this one has fancy glitter sewn into it. Then there is the big wad of money.

"Goodness," I say.

My heart laughs, and I feel guilty, slimy, cowardly. It should have been me. I don't like it, it's against everything about us. And plus, I don't like sharing him. I have these pictures in my head now. I want him to tell me all about it, at least so I have the right pictures in my head, but I know if I press him for details, he'll withdraw.

He says, "It was no big deal."

"Oh Danny," I say, and kiss his cheek and run my palm over his pretty green Mohawk, my eyes dribbling tears again, which I hate, but Danny is used to my silent dribbling. It don't mean anything. I've told him it's second nature for me, like sneezing, or feeling an itch somewhere on my body. I've been trying to cure myself of this for years.

"It was worth it," Danny says. "The experience alone, to have done that. I know what it's like now. I can write about it."

"That's naïve and silly," I say. "There is no power in that."

"Thanks," Danny says.

I've pissed him off. I want to sew my mouth shut with a needle and thread because all that comes out of it is garbage. "Forget I said that," I say, and stroke his Mohawk, my little pet, but he doesn't want me to love on him. He wants to work on his book. He is all geared up with his new material, and tries getting up, but I grab his arm.

"Stop," I say.

My heart sighs, and settles back down next to me. I kiss him, I don't even care, I just want him. I get his clothes off. There he is, a flat stretch of beautiful with legs, these long arms that I kiss all over. I look for signs that others have touched him, traces, the bread crumbs of monetary love. Danny senses what I'm doing, doesn't like this, and fights me, but I am strong. I hit him. I hold him down by the neck. He stops fighting and is mine, he belongs to me. I grab up his lovely sex and knock it around and put it in me and, fucking him, call him a bastard, even though what he really is, starting today, is a whore.

Grist for the mill. He can put this in his book if he wants, how his girlfriend raped him after he came home from having some guy jerk off in his face. I won't apologize. I'm sick of apologizing, sick of being the girl in the rain, a charity case, a gratuitous object of ridicule, an easy fuck, this thing who hopes and gives endlessly *you bastard*, and comes like a high flower above the bodies of unremembered men, never asking for anything in return. Can you see her? His wash of machine-gun fire punctures holes in her organs, exits her body a thousand different places, her eyes, her mouth, her breasts, her spine, releasing that sad ocean within her. Not dead, she wilts, falls down bloody and wet as the lifeline feeding her softens and withdraws, leaving her cold once more, self-sufficient, captured within the boundaries of her stupidity.

"I'm sorry," I say, breathing.

Danny looks like he's been stabbed.

"I'm filth," I say.

"I won't respond to that," my heart says.

"How did this happen to me, Danny? Won't it ever go away?"

"I told you, don't. I haven't the stomach. Listen, on the bus I saw this building by the Queensboro Bridge. I think we should check it out. On the walls were anti-war slogans and even some poems spray-painted."

"First forgive me and mean it."

"You want me to pretend to feel sorry for you?"

"Yes," I say, weeping. My eyes, there's something wrong with them, they overflow out of nowhere. My pesky dribblings fall onto Danny's face, into his mouth and eyes. "Pretend," I say.

Danny knocks me off him and slides into his underwear.

I don't blame him. I should have kept these parts of myself concealed, gone out of my way to be a good liar. As my heart dresses I grab the Camels off the floor, lean my bare back against the concrete wall and light up. It's my first smoke today. The gray smoke mixes with all the gray color of the doctor's walls, and even though they are made of concrete, his walls, I find myself searching out flaws, anything that might, upon closer inspection, be a hole. It's a bad habit. I do it wherever I go, whenever I'm in a room, I always look for holes. There is just something so obscene about it, that image of a hole with an eyeball behind it, detached like that, floating.

I feel momentarily flighty from all the nice smoke, assimilated, part of something less me. Up at the small window, pants cross the pane as Danny's juice creeps out from between my legs and pools against my asshole. Unlike those legs walking by with places to go, these microscopic tadpoles have nothing but dead-ends to look forward to. I am pregnant two months running. The legs come at intervals. I anticipate their appearance in the bright window, for their shadows announce them ahead of time. I find it mesmerizing, somewhat profound.

My heart writes in his black book, and while smoking I tell him that I am offended by the entrepreneurial spikes that shop owners place on their marquees to prevent pigeons from landing. "I mean, how would you like it if someone tried to stab you in the feet?" I say, and onward he writes. I say a lot of stupid things in passing, like, "Why do people even care about pigeon shit? I don't see what the big deal is. It's like frosting." Danny is used to it. I mention my recent craving for Strawberry Pop Tarts, my desire to fly in a balloon above the Florida everglades, and my colonized uterus. Danny looks at me then, his pen poised above his book, no expression on his face. He sees that I am not lying for attention, then continues writing till finally he says get dressed. It's time to romp in the world. "Goodie!" I say, and hit my balled fists together like kids do. In a snap I'm dressed in my slutty getup and we hit the stairs and wait for the bus out there. We ride the Q44 to Queens Boulevard, and then on the Q60 to Manhattan my heart, out of nowhere, says, "I can't believe you didn't tell me, Greta."

"Tell you?"

My heart slaps his forehead with both hands then pulls them away as if never in his life has he heard anything so dumb.

"It's nobody's," I say.

"Don't you think I deserved to know?"

"If it had something to do with you, you would have helped me earlier. I begged you to forgive me and all you did was humor me. It's my problem."

Danny's got this all-serious look. I have to laugh. Sweat beads his brow. He looks like he's actually feeling something, mustering up some concern for me. It's the same look my mom got when I told her I wanted my vulva burned off, like maybe I could self-cauterize it with a lug wrench pulled from a bonfire? But please! I'm twenty-five. I've had four abortions. My first was during the last century, when I was fifteen, and my stepbrother had already left for college at fucking Berkeley, 3000 miles away. Good for him. This will be my fifth. Since when did I try to hold somebody else responsible for these people that could have been? Me, I'm a fleshed machine who conceives for the purpose of ejecting what? Babies, babies, yucky yucky babies, I can't stand babies. Look at what they grow up into, these trivial, biting, clammy-looking women who push their babies along the sidewalks in expensive, super-constructed perambulators of reinforced alloy, two at a time, with hand-brakes, and pumpupable tires run on greased ball bearings. It's enough to make any sane person sick, and I am a sane woman. How anybody could find babies cute is beyond me. Babies can only be reminders of criminal activity.

There are too many people in the world!

Any woman who has a second child ought to be jailed for a year.

If she has a third, jailed for five years. A fourth, ten years.

Because since when was a baby born for reasons other than self-ishness?

Never.

Unless you believe Jesus was born to save the world.

Even then, do you think God, in this fairytale version of kingly sacrifice, is not concerned about whether or not people love him? To have fed his only begotten to pigs and jerks, to have allowed him to be tortured when all he had to do was snap his fingers to bring harmony to the world, it just emphasizes how greedy and heartless and ugly and stupid people are as a whole.

Ask me, any woman who has five children ought to be burned alive.

Whoredom? Having babies is whoredom. I think it's a horrible thing to do to anybody, to have them. I know it's a scary thing to do, but I really wish my mother had had the courage to abort me. It would have saved me so much trouble and pain.

I'm angry, sure. I could puke. Thinking about babies makes me this way, but I too can live life pleasantly. Call it blanket-blue, just blanket your mind in blue and forget the unfairness of things. Forget the endless times you hoped, only to have that hope dashed, and forget the many times your stepbrother fucked you, how he fucked you from behind on your mother's kitchen floor while his friends watched through the window, and forget your step-dad, and the horrible bitterness and fear you felt when you found the hole in the wall that he would watch you through. Forget it. Forget it, all the nastiness of the normal world, like what I saw Friday night in Brooklyn. Danny and I each paid eleven dollars to see Melt Banana. They were great, I loved them, but I started weeping. It was that dipshit girl out with her friends, these three boys. She kissed one, then another one, and the boys kept pretending to smash her face, like with their fists and elbows, balling their fists up and pretending to hit her, pretending to sideswipe her with their elbows and then laughing about it. The girl's face was messed up a little, like with acne pits, and she was drunk. For a minute she was even sitting on the green felt of the pool table with her legs apart, and when they weren't kissing her, out came her tongue, wiggling in the air as if to say who's next? By the time she finally left with those boys I really wanted to clock her myself.

"I think you'd make a great mother is all I'm saying," Danny says. "You act as if I'm not even allowed to care about you."

"I'm a whore," I say matter-of-factly.

"Still the martyr," Danny says. "Self-deprecation gets boring real fast, Greta."

"I know," I say, smiling at him, stroking his Mohawk of neon green, kissing him even on the cheek, which he likes. He likes being lavished with love, especially in public. I try not to abuse this power I have over him. It's been a nice bus ride so far. We've had our little talk, though nothing has been accomplished. I don't feel enlightened by Danny's "great mother" bullshit. I know that he is lying to me about that. What he's probably saying is that he thinks he'd make a great father, *hint hint*, and he would, I know, but who cares besides nobody? I just wish we were back in the doctor's basement so that we could fuck.

The Q60 lets us off near the East Channel. We pick up some beer at the corner store, and my heart leads me up the walk to this building that caught his eye earlier while riding to the city to have, in his own words, his youthful sexuality exploited. He thinks that by getting paid he can fight fire with fire, poor thing, but I love him, I do, he's the only boy who's ever gone to sleep with his fingers in my mouth. I feel good around him, like the two of us are brave warriors against oppression. I love his enthusiasm, how he gets excited and hyped up when people talk anarchy. I love how he talks to strangers. I love that he takes his writing seriously, that he feels protective of me.

The building is a big box, takes up the whole block. We count seven floors, lots of broken glinting windows up there. Up higher the blue sky all hollow and empty blankets the city with color and light, its massive uniformity making everything seem so complex down here in the simple world. Against the sky, every crack in the building, every sticking-out-nail in the ply-boards, each sash and stain, each bent mullion, the millions of paint flakes peeling away from the surface, it wants my attention—too much to deal with piece by piece, so I heap it all together and admire it as one. The possibilities amaze me, and I really want to hug the building, but stop myself, exercising an admirable degree of self-control. Were I to hug the building, I know I would look supremely stupid.

The entranceway is not boarded. We climb the stairwell into the dark, but are stopped by locked doors. There's a busted-out transom with light pouring through. Promising. Danny laces his fingers, cups my sneaker, lifts me up there and I push over and down, ripping my skirt and practically snapping my neck when I hit the floor. I cry out and Danny, my hero, says, "Break anything?"

"Only my self-esteem," I say, brushing the crud off my face.

"Your selfish steam?" Danny inquires, and though I can't see him, I know he's smirking behind the door, thinking he's darned clever, which he is.

"Man, it's great in here," I say. "All these windows. I wish I had my roller skates."

Danny tosses the six-pack of Miller tallboys over the transom. I catch it. Then Danny's round face pokes through the opening. He slips through and falls into my arms. I swing him and the beer round and round, and we get dizzy, and collapse in a pile of us, and we act retarded, and drool, I love this, these moments where mere motion makes me happy, where I am not obsessing over the life I have lived and the choices I could have made in this bizarre yet grossly compelling world that I live in. I lick him, kiss him. "You worm," I say. "You slipped through that hole like a little worm poking his head out of the ground because of the rain."

Danny slides away from me and wiggles and writhes. It is so funny. I'm laughing. I want to be a worm too. I hold my arms to my sides and do like Danny, rolling over and squirming and getting dust and grime all over me. "Watch out for the mama bird!" I cry, and in my mind see a massive owl swoop down and grab us, one in each claw. I scream, feeling what it feels like, and Danny screams. Then we're like, oh shit, we don't want to scare the other people who might live here, so taper off into quieter laughter, and Danny says, "If you could see yourself, like how you just acted just now, you would know what I'm talking about."

"No, I'm a psychotic monster," I say. "I'd probably choke the thing then sling it off a bridge."

"It's your time," Danny says, but screw him, it'll never happen.

What does happen is we hit the six-pack, peel off two talls, pop the tabs then drink a lot of the delicious stuff down.

"This place is killer," Danny says. "Look at those ancient presses, Greta. I wonder if they still work?"

"I love you," I say. "If you were a superhero there'd be a big O sewn into your costume. O for optimism."

"I hate seeing stuff go to waste," Danny says.

"Out with the old," I say.

There's lots of broken glass, and paper scraps, and graffiti: LISA CHONG SUX FAT COX 4 FREE. The bubbled names of bygone boys compete, overlapping tin plaques screwed to the walls: WARNING ASBESTOS. You find that in old buildings, but Danny says asbestos, like tobacco smoke, only hurts you if you're in constant contact with it, like for years, same thing as what happens to people when they live in so-called democracies. The lies enter through the ears and eyes, eat away at a person's capacity for compassion until there's nothing left but a corrupt package of hermetically sealed ignorance. Those are the wages of Imperialism, of Capitalism. Danny is a true believer in the power of Anarchism to change the world, and that is why we are in this building. Just think if this place was overrun by conscientious punks like us? It'd be one of the most killer places imaginable. The hard part is organizing, getting people to set down their trivial concerns to join the good fight.

We climb a dark stairwell and walk through crumbling halls. We peer into vandalized rooms, keeping a lookout for cool people, but find only trash, discarded clothes, beer cans, plastic sheets covered in pigeon shit. One floor is cluttered with coffee cups and kitchen stuff, broken plates, all these stainless steel tables that look really creepy in the semi-dark, like dead bodies are supposed to be on them. Grease is everywhere, forks, knives, the rugs are wet. I smell piss. We hear rats either fucking or fighting, take your pick. Another floor has a thousand cubicles in it, gaping Xerox machines and smashed computer screens. When we reach the seventh floor, it's like *Ah, the Promised Land has fallen.* Couches are lined against the windows overlooking the channel. We have a perfect view of the Manhattan skyline.

"Anybody home?" Danny calls out.

I feel as I do when I stumble across makeshift dwellings in the woods. Anticipation and dread and hope and fear. We are trespassers.

"Looks deserted," I say, but a nearly full gallon jug of water sits within reach of the plushiest of the three couches. Empty forty-ouncers are all over, and I see a can-pipe, and some old syringe-needles carefully placed against the wall where nobody will step on them in their bare feet. A den of drunks and druggies.

"I guess we're alone," Danny says.

We pop our last tallboy, make ourselves at home. Looking through the windows at the romantic view, two lovers, my thoughts grow soft, and we talk of the immeasurable beauty of the city. Not the city itself, the concrete miracle of what humans do when they put their heads together, but the humans within it, how fragile they are, how funny and sad and strange. A man runs stooped after his windblown yarmulke. A shrimp-faced woman snores while wide-awake. I wish I could be everybody in the world all at once, because I love them, I really do, even though I sometimes know for a fact that I despise them. They are here, though, so since they are here, what choice do I have but to love them? I love them until the bomb goes off inside my uterus. Seeing the splatter helps me keep tabs on reality. When the bomb goes off inside my uterus, I see myself, a burned up little girl who, getting into bed, finds a plastic dildo under her pillow.

Talking about the people we have seen in the streets, on the subways, in the libraries and corner stores and parks, I am pleased in that Danny sees in me a person who can appreciate others.

I like being thought of this way. I've noticed that the more I talk about how great people are, the more interest Danny shows in me, in my body and my intellect. When I talk about how children are these ugly, stupid, disgusting creatures that make me want to puke at the mere sound of their voices, Danny turns off. But is it not true that children are reflections of their parents? Is it not true that most parents are cruel arrogant blobs that make you wish you were dead? Is it not true that parents get off on the power they have over you? The reason parents belittle their children, I have discovered, is how else are they going to feel powerful in the face of something that has not yet been fully corrupted? They want their children to be stupid. They want their children to be ugly. They want their children to be willing containers for the poison juices that pulse within their hearts, their brains, overflowing from their loins.

There I go again, acting resentful over the fact that I'll never be able to forgive those people, my so-called family, especially my mother. The psychologist I saw in Virginia Beach said that since Mom was dead, I had to recognize Mom inside me, and forgive her that way, essentially forgive myself. I liked the psychologist. She was unbeguiling and smelled of pine sap, a clean woman with long flowing sensuous gray hair. She interviewed me in the subdued window light of her office, and I cried, of course, and was grateful for her expertise. She put her hand on my shoulder. When we hugged at the end of our session, I didn't want to let her go. I was open to anything then. Had she asked me to show her my cervix I would have done it gladly. I would have turned myself inside out for her because she really seemed to have all the answers, and she wanted to see me again, free of charge, she said. I suppose I should have gone back, just to see her, but I don't see the point in forgiving myself in order to forgive somebody else. That's just really stupid, if you ask me. All I did was be born.

Forget it.

I'm talking about how great people are, and mean every word I say. I say, "This little Chinese girl rode up to me on her bicycle the other day and she looked up at me and said, 'Have you ever been to the forest?' " Danny loves this. He leans in close, and I don't reach out to kiss him. In this, Danny's tongue slips into my mouth. He reaches up my skirt, I all the while miles from eager, just miles, for Danny doesn't like being told what to do. Tell him what to do, he thinks of Imperialism, and stops, does the opposite, and I want him to get me back for earlier when I forced myself on him during my desperate time of need. I threw his feelings to the side like trash. I've fucked guys all sorts of worse places than this. I want him to conquer me. I'm a primitive island back in the old days, ripe for colonial invasion. We are having a sweet moment here with our tongues. He has parted my legs, is rooting up against me, but a loud voice, as if from the ceiling, cries: "Give up, woman! Surrender yourself to the dark side of the force!"

We fall away from each other and stand up to find this very dignified-looking black man in an overcoat and black beret eying us from across the room. His nose appears to be bleeding from one nostril.

"Oh, hey!" Danny cries.

The man walks closer. He's got a closed umbrella in one hand, which seems to be his handy walking stick, and he stops in front of

John Oliver Hodges

us and just stands there staring, now and then licking the blood out of his mustache.

"We've been waiting for you," I say, and am unpleased with my voice.

Another black man appears from the doorway of the adjacent room, this one long-headed, bald up top, thirtyish, jerky. His head flips back and forth. He's barefoot, wears white cutoff shorts, and a pink shirt about three sizes too small. The shirt has puffy sleeves and the words SPOLIED BRAT on it, and doesn't come down all the way. As he approaches, I see that he's drawn around his bellybutton so that it looks like a eye—unless that's a tattoo. "We thought you was the Juice, man," he says. "Them boys come in here with baseball bats."

Danny laughs, and steps over with his hand outstretched. "I'm Danny from Virginia Beach," he says, and they shake.

"Hey, man, I'm Derek from Dallas. We thought you was the Juice, man. Then we saw you getting down and dirty on the couch. We didn't think it was right, you know what I'm saying?"

"Give up, woman!" the other man cries. "Surrender yourself to the dark side of the force!"

Derek laughs. "That's Hasad."

"Oh, is he Muslim?" Danny says.

"Shit no, he a scientist, man. He been all around the world, too, and he been to other planets and shit."

"I'm Greta," I say, and hold my hand out for a shake. Derek from Dallas screws his face up, but shakes my hand anyway. "We're looking for people like us," I say, "people who can live together in harmony and work together to change the world."

Derek wipes his hand on his shorts. He looks me up and down. "I don't go with no terrorists," he says.

I laugh, but don't feel it, it's just fake. "Take this building," I say, "all this room. We could fix the place up and get hundreds of people who care about being people to move in. You know how everybody seems to just want to dominate everybody else? How people always feel better if they can piss on you? That's life, right? Making money, not sharing it with others, doing stuff to them and messing them up. We're going to start a community where people see the good parts of themselves in others."

"Yes," Danny says.

"If enough of us get together, we can influence the course of history. Before you know it, the whole world will be happy, no war, nobody starving, nobody hungry, everybody with heat in the winter, nobody wishing they were dead all the time."

"I see what you're saying," Derek says, stroking his chin.

"Give up, woman!" Hasad shouts. "Surrender yourself to the dark side of the force!"

"I'm sure the Juice won't allow it," Derek says.

"They won't have any choice if we fight them," Danny says.

I'm thinking, God, Danny, give it up.

But Danny starts talking all about Fidel and Che, how these two courageous dudes got together and performed a miracle without God's help. Derek nods his head, agreeing with everything Danny says, but finally gets bored listening and runs back to the other room to get his jug of red wine. Soon the four of us are on the couch drinking and smoking cigarettes, and in just a bit Derek starts bragging about how he stopped us from putting on a free sex show. He says it didn't feel right to him, seeing us, that it made him feel like a Peeping Tom, but now that he knows us, he says, if we want to be nasty, he won't mind.

I look to my heart, letting him know that if he wants to, I'm okay with it. Danny is insulted by my suggestion. It's simply out of the question, but I don't see why it should matter to him. This morning he took some guy's member into his throat, didn't he? That was for money, for the dream. Everything with Danny is all about the dream. I look back at Derek from Dallas with his weird long bald head that is a lighter shade of brown on the very top. Derek won't look me in the eyes.

"She was hot to go," Derek says, shaking his squirrelly head, and he slaps his chest with both hands. "I mean, she was begging you to pop that cherry."

"Oh my God, my cherry!" I say.

Derek laughs his long head off, cackles and slaps himself.

This seems to make Hasad nervous. He stands up and, looking out the window at the awesome city, says, "Give up, woman! Surrender yourself to the dark side of the force!"

"I wanna see you pop that pussy!" Derek shouts.

Danny is not amused by this talk. He is itching to say something about how in the new world, the world that we have been imagining together each night as we fall asleep, the world where all human beings and animals are considered equal, and where sexist comments have no reason for being, Derek might be more interested in building a greenhouse than sex. Danny is formulating a sentence when Hasad, for no apparent reason, decides to poke me with his umbrella, not hard. He simply presses the metal tip against my belly. When Danny sees this, he smacks the umbrella, and it flips up and smacks Hasad in the face, knocks off his beret.

"Hey now, don't mess with Hasad!" Derek shouts, and jumps up, and I'm so bored because Jesus, they always do this, boys, men, the interminable interchange. I really want to yawn, but I feel something tearing inside me.

"Hasad shouldn't poke people with umbrellas," Danny informs Derek.

"You know what?" Derek says.

"What?" Danny says.

"You talk big for a white boy."

"What difference does it make if I'm white or black?"

My heart is so broken.

"The Juice are white," Derek says. "If you wasn't a spy for the Juice you might would pop her pussy!"

"I think you might be schizophrenic, Derek. You're talking crazy."

"Oh, I'm schizophrenic, am I? I'm crazy? Is that what you think? Have you already forgot that I stopped you from tearing it up? Do crazy people do that? Do they? Are you a Juice!"

"Will you please stop calling them the Juice!" Danny screams. "The word is Jew! They are Jews, understand?"

"Woman, give up!" Hasad yells, unfazed by Danny and Derek's yelling. I get the impression that he would yell his refrain even if I, a woman, was not in the room. He is somebody's father, I think, somebody's husband. I do wish he'd put his black beret back on though. Without it on his head, something is amiss. I think I'll pick it up for him, but when I lean over to grab it off the floor, I realize that I too am bleeding. I lift my skirt to see that my panties are soaked through. I should feel relief now, but my heart starts to beat really fast. "I'm sorry," I say to Hasad, and he looks at me as if he understands. He stoops to pick up his umbrella, then sits down on the couch beside me. I scoot up close to him, right next to him so that our bodies touch. When he drapes his arm across my shoulder, I become less afraid, but carefully I draw out my underpants. I lift my sneakers up through the holes, one by one, and then together Hasad and I stare into the red cup of panty where, if I'm not mistaken, a tiny foot pokes up, a hand, a spray of soft ribs poking through diaphanous skin.

Chromosomes are tiny string-like structures in cells of the body, I remember from high school, and guess I could write a poem like women do. All I want, though, is to apologize to the little guy. "I'm sorry," I say, and a drop of Hasad's blood falls into this piece of me as the city grows dark beyond the river.

NEGATIVES

The kitchen scrubber was useless. The soap was useless. The hot water was useless. Uselessness was the theme of her life, was her middle name. Her last name was Retarded. See her introduced at the American Convention for Retarded People: "And now give a big hand for Karen Uselessness Retarded." Everybody cheers, and Karen steps out from behind the curtain with red stains all over her naked body, red hearts, red dashes, clubs, and what looked to her like a horse with an exploding head. Well, she'd tried. She put a dress on and sat on the couch and when her husband returned from his bimbos and said, "Wow," began to cry. The dress covered some of the red, but her arms and face were hopeless. "Mops," she said. Hubby chuckled. "Is under the tree," she said. Hubby sat down beside her. She said, "His mouth was open, I saw his tooth."

Hubby drove her to Lowe's, left her in the car. He returned with a gallon jug of thinner. On the drive home he spoke of his upcoming show at the Daytona Museum of Art. There was going to be a poster. "Aren't you excited?" he said. "One of these days we'll move to New York City. That's the picture capital of the world!"

Back at the apartment, she slipped off her dress and climbed into the tub. He poured thinner on her. Wearing a pair of rubber darkroom gloves, he rubbed the thinner around on her. The red on her skin loosened, it came undone, and she closed her eyes. The fumes curled around inside her nose. It was awful. It was too much. "Won't this burn my skin?" she said, and opened her eyes. The red horse had turned a watery pink color, its original lines barely visible. The horse and the clubs were sliding around on her. She was turning pink.

"Cool," he said. "But keep your eyes closed. I don't want them to get spirits in them. Hang on. I'll be right back."

She closed her eyes. She heard his footsteps hurry off. She heard his hurried footsteps hurry back. Then something cold and thick touched her solar plexus. She opened her eyes. She saw the red spout coming down from the can of paint he held above her. Before she could say anything, he stopped pouring. "Don't!" he said, and, using an old toilet paper roll, spread the red paint across her breasts, smeared the red paint around on her stomach, and he smeared the red paint down her legs.

She groaned. She screamed.

"Great!" he said, and tossed the toilet paper roll in the wastebasket under the sink. He grabbed his Leica off the commode, and snapped pictures of her. "It won't kill you. I promise," he said.

"No no, why did you do that?" she sobbed.

He splashed more thinner on her. "A hundred percent mineral

spirits," he said. "And look, it says Smart," he said, reading the brand name. "Do you think anything branded Smart could hurt you?"

She looked at the plastic jug in his hands and saw the words DANGER, HARMFUL, FATAL, in green. "It stinks," she said. "Hurry, I can't stand this." She was beginning to panic. She started to get up. He pressed her back.

"Little girl," he said. He poured thinner in her hair. "Trust me," he said. "Untense your nerves," he said. "Don't you even know what you most need?"

"What do you mean?"

"You need to listen, carefully, to everything I say."

"I've listened to you too much."

He laughed. "Turn over," he said.

"What?"

"Don't act like this."

"There isn't any on my back," she said.

"Irrelevant. Look," he said, "do you want me to help you or not?"

She turned over. He rubbed the red all over her back. He rubbed the red all over her hips. He peeled off the rubber gloves. He tossed the rubber gloves into the wastebasket under the sink. He snapped more pictures. "Act sexy," he said.

"I gotta get this stuff off me," she said. "I'm turning on the water now."

"Wait," he said, "I've got color film in here, don't you get it? It's perfect. I might be able to use this stuff for my show."

"No," she said.

"Put your hands on your hips."

"No," she said, but he kept snapping and snapping, and then he was laughing as he snapped more pictures. She curled up in the tub, red and pink all over, gross. It was now that he turned on the shower, snapping pictures of her all the while, as she stood up, screaming for him to stop, please, the monster. When he would not stop, she got back down in the tub, curled up, and waited for him to leave, which he did, finally, but not without shutting the door with just the right amount of slam. He wanted her to confront him on this later, get upset about it, bring it up, accuse him of slamming the door during her mental breakdown. He wanted to throw the slam in her face, make her look foolish in front of him, make her need him, depend on him. He wanted her to feel as if she was trying to ruin his career as a photographer. He could be the new Robert Mapplethorpe, the new Richard Kern, but here she was trying to press the eject button on his talent, on his positive energy, on his fame.

Getting the red paint off her skin was a chore. It took so long, over thirty minutes, but finally, after rinsing, after using more paint thinner on her body, after shampooing, after soaping and rinsing again and again, she managed to rid herself of most of the red. She toweled dry. She picked her nightgown off the nail on the door and draped it around her. She left the bathroom, smelled pizza. He was on the couch. He was watching *Wheel of Fortune*, the opened pizza box and the shaker of Louisiana Hot Sauce laid out on the coffee table before him, where he had one of his feet propped up.

"I still smell it," she said. "It burns."

"Patchouliish, ain't it?" he said.

She sat beside him, peeled off a slice, splashed it with hot sauce, took a bite. It was soggy, the pizza, much too greasy. She did not like it, the pizza, so set her slice back in the cardboard box.

The lady turned some letters.

"Queen of hearts," she said.

"You got it right," he said. He said, "You know, it's always amazed me how you can go from screaming like a crazy woman who belongs in an insane asylum to all the sudden pleased and perfect. I wish I was like you."

"No you don't," she said, and went to the bedroom, turned off the lights, slipped under the covers and fell asleep. When she opened her eyes a few hours later, she heard rushing water in the kitchen, that familiar watery rushing sound that meant her husband was processing his black and white film. She had to pee, but Hubby did not like her going into the bathroom when he was doing his film things. It was forbidden. This was a bodily matter though. She was not going to pee in a coffee can again. She did not care, not anymore. She went in there, sat down. She peed, and while peeing, looked at the hanging strips of wet film, dark stripes laid against the air. There were eight strips, and Hubby had more on the way. The bottoms of the strips were pinched with clothespins and dripped residual chemicals slowly into the tub, which still smelled like paint thinner.

When she finished peeing, she stepped up close to his negatives and took a peek at his bimbos, candid shots of girls and women caught outside in the sunny world, checking their tans, entering Laundromats, shopping, looking over their shoulders while stepping off curbs etcetera. Other bimbos looked straight into his lens, not smiling—that was a trademark of serious photographers. If somebody smiled, that was an indicator that what you were looking at was cheap and amateur, so he'd told her. This show of his was going to be the biggest embarrassment of her life. He was going to hang pictures of her right alongside *them*. Pictures of her that she would regret forever, but he always had a way of explaining things, making it seem like she was too dumb to understand. "Nothing in the world is more beautiful than the female body," he would say. "The whole thing of girls is beautiful, women, old ladies, it doesn't matter what shape you put them into, they will always be beautiful. My life's ambition is to take an ugly picture of a woman."

Once, he'd busted open the door of this shrine thing in the cemetery where an empty coffin was propped on a slab below a large stained glass window of Jesus walking on the water. She right away thought it would be neat to get in the coffin and he could take her picture. "That's too obvious," he said, and said, "We need to make something extremely vulgar. It's the only way I'm ever going to make any headway in this business. When Robert Mapplethorpe stuck that whip up his asshole, he wasn't thinking in terms of titillating anybody's senses. He was grabbing the world by the throat."

She went back to bed. She slept, but then he was shaking her, waking her up to tell her she'd forgotten to flush the toilet when she went in and looked at his negatives.

"I want a divorce," she said.

He laughed. "Sure," he said, "maybe I should unbury Mops and put him back where you left him. Let you take care of Mops."

"You buried him?"

"Hey," he said, pressing her back onto the pillow. "I thought you were sleeping. Go back to sleep. You can pretend it never happened." He started stroking her forehead.

"Stop," she said.

"Nasty girl," he said.

"What did you do?"

"I buried his ass, all for you. I'll unbury him and put him in the bed with you. Would you like that? You can use his leg as a dildo. I'll take a picture."

"Go away," she said. "I'm sleeping."

He left.

In the morning, she went to the bushy tree, and it was true, Mops was gone. That dog, she should never have brought him home from the humane society. She should have let him be. Euthanasia would have been better for Mops. Her husband, upon returning from his bimbos two days before, seeing Mops in the couch with her, called her wicked, accused her of using a sentient being to make a point. What point? The same point that she always in her bitterness and bitchiness pursued. The point that she too, like him with his bimbos, could have interests in the world. Then, coming home from work the very next day, she ran over him. It didn't kill him though. She tried to put him out of his misery by slamming an old can of paint against his head, but changed her mind at the last second. She directed the can onto the sidewalk. The can exploded and she was attacked by the red paint.

She looked around the yard for dug places, places that her husband might have buried Mops, but there weren't any dug places that she could see.

So she got in her car, drove to work. Mrs. Arnold was waiting for her, with her twins, her Georgia Peaches as she always called them, Cindy and Celeste. As soon as she pulled out her scissors, both little girls started bawling. Mrs. Arnold said, "In some ways it's adorable, but I'm glad it's not an everyday thing."

She could have sworn their hairs, each hair, had feelings in them. Whenever she cut a strand, the child screamed. Today, she gave Celeste a hard look. "Hair does not feel," she told the brat.

"Oh," Mrs. Arnold piped in, "you should see them in front of a camera! They're absolutely wild. When they had their Christmas pictures snapped last year they tore the ball off the photographer's Santa cap."

She was glad when they were gone. She was glad to see them go, but there was another head waiting for her.

Later, when she pulled up to the apartment building, she passed the paint-stained sidewalk without looking at it, but she saw it, yes, in the corner of her eye, the red stain. She drove into the lot and parked. When she got up to the kitchen she slid some pizza slices into the toaster oven and went to the bathroom. The last four strips of his negatives still hung while he, she guessed, was off taking pictures of bimbos. Or printing in the darkroom at school, talking to whatever bimbo happened to be in the darkroom with him.

She stood close to the strips. She looked at the shapes on the rectangles that made up the strips.

At first she did not want to believe what she saw, Mops propped up on little branches in the middle of the sidewalk, looking like he was walking along with crutches. But that's what it was. She looked harder. Underneath Mops, all around him, were those wooden chess pieces he had that had faces of Richard Nixon carved into each one, with grumpy and pissed-off expressions. God he was weird!

She stopped looking and sat down, peed.

A shriek came from the kitchen.

She kept peeing.

It was the fire alarm.

She wiped and flushed.

She went to the kitchen. The toaster oven was in flames, and there was a lot of smoke. She pulled a chair to the middle of the room, stood on it and pulled the battery out of the alarm. Then she watched the flames move onto the wall. The wall crackled, and she watched the design the flames made on the wall as they traveled upward. They were like some very stylish bangs, she thought, fluid and bright, colorful, a perfect blend of orange, yellow and red, and even blue and emerald.

The flames took hold of the ceiling. She went to the living room. She pulled the phone book from under the couch. She opened it, the phone book, and there, there on the first page of the phone book, was: IMPORTANT INFORMATION, beneath which a drawing of a fire was, a drawing of a badge was, and a drawing of one of those freaky snake-looking things was.

She looked through the next several pages of the phone book. She found a map of the different time zones, which was pretty neat, because if she was on Alabama time, the fire wouldn't even be happening now.

She turned the page. She looked at some of the area codes. Birmingham was 205, Mobile 334. Alaska, all locations, 907. The area code for the Virgin Islands was 340. On the next page there was a HOW TO section, and a WHERE TO FIND section. She looked at these numbers until her eyes hurt from the smoke. She started to cough. She held the phone to her ear, and pressed the buttons.

* * *

He'd been taking pictures at the beach all day, at the boardwalk, and in front of the arcades. Got a good one of this dude, about the skinniest man he'd ever seen, in a bikini bottom. The dude flexed his muscles in classic poses, his tendons and bones outlined sharply against his skin—or hide, that was more like it—that was all brown and tough. Some girl walking along ran up next to him and struck the same pose. She'd seen the camera and was inspired to do that. At first the dude thought it was neat, but his face took on a look of humility. He was being downplayed, his musculature brittle next to this fleshy random woman.

He got a lot of other good pictures too, especially of that family walking up the steps from the beach, the way they appeared to be floating, tumbling upwards toward the arcades and flashing lights, their bodies so light and bouncy and fluid. It had been a marvelous sight. His first one-man-show would be a success, though he sometimes wondered if he was making a mistake by having his name put out there as a documentary photographer when for the last five months or so his main interest had been the female nude—he loved warping it out of shape, objectifying it, animalizing it, exploding it into nature. The controlling idea behind his work was that, not only could the female body be bent to represent anything under the sun, it was everything under the sun. It was roads and sky and roots and metal. In his pictures, the female body was everything, was God. He loved photographing his wife, and there were girls from the college that would go with him into the woods for photo shoots. On several occasions he'd paid prostitutes to pose. Word had gotten around, and now, instead of him going to them, they often came to him. For some strange reason they all wanted pictures of themselves. He was always glad to oblige.

He was five blocks from home when he saw those puffs billowing up into the sky. He loved a good fire, had taken many good pictures in front of fires. Was always on the lookout for catastrophe and violence, like that fight at Bike Week, or the time some girl fell out of a sixth floor balcony of the Mariton Hotel. She'd landed on the driveway leading down to the underground parking lot. It was the strangest thing. There she was, a dead girl flat on her face, all this blood seeping downhill from her head. The sight had given him a scare. He'd frozen up, and had been afraid to take any pictures. Instead he took pictures of the people standing around watching her. He'd never forgiven himself for being such a coward in the face of death. After that, he promised himself never to balk at what promised to be an amazing picture.

The smoke sure looked a lot to be coming from about the place his apartment building was. He thought of his negatives and started running, holding the camera bag up close to his side so that he could run faster. He turned the corner onto Hollywood and saw the fire engine down there and ran. He ran, passing his wife on the sidewalk, and ran around to the back of the building and took the stairs, which were on fire. As he approached the landing he slowed. Long fiery arms reached through the windows, flapping crazily. He took another step and the staircase gave way. He hit the ground hard, couldn't breathe. Burning boards fell on him. He rolled out of it, and looked up at the building, thinking of his negatives, his pictures.

He walked around front, ignoring his burns and cracked ribs. He walked up to his wife and stood beside her, watching the building burn. His wife tried hugging him, but he did not, he just did not want to deal with her now. She kept trying to show him the little kitty she'd picked out of the inside stairwell as she'd evacuated the building.

THE LOVE BOX

In her wax box green and red grape clusters drooled over a banana heap, and I saw rounds of cottage cheese in there, and some canned goods *sans labél*. When I cleared my throat she jerked her face my way, and said, "You scared me. I thought you were the butcher." Her hair was a ratty gold color, her face large and round and greasy. Stitches traveled like centipedes through a stretchy material that hugged her body tight in subdued grays and browns, all but for her arms that emerged naked from their holes. This getup made her look built of the parts of different people, different women. Her face was wet.

"Nice catch," I said.

"Really?" she said.

"Some fancy fish in there. Good thing I'm not the butcher. I'd make you throw everything back. Have you noticed that he tucks his pants into his socks?"

The woman started to laugh.

"He'd look good on a horse, don't you think?" I said.

Her laughter rose up strong as she thought of him astride a horse, poor guy, and then ended with a pleased sigh. She reached her hand through the dumpster window. We shook and exchanged names. She was putting together a book called *The Joy of Dumpster Diving*. Would I take pictures of her collecting the food? Sure, no problemo. She unclipped the digital camera from her cozy bodysuit, handed it over, and I photographed her parting garbage with fingers, digging, reaching down toward the lower depths where who knew what lurked. I wanted to tell her don't, don't do that, but she pulled up TV dinners, moon pies, rolls of BUY ONE GET ONE FREE stickers. She handed me the boxes and I carried them to her pickup. I photographed her climbing out of the dumpster.

Once on the tarmac, she brushed her hands along her suit, and I noticed, again, the large pads of crinkled hair in the pits of her arms, these gold nests both brittle and soft. I have always been a connoisseur of the female form, its outbursts and irregularities. Discerning beauty in all its forms was a crucial aspect of my job up until I left Atlanta. This woman, Jane Mayfly as she called herself, was a runaway waterfall, a feast of wanton color. "Thanks a ton, Dave," she said, just as if we were old buddies. She climbed into her beat Isuzu. I watched her drive over the speed bumps without slowing.

Jane gone, I felt what I'd sworn away, a stir only, but it left me too nervous to steal off with my usual dumpster goodies. I hit the corner of Magnolia and Mahan, unfolded my beggar's sign, and smiled at traffic, bowed and God-blessed folks and, come six when the bustle had died down to a trickle, bought a bottle at Mack's and hit my tent in the kudzu and got drunk. Or tried to get drunk. Stuff wasn't working. My mind was on Jane.

Next day I hung out in the woods by the dumpster till noon and smoked. While waiting for the Isuzu I wondered what I'd do if she actually showed. I'm a skilled manipulator. Tell a woman what she wants to hear, as odious as this sounds, you can generally, in time, get her to submit to your will. It's a mathematical certainty. The world belongs to him who would claim it.

Jane did not show. I felt sad and stupid. I watched the grocery clerks unload their carts, heaving sacks of food over the dumpster rim as the butcher supervised. Looked like a lot of pineapples today. I wasn't hungry. I left the woods and made for my tent, thinking I'd once more sleep the sleep of the wayward. As I walked down Lafayette, though, the Isuzu appeared. I wanted to go poof and be gone from the sight of the world. I could have turned my ass backwards, ran up the hill and hooked a right into the first driveway, but it was too late. I knew I'd been spotted. She slowed, stopped and leaned over to see me through the passenger window. She said, "What up, Dave?"

I raised my eyes to the skies.

"What do you see up there, Dave?"

"Rubied walls against a crystal sea. I see fancy fish and whales and angels."

"Hop in, buddy. I'm on my way."

"To the dumpster?" I asked.

"The place with the grace," Jane said, and I hopped in beside her. She drove us up the hill and around the bend and once again I shot her dragging up treasures from the depths: fruit juices and jars of peanut butter and half a dozen bags of gourmet coffee beans coated in macaroni and cheese. The pictures whopped along swimmingly, but imagine my surprise when Jane Mayfly licked a bunch of macaroni and cheese off her wrist.

She was taking the whole "joy" theme a bit far here, I thought.

"Is it good?" I asked.

"You want some?" She stuck her hand through the dumpster window.

I licked it out of her palm.

"Is it good?" she asked.

"Divine," I said, and wanted this taste test to keep going and going, but she pulled her hand back through the window, and I was flooded with a cruel desire. My despair was magnified by the iron, that huge hard sheet that separated me from the object of my greed. I felt bereft, but acted casual and climbed the dumpster and hopped down into the garbage with her.

"Isn't this great?" Jane said. She ripped the wrapper off a cream pie with her teeth. I photographed her eating it sweetly, all that cream in her mouth. As before, she was dressed in the homemade bodysuit. She smelled of woman sweat and laundry detergent, and maybe a little patchouli. Her smell went well with the deeper hot rank of the dumpster.

"More," I said.

"More what, Dave?"

"Macaroni and cheese."

Jane shifted onto her stomach and reached downward, pulled up a large handful of sloppy orange pasta curlies, then sat with her back against the hot wall. I crawled up and ate from her palm, licking the cheese off her fingers and swallowing all that color. Then I licked her arm. It felt natural, this. Jane ran fingers through my hair, and when I nudged up closer, spread her legs to make way for me. She appeared to be in a trance, and I pressed my mouth to hers. Amidst the boxes half-filled with food our tongues touched, the heat raining down upon us—it knocked us over and we shifted and slithered, and I guess I dissolved into Jane while vaguely, in some censorious corner of my mind, I was aware of the open dumpster window. Anybody walking by could look in and see us, but screw it, I said nothing, I licked up the spit that escaped Jane's face. Her bodysuit, whose various pieces were held together by Velcro, came apart in my hands. At her waist appeared a swirly outcropping of spun gold. There was cottage cheese in Jane's hair.

* * *

"That was the most remarkable moment of my life so far," my great new friend said, not slowing for the speed bumps. I felt as if we'd pulled off a heist. This was the getaway. "The only other thing I can think of, out of twenty-eight years, was the time a manatee came up to me in the Saint Marks River. I grabbed onto him and he pulled me through the water."

"You have a wild, runaway beauty," I said, and I said, "That's one of the things I like about you, Jane. Of course, if you were a little more tame you'd have lawyers and senators trying to fly you to Japan at three in the morning."

"Japan? What would I do in Japan?"

"Speak Japanese."

"Oh, and you're just some homeless dude, huh? How should I explain this to my conscience? What should I tell Chance?"

"You know, I once owned an art gallery in Atlanta."

"Are you trying to charm me, Dave?"

"I don't want you thinking you made love to a complete social outcast, that's all."

"Did we really do what I think we did?"

"I think we might should pretend we didn't. My feelings are not going to be happy with me."

"I don't even know you," Jane marveled. "You could be an escaped murderer."

"I could have any kind of disease. You could be pregnant with my child. I'm worried that you're going to kill me."

"Stop that," Jane said, and my heart overflowed with greasy love. Greasy love poured out of my eyeballs and ears and soaked Jane's hair and coated her body and her uncanny self-made clothes. I noticed that one of her Velcro flaps had come free, revealing a sliver of golden stomach that I wanted to bite into like I would a ripe peach.

"I'm not joking," I said. "I'm afraid you might kill me."

"That's ridiculous, Dave," Jane said, and she said, "Aren't you worried that I could've given you a nasty disease? You're foolish to go around fucking strange girls in dumpsters."

"I already have a nasty disease," I said, "but it's in my mind, and death may be just what the doctor ordered."

"Stop that."

"Am I lying?"

"Will you do me a favor, Dave?" Jane said.

"You want me to pretend that I don't feel a connection with you?"

"Yes, don't get funky on me, Dave."

"I lost my gallery and my woman and everything I owned because of stupid love."

"So you really did own a art gallery?"

"Lucrative and respected."

"I'm a artist."

"How could I not know that?"

"I make little houses and people out of cardboard. I make these awesome sculptures out of shit people throw away."

"Have you shown them around?"

"It's all for me, I'm selfish," Jane said. "My stuff is too unique for people to admire. I tried a few places. They said my stuff was chintzy, that's a word one lady used. But I don't want to talk about me. What happened to you that made you into a homeless dude? Did your wife mess around?"

"All she did was talk to other people and look at other people. Other people looked at her, and even that was too much for me. I couldn't bear it. I became a nuisance because each time I looked at her, each time I thought of her, I was filled with an inexplicable yearning, one so strong that all it ever brought me was pain. It was intolerable, I mean, we lived together, her and I, yet I could not get enough of her. I felt like a damn cannibal. I went out and did stupid shit to fix myself. I was jealous of the baby in her. Whenever I thought of her giving love to the baby that hadn't even been born yet, I wanted to vomit, and once did."

"You're cuckoo, Dave. You know that, don't you?"

"I became a drug fiend, Jane. I insulted the mayor, made a ass of myself in all the important circles. I considered suicide, but a different solution came to me. I snapped my fingers."

"Then I came along," Jane said.

"Yep." I didn't want to freak Jane out, but my hands had little brains in them, little minds of their own. As Jane drove along they snuck up on her and felt her arm and leg. She turned quiet like she'd done in the dumpster. She was easy to hypnotize, Jane, but I peeled myself away. "Pull over," I said.

"What?"

"Right here. Pull over."

"But I want to show you my house," Jane said. "It's a shotgun shack, I'm very proud of it. That guy Famous Amos was born in it. Don't you want to see it, Dave?"

"No," I said.

"Shit, dude, calm down," Jane said, quite pissed off by the look of her. She pulled into the Books-A-Million parking lot.

"I don't love you," I said, and got out and slammed the door and walked into the store where the smell of coffee hit me. Even coffee I was jealous of. Could Alice Boot, my dearly beloved, love coffee too? No, it was unacceptable. It wasn't fair. There was no room for coffee or for anything else in the love we shared. Love turned me into a freak, man. The only solution was to snap my fingers and disappear. Only now, staring across the sea of books, it started again, these eyes began to leak. I was embarrassed, so moved along as if I had a destination. I ducked into an aisle, looked at the spines, told myself let it go, you stupid jerk, you have the power, you did it before, but *Oh Jane*, my mind yowled, *I floated in that lovely ocean of light and spoil-*

ing food, on you! You were my boat. We were blameless neutral toilers of suck. Your breast filled my mouth in its entirety, all of it packed inside me like a buoy, a lifesaver that I clung to with all my teeth, there in our love box.

* * *

Once at my tent I lit a fire to ward off mosquitoes and folded my legs up lotus style and prayed. I said, "Father God, I don't deserve to be heard, but bless all in the world who suffer. Is it all right if I include myself here as once I did, and ask yet again that my insane sensibility be tempered? Please, Father, help me. I worry so much over my stupid idiot self. Keep me whole and sanctify my putrid ugliness, Father. In the name of your son who died on Calvary, taking upon his own precious shoulders all the crap mankind could dish out, fill me with a dull equanimity. Make me even. And please, Father, throw your pearls into Jane Mayfly while you're at it. My request is that you slam her with your power, that you make Jane fly like an angel to spread common sense throughout the land and that in doing so she is praised for it by influential people and is made to feel pride in all her worldly pursuits. Let people appreciate her art, Father God. As for me, if it suits you to bestow upon a worthless stupid a middling keepsake attesting to your omnipotence, benevolence and every other kind of -ence, allow that I be neutral in the world. Please wipe love off the face of my ability to experience it!"

In the morning I felt cured. My heart beat steady. I was not wracked with idiot yearning. I felt equal to the task of existing in daylight. I felt no need to stay hidden from the eyes of mankind. I was high on the chirping birds, the humid creeping heat—that was enough to live off—and the close greenery drooped about and for all I knew I was in a jungle in the middle of Africa. Foxes lilted by. I saw a possum. Yes, I told myself, I could love Jane without losing my mind. I'd been homeless for a year and a half now, and this was a challenge about which I needed to be tested. I needed to know, because what did I think? That I would remain this way forever? Getting rained on in the cold, being hungry and frowned upon, having no place to be alone, no place to call my own? There were some good things to being a social reject and outcast, but the cons outweighed the pros. It could be downright humiliating, this kind of life. I hated what people screamed out their windows at me: *Get a job!* and *God bless your mama!* and, once: *I'm going to cut off your toes tonight and shove them up your rectum!* That's all good grist for your general sense of well-being. When I lived in Jacksonville, I picked up crabs from the homeless shelter. I was shaving my crotch by a little stream in the woods, lost in the sweeping motion of the blue razor. A young woman in fishnet stockings and combat boots dropped down from the trees behind me. She had pink hair and was walking a small black and white dog. She didn't say a thing—what could she say?—but I about died of embarrassment. Even the dog turned its nose up at me. That very day I caught a coal car to Tallahassee, just to distance myself from that awful moment.

Oh, I felt some lingering questions. Snapping your fingers was a hard thing to do, a dream thing more than a reality thing. I was pretty disgusted with myself, so walked up to the dumpster and hung out on the knoll. When the Isuzu arrived I ran down there, closed the iron window, hopped over the top, and let out the love that had been cooped up inside me. It was like a zipper ran between my Adam's apple and my groin. The dumpster gave me permission to rip that shit open, open my solar plexus up. That's what I did. My guts and organs tumbled out of me to run slimy all over Jane, and pretty much yanked me down on top of her body.

We didn't speak. Of each other we knew what we needed, but my conscience bothered me, for Jane was neglecting her project, *The Joy of Dumpster Diving*. That book stood to be a best-selling classic. I was guilty of derailing her. That's how selfish I was when I was in the dumpster, when I was given permission. I just wanted that soft warm breast inside me, filling my mouth and lifting me up high, and higher, into the ether. I wanted myself inside her while that part of her was inside me, filling me. Was I playing tricks on me? When my me wasn't in the dumpster my me didn't want her, so the dumpster became a me-beacon. I would think of the dumpster as if what it represented for me was not my pleasure and my need for lovesome expression. The dumpster was merely a box that held the nourishment needed for survival, the white calcium, the red iron, the yellow vitamin C and orange carotene.

We kept a schedule. It was Mondays, Wednesdays, and Fridays. For three weeks we kept it up, two mute strangers tangled in fleeting animal passions, but I missed a day on purpose for Jane to work on her book. The following Monday Jane was late. I was in the dumpster. When she jumped down beside me all we did was talk. She said she read about me in *Art Papers*, this article entitled "Runaway Dave," about a man who disappeared.

"I snapped my fingers," I said.

"You're a legend, Dave. I had no idea that you loved art so passionate, that you discovered Gertha Plum and so many great outsider artists. People think of you as a hero in the art world. A theory says you might be dead. The dude who shanked your wife was a suspect but they let him go."

"Beautiful," I said.

"I'm trying to push your buttons, Dave."

"I love you, Jane," I said, and the brains in my hands began to think. They peeled down Jane's leg-sleeves and ripped back Velcro patches, pieces of her body spilling out, appearing like islands in the sunshine. As we kissed, time ebbed away, elongating into a briny ocean that covered the world, foaming in our ears. I'd told my bum friends of Jane. They may have been watching our box from up on the knoll, knowing what we were doing inside of it. They were supportive of my situation, patted me on the back and all, and told their own true stories that I thought were wonderful.

So the dumpster was our safe place, our haven where we loved without consequence. In the dumpster we felt immune to harm, but I knew it couldn't last. On one occasion we had just separated and were on our backs on a bed of thawing steaks, staring up at the wide blue sky. That's when Jane told me. She said, "Chance is back."

"Chance?"

"From his tour, you know, he plays electric mandolin in a band. I told him about you. I didn't want him in the dark."

I eyed the white stream of a silver bullet slicing the sky in two.

"He's a prince, you know?"

"A prince?"

"From a tribe in Cameroon. Where Chance comes from a man's entitled to as many wives as he wants."

"Chance is black?"

"Who cares besides nobody?"

"I didn't know you had a black boyfriend, Jane."

"What difference does it make, Dave?"

"It makes you more special."

"He was quiet at first," Jane said. "He was put off by it, but then he started smiling and telling me about all the women he fucked on the road. He hadn't planned on telling me, is that low? Shit pissed me off."

"He was willing to jeopardize your health over his own selfish way of looking at the world," I told Jane. "A lot of people are like that. They squeeze life instead of cradle it."

"Chance is a squeezer," Jane said, and leaned back my way, nudged her face against my shoulder and draped my midsection with her leg, adorning me with her smooth gold glorious—what else to call it?—river of womanly music and delight. "I love you, baby," she said, and told me that she and Chance broke up, that she was tired of meeting me only in the dumpster. She wanted us to take our love outside of the box, she said, and moved her hand up and down my chest, closing her fingers on the hair and pulling it. I watched the plane disappear beyond the dumpster wall.

I thought about it. I opened my mouth to tell her forget it, drop it, remove it from your list of possibilities. Don't use me to forget your African mandolin player, Jesus, but when I opened my mouth, all to come out was the steady rhythmic clack of the warehouse door. The grocery clerks were coming out. We heard them wheeling shopping carts filled with groceries across the concrete dock, so we burrowed down into the hamburger meats and apple pies and cookies and greens and things. We covered ourselves with loose Delmonico steaks and fish heads, all these boxes and sacks. "Don't move," Jane whispered. We held our breath. A pinch later the sky erupted in a squall of loose vegetables and flowers and pastries. It was comforting, but somebody shouted, "A foot!" in a high-pitched nasally voice.

"The butcher," Jane whispered.

I hugged Jane tighter.

"Call the cops!" the butcher cried.

We scrambled to right ourselves. Looking up we saw the face of the butcher and a large huge black man's face.

"I was looking for my diamond pendant," Jane said, shaking one long sexy leg into her homemade tights. On her thigh was a smear of composting spinach.

The butcher looked like he was tasting some new and possibly dangerous substance. When a decision softened his face he jumped off the loading dock in his bloody apron. A few seconds later the plastic lid came down above us. I heard the curled padlock finger slither through the hole and snap. The iron window closed then, and was locked. Sporadic light beams reached through the crevices into the darkness of us, where we fed each other Little Debbie's Hoho cakes.

The cops came. We heard the butcher out there. He said, "I tell you I couldn't believe it when I seen it. A foot! I thought somebody was disposed of, but the foot moved. I seen then the woman's face, and I said to myself, I recognize you, you sonofabitch. I'd caught her stealing yogurt and cheese, but this time she was nekid. I want you to arrest her."

"Why were they naked?" we heard the police officer say. It was a woman police officer's voice, and I liked this, and I wanted to hear what the answer to her question would be.

"I didn't see no nekid peoples," the black guy said.

"What are you saying, Antonio? You saw them plain as day, same as I."

"I didn't see no nekid peoples," Antonio repeated. "To be nekid you gots to have not a stitch to your name on your body. All I seed was bits and pieces, baby. I didn't see no piece uncovered that I wouldn't see uncovered right there on aisle seven where the peoples buys the coffee."

* * *

Jane Mayfly and I were given a warning. That may have been because Jane acted like we were a couple. "We're artists," she told the cops, and held my arm. I wasn't a homeless dude anymore, but a citizen. To better explore this new feeling I let Jane drive me to her shotgun shack, and Lord, what a treat. Jane turned out to be an artist quite deserving of professional representation. Even though I had given up my professional life, I kept up with what was happening in the art world. When you're homeless, you feel the need to read, to work on your mind if nothing else.

What I saw in Jane was an outsider artist of the occasional accidental insight. In her cluttered shack were the bizarre out-of-whack sculptures she'd worked on without hope for reward for the last eight years, ever since her graduate application was rejected on the basis that her work showed "no unity of vision." Her cardboard tableaus, even though I am one to turn his nose up at throwaway art, were redeemable, I thought, in how precious they were, just stick figure people stuck into regular old cardboard sheets, old vacuum cleaner boxes and boxes that once housed vodka bottles or coffee pots, with toothpicks dispensed—somehow this detail was important to

Jane—from Chinese buffet restaurants and from sandwiches that she had personally eaten. If a toothpick could hold a garden sandwich together, why not a work of art?

As for Jane's junk sculptures, she had fashioned them out of brooms and bike parts and thrown-out exercise contraptions, old lamps and broke umbrellas. It was intriguing how she had placed the things, her decisions in relation to her titles—who knew what came first, the titles or the placements—but how many times had I seen this? They were awful, just embarrassing pieces of junk, but who, I thought, was I, to cast judgment, especially now that I had sworn it all away? Besides that, wasn't art a thing done for joy? Did art have to be good? Did art have to defy all creation to be new? Of her sculptures, I said, "These are something else."

"Really?" she said, looking to Runaway Dave, the expert, for further elucidation.

"They are like cocoons," I said, "compressions of where we would like to be when life assaults us with its crazy demands."

"That's it, that's what I'm trying to say!" Jane said. "I never could express it, but you just said the whole thing of what I'm trying to do. You are such a genius, Dave."

In the days to follow I found a bit out about Jane. Jane's artistic journey, it seemed, was launched from an incident involving her dad. While a high school girl down in Key Largo where she grew up, she fell in love with a boy named Ontario Mills. Her father was a successful tractor salesman. He watched football on the weekends. What he liked about black men was that black men gave the team of his Alma matter "speed." Upon hearing that his daughter was invited to the prom by a kid named Ontario Mills, he forbade it, and locked her in her room for a day and a half. Jane ended up going to the prom with some white jerk she hated. That messed her up forever, the worst of it being the part where she had to lie to Ontario, telling Ontario that she didn't feel any kind of connection with him, that that was the reason she didn't want to hang out with him. Her dad had made her a liar, even though her dad was Episcopalian and claimed to hate liars. Instead of rejecting her father for this assault and for his hypocrisy, or rejecting her mother who supported him, she went on to make junk sculptures, and live her life in a manner that they could not ever approve of. She showered seldom, had sex with black men, ate food out of dumpsters, sewed her own clothes and combed her hair only with her fingers. Whenever they visited, they brought along bras for her to wear, new panties, underarm deodorants and boxes of Wheat Thins, gifts for their cherished daughter who, from their way of thinking, was plain weird.

I felt pretty in control these new days of my life with Jane. I took a chance and forswore my vows to never love again. I asked Jane Mayfly to marry me. Jane said, "Hell yes, Dave!"

Though I had sworn Alice off, mentally, I knew there were emotions that I could never be free of. Was I marrying Jane to abolish the love I'd held for another woman? Was I marrying Jane to prove to myself that I could love without going crazy? Didn't I have a daughter now? Her name was Prudence. I wanted to be her daddy, but I was untrustworthy, wasn't I? As a daddy I would have been way too controlling. I did not want to ruin my daughter's life by making myself known to her. I needed to be, for her and for Alice, dead.

* * *

We found a certified minister in the yellow pages. On the phone I explained to him that we wanted to be married in the dumpster behind Winn Dixie.

"I never married anybody in a dumpster before," the certified minister said, sounding a bit Elvisy to my ear, like he might very well have been an Elvis impersonator.

"We're artistic," I told him.

"Hey, I'm an artist too," he said. "I'm a talented fountain installer. I installed a fountain for ex-governor Bob Graham, know who that is?"

"The ex-governor?"

"He's a great man, everybody says so. I had lots of personal contact with Bobby. Would you like me to dress like Elvis?"

"Sure," I said.

"It's fifty dollars extra. That makes a hundred dollars together. You want standard vows, or do you have your own personal vows?"

"Thanks for asking. We'll come up with our own."

Jane worked on her wedding dress all that week. She ransacked the Battered Women's Thrift Store dumpster up the hill, and came home with a heap of materials. On the day of our wedding, when she put the thing on, what an adorable eyesore! The dress was white in the way of wedding dresses and layered, but here and there you saw a patch of a man's Izod shirt, or a patch of a woman's panties. There were sugar cones, like what you eat ice cream out of, sewn into the shoulders, poking upward.

Our esteemed notary, true to his word, arrived dressed like Elvis, hair dyed black and slicked back with brilliantine. He read our vows in the parking lot, looking up now and then through the dumpster window at my bride and I standing barefoot on a lot of bananas. His mother, who was confined to a wheelchair, was with him, as were seven bums, all friends of mine who'd stepped down from the knoll to serve as our witnesses. Once married, I kissed my lovely bride for all to see, then watched her straddle the crusty upper rim of the dumpster.

"Don't move!" Elvis's mother shrieked from her wheelchair, and snapped a picture.

I was dressed, according to Jane's desire, in a tuxedo scarfed from a dumpster. This tux Jane had altered to fit me tight. I felt mummy-like. In the July heat I was a sweaty something you didn't want to be, unless you were me. All around us the awesome humidity wiggled, if humidity can be said to wiggle. It was just awful humid is all, and as we stood drinking our champagne down the supermarket door rolled upward, and we were caught red-handed again.

The butcher's white apron was spotless today. As always, the butcher had his pants tucked into his socks and looked ridiculous and officious. Seeing Elvis coruscate in the sun, and the bums and the old lady with her oxygen tank, he figured out what was going on here, and to our surprise returned to the supermarket and came back a second later with a dozen expired filet mignons. That was the butcher's gift to us, but we gave them to Elvis, our feet stinging against the asphalt.

* * *

We've been married three weeks now. My fear that I would miss the outdoors and the pressure given over by Nature was unfounded. Come to find out it's no trouble. I feel no bitterness over my life in a box. No sense here of being closed in. I'll be looking at Jane across the room hunched over her sewing machine, her bare legs on either side of it, and the room around her will darken. I can watch her without feeling the old craziness bubble up inside me, that desperate longing and the feeling that without her I could suffocate. I know now that life itself does not depend upon the thing's closeness, the woman, her loyalty, her exclusivity—how selfish! What I felt for Alice may not have been love at all. Maybe love is a quiet spirited fish whose shadow clouds a room but for the cherished object of the lover's devotion.

Jane, I've noticed, is a little bit simple. She says that fate brought us together.

Either way, I feel as if I am cured of what has ailed me for so long.

And Jane says I should be an art dealer again, move the world. She hints that if I love her I will not let her talent molder in the shoulder of art's frenetic highway. "My passions need seeing," she implores. "When my passions are seen, I'll be famous."

I smile. Jane accepts my encouragement, but in truth I am against it. There was a time that I moved art like it was water, channeling it from artist to buyer and taking my cut. Elton John was a regular customer of mine, and I sold a Gertha Plum to the great dancer Baryshnikov, who is very fond of outsider art. I felt like a pimp. I don't think I could have paid Baryshnikov to put one of Jane's tableaus in his trunk. Art, all art, it doesn't matter what kind of art, requires, I believe this, a purity that can only be had through a disavowal, even disgust of all art ever created. The furthest thing from any true artist's mind is always art. In a word, true art is never self-conscious or money-minded. True art is untainted by the world of ideas, by preconceived force-feedings about the criteria for beauty.

On the weekends, and on weekdays too, we collect junk from the sides of the roads, garbage cans and frying pans of scratched Teflon. There's just tons of stuff to find when you're looking. Tossed colognes? Half-eaten bags of roasted peanuts still in their shells? Yes, Jane cracks them, eats them as she steers the Isuzu, asking me if I want one. Sure, I say, and she pours me out a handful.

Best of all is that we have decided to pursue Jane's dream of publishing a book entitled *The Joy of Dumpster Diving*. Her dream is my dream. Part of our days we spend cooking, trying out different combinations of food, and writing recipes. When we drive to the coast to collect shells for Jane's sculptures, we gather comestibles all along the way. We always have an excess of food, and we just throw it into the compost heap if it starts to spoil. At any given time we can feed a few dozen souls. We've dreamed of opening a free restaurant. We take pictures of each other naked in the dumpster, and arrange our yields in pleasing compositions on a quilt in the yard. I have photographed Jane draped in sausage links while meditating in the lotus position.

We upload our pictures of ourselves onto Jane's computer. Jane has suggested that we start a website called *Dumpster Love*, which I think is a grand idea. We drink tallboy Millers in the afternoons, write dumpster reminiscences, dumpster poems and dumpster songs. I have tape-recorded my friends, the bums up on the hill, documenting their dumpster stories. Our collection is growing. At night, as I drift off to sleep, I see a dumpster overflowing, a cornucopia flooding the world with love.

ACKNOWLEDGMENTS

To those for whom association with the author of this collection is no offense, I would like to express gratitude, beginning with my homeboys: Kevin Norton, Tim Heron, John Henry Fountain, and David Silas. I extend a heartfelt salute to my home-girls: Goldberry Burton, Hilary Klein, and Sarah Wagoner. While at the University of Mississippi, new friends gave generously of themselves; allow me to recite their names: Tim Earley, Elizabeth Kaiser, Anya Groner, Tracy Morin, Bill Boyl, Burke Nixon, Doug McClain, Herman King, Jamie Paige, Alex Taylor, Tom Bennitt, Clarissa Romano, Anne Corbitt, Kris Kammerud, David Swider, Rachel Smith, Michael Bible, Seth Borgen, Abigail Greenbaum, Emily Green, Jacqui Bazarte, Will McIntosh, Wendy Buffington, Travis Blankenship, Jenny Linscott, David Hargrove and Josh Camp Brown. The editors who chose these stories for original publication have my thanks, in particular Rebecca Bengal at *American Short Fiction*. Thank you Leslie Jill Patterson at *Iron Horse Literary Review* and Lawrence Hetrick at the *Chattahoochee Review*. Other editors include: Brooks Steritt, Jackie Corley, Ed Winstead, Simon Moon, Jarrid Deaton, Sheldon Lee Compton, Mina Proctor, Darcy Cosper, Brian Schott, Tessa Smith McGovern, and Katrina Gray. The humanity and patience of my estimable professors at Ole Miss still amazes me, so thank you Tom Franklin, John Brandon, Jack Pendarvis, Mary Hayes, Gary Short and Annette Trefzer. Thanks go to my wise and kind Florida State University professors as well: Jim Roche, Virgil Suarez, Mark Winegardner, Barry Faulk, Susan Taylor, Jerrilyn McGregory and Stanley E. Gontarski. To my students Hannah May Christian, Drew Ciccolo, Johnny Muller, Krystal Perez, Nancy Chung, Clyde Christopher and Fairest Miko—thanks y'all. Thank you Brenda Robertson at the Ole Miss Writing Center; David Galef and Emily Isaacs at Mont-

John Oliver Hodges

clair State University; Ray Potes at Hamburger Eyes; Jeffrey Hoone at Light Work; Alex Steele at the Gotham Writers' Workshop; and Eric Breitenbach at the Southeast Center for Photographic Studies in Daytona Beach. Adem Geraghty and Sylvia Borkowska have my thanks for the cool pad in Brooklyn; and thank you Ernest and Hardy, my brothers. Thank you Brady Miller and Rick Reid, Brooklyn friends who have greatly enriched my life. I owe thanks to my Alaskan pals McClain Steadman, David Thomas, Jeff Irwin, Tom Regal, the Quigleys, and a guy named Brian. This book honors the memory of Jerome Stern; and I thank Gordon Lish for doing what he could for bumbling stumbling mumbling me. The Sewanee Writers' Conference gave support in the way of a Tennessee Williams Scholarship, during which time the title story of this collection was workshopped under the direction of Tim O'Brien. Tremendous thanks goes to Hee Jung Woo. And thank you Joe Taylor and the Livingston Press crew for making this book happen, and for the invaluable intent behind the Tartt First Fiction series. Lastly, for his impeccable finesse and friendship in life and in death, his goodness, editorial input and guidance, I thank Barry Hannah.

author photo: Brady Miller

JOHN OLIVER HODGES was born in Florida. His first published story was about a guy who steals a baby in a jar of formaldehyde from a college biology lab. His girlfriend starts talking to the baby, and treats it like a real baby, so the guy tries putting a stop to the craziness. In the tussle that follows the jar drops and breaks and the baby sloshes across the floor in the glass and liquid. Since then his fictions have appeared in many online and print journals. He currently lives in New York City.